The Rose and the Mask

A Beauty and the Beast Retelling

First published 2017

2

ISBN: 978-1542856423

www.VictoriaLeybourne.com

Sorcerers have never existed; but their power has, for those who have had the talent to make others believe they were sorcerers.

—Giacomo Casanova, *The Story Of My Life*

Prologue

VENICE, 1752

The shutters on the little window clattered open in a puff of dust, and Faustina Casanova leaned out, helping herself to a few lungfuls of night air. Sounds of celebration wafted up from elsewhere in the palazzo and the surrounding San Marco streets, but the canal below was still and calm. Faustina, on the other hand, was neither.

It was a *very* small window, and Faustina, being tall and not particularly narrow, was disappointed in it. She drummed her fingernails thoughtfully against the wooden frame, casting about for alternative options. There weren't any. The room was not a large one and, being situated on the top floor and towards the unlovely rear of the house, had very little to offer the would-be escapist. The door would have been an obvious choice but she had ruled that out early in the proceedings by locking it between herself and the palazzo's owner, a very wealthy merchant with surprisingly good reflexes. She had gathered from his remarks, during a brief chase, that he knew about the jewellery she had stashed about her person and would very much like it back.

The hammering on the door was intensifying. She thought she heard something give.

"Open this door!" bellowed Signor Sourosin. "You don't know who you're dealing with. When I get my hands on you, thief, I'll make you rue the day you were whelped!"

Faustina raised her eyebrows, so that her forehead crinkled behind the satin mask that covered the upper half of her face. *Whelped?* There was no call for that.

"That sounds very nice," she shouted back, "but I think I prefer the door the way it is, if it's all the same to you."

Ignoring his response—which, in any case, was more of an incoherent roar than anything intelligible—she looked out of the window again, then contemplated her gown. She hadn't come dressed for burglary. The original plan for the evening had been to slip unnoticed into the rather splendid *Carnevale* ball Signor Sourosin was holding downstairs, help herself to food, drink and perhaps a few dances with anonymous strangers, then slip back out again. For that purpose, this scarlet silk gown, liberated from a dressmaker's earlier that week, had been perfect. But, as the evening had worn on, she'd happened to spot an unguarded staircase, then an unguarded doorway, then an unguarded jewellery box, and one thing had led quite naturally to several others.

She heard footsteps and more voices beyond the door, then a couple of very meaningful blows with some hard implement. The wood began to split.

The time for hesitation had passed. Bunching up her ample skirts as best she could in one hand, she scrambled up onto the windowsill. She paused there for a moment, hunched like a gargoyle and contemplating human mortality, then began to haul herself through the window, out and up.

The window frame held tight about her hips, as she had anticipated, but, with concentrated effort, she wriggled through. Scrambling, she managed to gain purchase first on the decorative stone ridge over the window, then the sill of the next window, above that. Inside, she heard a final, decisive crash, and the door disintegrated. It was now or never. Mustering all her strength, she held fast to the upper window, lifting first one foot and then the other onto the ridge. Below, Sourosin thrust a red face out into the night.

"Get back here!" he screamed. It wasn't much of an invitation.

The shutters of the window above were open. Faustina caught hold of the inside of the window frame then, in a last burst of energy, kicked away her perch on the lower window and threw herself through the new one, landing in an undignified heap on the floor. She had secreted the jewellery in the top of her dress—another decision she might have made differently, had she known what was to come—and some of it spilled out onto the floor. She scooped it hastily back up before scrambling to her feet.

This room was a bedroom, mercifully unoccupied. She

didn't stop to admire the decor, preferring instead to make briskly for the servants' staircase, which she had taken the precaution of locating earlier in the evening. It was a cold, bare-stoned affair, seemingly interminable, and she lamented the wear on a rather fine pair of satin slippers as she raced down it. She readied a palmful of coins as she neared the bottom. These she slipped into the hands of a surprised butler, pressing a finger to her lips to indicate that his discretion would be appreciated. From there, it was a relatively simple matter of exiting via the side door and blending into the crowd beyond it.

And when Venice did crowds, it did them properly. Everywhere Faustina looked she saw people: twirling, laughing, dancing people, their lurid costumes seeming to glow even in the grey moonlight. The clothes were overshadowed only by the masks. Every face she saw was artificial. Some were beautiful constructions in silk, lace and feathers, others stark and unadorned. The wearing of masks was permitted in Venice throughout *Carnevale* and embraced whole-heartedly by the populace. Just about everyone could find some use for anonymity.

Despite the peril from which she had so recently extracted herself, Faustina couldn't help but smile a little. *Carnevale*. She had been feeling it all day, the change in the city's rhythm. Venice overflowed with life and beauty even in her darkest times, but she was always at her best during the carnival season. From now until Shrove Tuesday, the streets and canals would be flooded with colour and celebration, the people at once concealed and conspicuous in their magnificent disguises. Under these circumstances, no Venetian could pity herself too greatly.

Indeed, by the time she had traversed Rio de San Moisè and was approaching St Mark's Square, Faustina felt almost elated.

She knew now that her disappearance was complete. She couldn't have stood out here if she'd wanted to. The Square was the beating heart of Venice, the place all the people, colour and intrigue flowed to and ebbed from. Here, the power and splendour of *La Serenissima*—the Serene Republic of Venice—could be seen in their most concentrated form. To the east, the opulent Basilica pushed domes and spires up into the sky, so rich in gold and jewels liberated from distant lands that it had earned the nickname *Chiesa d'Oro*—Church of Gold. It was crowned by a winged lion, the symbol of the republic, picked out in bright relief. To the south of the Basilica, overlooking the smaller *Piazetta* and the Grand Canal, stood the Doge's Palace, the seat of power in the city, built of arches upon arches in the fusion of eastern and western styles that made Venice unique.

Despite the immeasurable beauty and grandeur of the architecture, it was the vibrant swirl of people who met, talked and did business there that really made the Square shine. Tonight, the numerous *Carnevale* celebrations being held throughout the city had spilled out onto the streets, and now the square was a riot of human activity.

Faustina was still blissfully soaking up the atmosphere when roughly six-and-a-half feet of this human activity collided with her left shoulder blade. She stumbled, which dislodged a bracelet from somewhere in the vicinity of her breasts and sent it spinning across the paving.

"I'm so sorry!" It was a man's voice, deep and rich and smooth, and it belonged to the figure who now hastened to retrieve the bracelet and hand it back to her. "Here." He spoke earnestly, which made the fact that he was wearing a mask in the stylised shape of a goat's head all the more amusing. It began with a relatively understated nosepiece, sticking out above his upper lip, but quickly became, around the forehead, something rather less subtle. Two enormous horns spiralled out north of his ears and the eyeholes were deep-set, which no doubt affected his peripheral vision. Despite the collision, Faustina felt herself warming to him.

"Thank you," she said, flashing him a smile. "And you're forgiven." She stopped herself just in time from returning the bracelet to her cleavage—a move probably likely to cause, at the very least, a certain amount of bemusement—and slipped it on her wrist instead. It was comprised of two simple strings of white pearls, clasping a tiny but exquisitely-detailed cameo painting of a blood-red rose. Overall, it was quite an attractive piece, and she realised after a moment or two that she had been looking at it rather too long for someone who supposedly owned it. She glanced back up at her new acquaintance, who was looking at her with gently-twinkling eyes. It was quite difficult to tell, under the goat mask, but Faustina had a lifetime's experience—all twenty-one years of it—of guessing at the handsomeness of faces half-hidden by masks, and his square, set jaw and smooth, full lips suggested that he might also be quite an attractive piece.

"Where were you going in such a hurry?" she asked him.

"I was on my way to meet someone." He was looking at her so intensely that she was beginning to suspect that he was every bit as impressed by what he was seeing as she was. She doubted that her own, rather plain mask could be the culprit.

She narrowed her eyes a little, turning up the corners of her mouth in a teasing smile. "Well, you met me."

"Yes, I suppose I did."

He smiled, lighting up what was visible of his face, and Faustina felt temptation claim her. This was *Carnevale,* after all, where indiscretions could be as indiscreet as one liked, and anonymity made anything possible.

She took a chance. "I suppose you wouldn't like to meet me again in about five minutes? I know a wonderful little place nearby." It wasn't so much "wonderful" as it was "somewhere a person could readily dispose of stolen jewellery", but Faustina preferred not to linger over these minor details.

"I'd like that very much." It really was a spectacular smile.

"And I further suppose," she went on, "that you wouldn't like to walk there together?"

"I respectfully disagree," he said, and he offered her his arm.

The Osteria Del Cacciatore was not one of Venice's most salubrious drinking establishments. The discerning visitor might have noted that it lacked a certain *je ne sais quoi,* if *je ne sais quoi* meant natural light, tables with a full complement of legs and an absence of suspicious smells. What the place did have, however, was atmosphere. The air was thick with atmosphere. One could have scraped it off the walls.

"Are you sure this is the place?" The half of the stranger's face that wasn't caprine was a picture of bemusement. Someone lurched into him and then apologised profusely to his shoes.

"Don't worry," Faustina said, cheerily, "you'll get used to it."

Wild eyes darted around beneath the horns. "If you say so. Perhaps you could find somewhere to sit while I get us something to drink?"

"Of course." She flashed him her brightest smile. The moment his back was turned, she dodged nimbly around the lurcher, who seemed to be deep in contemplation of some philosophical matter, and made for the *osteria*'s furthest and darkest corner.

Women were not always welcome in public houses, but the owner of this establishment—a grizzled individual who answered to Lupo and was rumoured to have once bitten off a man's ear—took a broad view on the matter. Lupo took a broad view on most matters. As long as money made its way into his pockets, he didn't much care who was putting it there or how they'd acquired it. It was a commendable attitude, in Faustina's opinion, and one that attracted a number of like-minded individuals to do business in the *osteria*'s shadowy back room. It was there that Faustina found her contact, sitting in his usual spot and wearing his usual cowl, a defence against the possibility that someone might recognise him through the near-darkness and the fog of pipe smoke he was marinating in.

"*Buona sera*," was her cordial greeting.

"Put it on the table."

It was closer to a grunt than human speech, but she took his meaning. Turning away from him a little for the sake of modesty, she rummaged in her clothing and produced her tangled, glittering haul, which she laid on the table with a flourish.

"I'll take fifty," she said, airily.

"*Soldi*?"

"Ha ha," she said, without actually laughing. "No. *Lire*."

A hand darted from the darkness and turned over the jewellery for examination. "I won't sell it for more than that. Not if the rightful owner's still looking for it. I take it they *are* going to be looking for it?"

Faustina cocked her head. "Maybe. Maybe not. You know these nobles. Very short attention spans."

"Hmm. How long ago did you steal it?"

Faustina bit a hangnail on her thumb, scrunching up her face. "About twenty minutes?"

There came a barking laugh. "I'll give you thirty *lire*. That's my final offer."

"That was your first offer."

"I call that efficiency. Do we have a deal?"

Faustina looked over her shoulder. The jewellery was worth more than that, much more, but all the buyers she knew were either discreet *or* fair, never both. And besides, there was a very handsome goat waiting for her. "Deal," she said, and held out her hand.

"Don't you want to sell that?" A bony finger extended towards her wrist. "I'll give you another five for it."

Faustina looked down. She'd almost forgotten the rose bracelet. She made to take it off, then stopped herself. Her handsome stranger might notice that it was missing, which would lead to some rather uncomfortable questions. Besides, she rather liked it.

"No, thank you," she said, "I'll keep the bracelet."

A rustling sound indicated what might have been a shrug and, a moment later, the hand pushed a pile of coins across the table to her.

"Nice doing business with you," said Faustina, and she scooped them up. She received another throaty grunt in response.

The *osteria*'s front room seemed almost airy, relatively speaking, when she returned to it. It was crowded but, as luck would have it, a group was preparing to take what looked like a fairly promising fight outside. Having loitered out of range until the opportune moment, Faustina managed to secure two seats just as the man in the goat mask returned with two foaming tankards.

"They didn't have any wine," he said, sounding perturbed. "So I got this instead."

Faustina accepted a tankard and peered curiously at its contents. In fact, "foam" was rather too generous a description of what was floating on top of it. "Scum" would have been more to the point. She cleared her throat. "What is it?"

"I didn't like to ask." He sat down. "The gentleman who sold it to me kept looking at my ears in a manner I didn't much like."

Faustina suppressed a giggle. "He was probably admiring your horns."

He looked up at her with confusion for a moment, then his face cleared and he touched the mask. "Oh! I'd forgotten I was wearing this thing." He put down his drink. "What do you think of it?"

"It draws the eye," Faustina noted, tactfully.

"That was the idea. Still—" he looked around "—I'm beginning to think there might be a time and a place for drawing eyes, and that this isn't it." He reached behind his head and loosened a cord, allowing the goat mask to come away in his hands. "That's better."

Faustina took a cautious sip of her drink, allowing herself to survey his face at her leisure. Her instincts had not led her astray—he was *very* attractive. His strong jaw was matched by high, prominent cheekbones, and his olive skin was smooth and clean-shaven.

"Would you like to take yours off too?" he asked.

She gave an amused half-smile, widening her eyes at him. "And be seen alone with a strange man? Certainly not. Think of the risk to my reputation!"

It was a joke, of course. Having hauled this stranger off to a dubious drinking hole on a moment's acquaintance, she had, she felt, demonstrated quite clearly that her reputation was not of utmost importance to her. But he seemed to take her remark very seriously.

"Oh, of course. Do you think I ought to put mine back on?"

Faustina took another swig from her tankard. The liquid inside wasn't as bad as it looked—although that wasn't saying much. "If you like," she said. "But I wish you wouldn't. You're really quite pleasant to look at."

He smiled, and the corners of his eyes crinkled.

"Thank you. I'll leave it off then, if that would please you. And, if I may say, the lower part of your face, at least, is very attractive."

"What a charmingly specific compliment." She shot him a smiling, sidelong look. "Would you like to dance?"

He frowned. "There isn't any—"

But he was interrupted. Behind him, though in Faustina's eye line, Lupo was tuning a fiddle, causing it to emit an unpleasant screech. A handful of the *osteria*'s patrons had noted, over the years, a certain incongruity between Lupo's faintly murderous persona and his fondness for this stringed instrument, but always very, *very* quietly.

A moment later, the barkeeper's gnarled and scabby fingers were flying over the strings. There was little about Lupo that suggested either artistry or joy, but, in his music, there was both. It was a buoyant tune, and irresistible. Already half the drinkers in the room had begun to sing or clap their hands, including some who had been showing only very minimal signs of life until then.

Faustina leapt to her feet. "Come on!"

The stranger looked around for a moment, then shrugged and stood. He took her outstretched hand, pressing soft, warm skin against hers.

They were the first to take to the floor, though they were not alone for long. Only a few bars later, they were in the midst of a seething, stamping crowd. They whirled and jumped, weaving inexpertly around their equally inexpert fellow dancers. No two couples danced the same dance but, somehow, the overall effect was of happy unity, and contusions were kept to a bare minimum. The beat seemed to grow faster and faster, until Faustina felt that she wasn't so much dancing to the tune as flying to it. For every time the dance pulled her and her stranger apart, it threw them back together, and each time his eyes looked brighter and his hands felt more welcoming.

Finally, the music stopped. They were left together, hands clasped. The skin beneath Faustina's mask was slicked with sweat, but she was exhilarated. The stranger was beaming down at her.

"Would you like some fresh air?" he asked.

She nodded. Pausing only to collect his mask from the table, the stranger led her back out into the quiet alley outside. She found her arm caught up in his, though she couldn't remember how it had got there. They walked together in silver moonlight, watching reflected stars shimmer on the gently rippling surface of a canal. When they came to a bridge, the stranger made to lead her across it. She stopped suddenly and pulled him back.

He frowned, seeming about to ask a question. She didn't let him. Instead, she reached for his neck and guided him down to her lips. They kissed. It was chaste, a soft brush of skin against skin, but it held promise.

When they parted, he looked surprised, though not unpleasantly so.

"You're not at all what I expected," he said.

She was puzzled but, with cool air flooding her lungs and happiness swelling in her chest, puzzlement made her feel like laughing, so she did. "What do you mean?"

"I don't know." He gestured expansively, the mask still in his hand. "Tonight, that tavern, the dancing… I've never done anything like this before. It makes all the society balls seem frightfully stuffy, doesn't it?"

Faustina didn't answer, stretching up instead for another kiss. She got it.

Contentment washed over her. This was exactly what she had been hoping for: a fun night spent in attractive company. No names, no attachments: it was, as far as she was concerned, exactly what *Carnevale* was all about.

"You know," the stranger said, softly, "I think I'm going to like being married to you."

Faustina took an involuntary step backwards, blinking slowly as a chill rushed down her spine. It was tempting to start running, as far and as fast as possible, but it occurred to her that he might have been joking. She tried a joke in return: "If you want to marry me," she said, "you'll have to buy me at least one more drink, first."

He laughed. "The betrothal isn't enough, then?"

Faustina stared at him, her eyebrows contorted in confusion. "Who… who do you think I am?"

A diverse range of expressions now flashed across the stranger's face: amusement, bemusement, then sudden realisation. His hand darted towards her. Before she could react, he had grabbed her wrist.

"Where did you get this bracelet?" He had raised his voice now, enough to attract the attention of a small crowd that had spilled out of a party on the other side of the canal.

The temptation to run became overwhelming, so Faustina stopped resisting it. She paused only briefly, to yank her hand free and to flash him a final, quick smile.

"It was nice meeting you," she said. And then she ran.

ONE

1753—ONE YEAR LATER

Evening toppled gently over the *Laguna Veneta*. From the roof of his island palazzo, Benedetto Bellini watched the building's shadow lengthen to the east, cloaking a lawn in a jagged expanse of grey. To the south-west, the last tendrils of golden sunlight played out across the distant domes and gleaming spires of Venice—a final blaze of beauty before darkness fell. It was a perfect sunset, the sort that so often turned otherwise blameless people into poets. Benedetto, however, was unmoved by it. If the sun wasn't going to crash into the Earth and destroy it, the way any merciful celestial body would have, then there was little in its activities to interest him.

He looked down again at the sheet of paper that creased in his gloved hand. He'd copied the instructions exactly as they'd appeared in the book, he was sure of that, and he'd followed them to the letter. He'd gone to high ground—well, perhaps whether or not the roof counted as "ground" was a matter for debate, but this was a small island and didn't offer much in the way of topography. He'd spent most of the afternoon fighting to keep a rather distressing number of candles alight in the face of a stiff breeze. And he must have shouted the incantation into the unfeeling air several dozen times, if the soreness of his throat was any indicator. Nothing had happened.

He wasn't terribly surprised. After all, "nothing" pretty much summed up the outcome of every other attempt he'd made to free himself from his current predicament, and there had been no reason to expect this one to be any different. At least this spell hadn't involved a poultice. Benedetto had had enough of poultices. He'd smeared things on his skin he would have preferred never to have even heard of.

He crumpled the copied page into a ball and, for a moment, toyed with the idea of hurling it into the lagoon. He decided not to. It was unlikely he'd be able to throw it hard enough, and he'd just have to go down to the garden to pick it up. He sighed deeply, then put a hand to his face—or rather, to the mask that covered it, reflexively checking that it was still secure. Then he turned his back on the city and withdrew his pocket watch. Having registered the time—six o'clock—he put the watch back, then set about gathering up what was left of the candles. As he did so, he made an effort to compose himself. He was expecting guests.

Carnevale had returned to Venice for another year, and Faustina was climbing through another window. If she had refrained from doing so in the intervening time, the thing would have looked like a coincidence. In actual fact, she had been making rather a habit of it—particularly when entering her own quarters—as she was doing now. She had refined the art of avoiding Ersilia, her landlady, so extensively that it had become second nature. The idea of using the front door, which opened onto the same narrow passageway as Ersilia's own quarters, now seemed all but unthinkable.

A chunk of the windowsill came away in Faustina's hand as she scrambled over it. She grunted and dropped it on the floor, wiping her hand on her skirt. She had heard Ersilia describe this building, in cold blood, as a "boarding house", but Faustina would have substituted the term "hovel". It wasn't the only point on which they disagreed. For instance, while Faustina thought of herself as a flawed but interesting young woman with a bright future ahead of her, Ersilia had her down as an appalling waste of good city air who would wind up in the gutter—and sooner rather than later, if she didn't come up with some rent.

Rent. Faustina rolled the hated word around in her head a few times as she crossed the room. She had spent a little time as a guest of the Venetian authorities earlier that year following a misunderstanding over the ownership of a very chic pair of soft leather boots and, ever since, it had been a struggle to gain access to any of the establishments where she had previously enjoyed her customary five-finger discount. As a consequence, she was experiencing something of a cash flow problem. Ersilia—who was nothing if not enterprising—had proposed another form of payment.

Faustina knelt beside a wooden chest, pushed up against the wall in the darkest corner of a generally dingy room. The chest had a large and reassuringly sturdy keyhole, and she kept the key on a chain around her neck. She slipped it off now and slid it into the lock, before lifting the chest's heavy lid. Reaching inside, she withdrew a small box of paints and brushes, a palette, and a section of sailcloth that had been rolled up into a tube. Then she started to stand.

"*Ciao!*" It was a cheery little voice in the darkness behind her.

Faustina squawked, scattering brushes over the floor as she turned to look.

A figure waved at her from the end of her bed. "I'm sorry, I thought you'd seen me when you came in, then you walked across the room and I realised you hadn't, and then I kind of panicked."

The speaker was a small, slender girl, around Faustina's age but about two-thirds of her height, with gently-curling blonde hair and a pretty, delicately-featured face that bore a permanent expression of mild worry. Her name was Chiara Idoni and she was Faustina's best friend—although, just at the moment, Faustina was struggling not to throw anything at her.

"*Zio bestia,* Chiara! You nearly scared me to death.

What are you doing here?"

"It's *Carnevale*!" Chiara waved a half-face mask, cut in the shape of the moon and painted with a night sky full of constellations. "I was hoping you'd take me to whatever party you're going to."

Faustina dumped the rest of what she was holding on the bed and bent to pick up her brushes. "Your stepmother let you out for the evening? Has she been taken ill? Replaced by an imposter? Whatever you do, don't tell anyone, they might go looking for the real one."

Chiara laughed, then abruptly stopped, looking guilty. "She's not that bad."

"So she did let you out?"

"No, not exactly." Chiara fiddled with the mask. "*Matrigna* and the girls left for an appointment in Verona. They're going to see a matchmaker for Teodora."

Faustina felt her eyebrows shoot up to her hairline. "So, she has you working in that house like a servant, but she can afford to go to Verona to marry off one of those awful daughters of hers?"

Chiara sagged back against the wall. "You can't blame her for wanting the best for her daughters. Her own daughters, I mean."

"Yes I can," Faustina muttered, "and so should you." But she knew it was a lost cause. She'd had this conversation with Chiara a hundred times, and she could never get her to stop defending the family who had been mistreating her ever since her father died.

Chiara changed the subject. "So, the party—where are you going?"

Faustina turned a rueful gaze on her. "Nowhere, not

tonight. I've got work to do."

She picked up the tube and unrolled it, revealing a painting of a horse. She looked at it dispassionately, then held it up to show Chiara.

"It's a horse," said Chiara.

"I know."

Faustina's tone was scathing, though her malice was intended solely for the equine in question. Like many Venetians, Faustina was not fond of horses. The great, clattering beasts were not permitted in the city, and there would have been little use for them if they had been. Horses, as she understood it, were out of their element where canals were concerned, and the lumbering carts they pulled would not have fitted down the city's narrow alleys. On the mainland, however, people were apparently quite fond of horses—fond enough to pay outrageous sums for images of them, especially if they were by famous painters. Or so Ersilia said. That was why she wanted the painting copied. The one she had given Faustina was itself a copy, since people tended not to trust small-time criminals with priceless originals, but Faustina was doing her best with it. It probably didn't matter all that much. On some level, people who purchased rare works of art in dark alleyways presumably knew that they were taking a risk.

Faustina did not particularly like duplicating other people's paintings, nor had she grown any fonder of the sight of this horse over the four or five times she had already painted it. Sometimes she regretted ever letting Ersilia discover that she had any artistic talent. Then again, it was difficult to keep things from Ersilia. She had what might diplomatically have been termed a "strong personality". She also had a strong forearm, which was generally to be found gripping some household implement with a degree of menace. Faustina had heard legends of boarding house residents who had defied her, but never first-hand. The protagonists of those stories never seemed to stick around to tell them.

Besides, doing the paintings meant that Ersilia provided paints and brushes—which, very occasionally, Faustina found time to use for paintings of her own.

Faustina explained all of this to Chiara, who looked disappointed.

"That's all right," she said, sighing. "I understand."

Guilt twisted Faustina's stomach. "I'll do the fetlocks and then we'll go, how about that?"

Chiara squealed incomprehensibly, which Faustina took as agreement. She was about to speak again when there was a knock at the door.

Faustina swore. "I'll have another one ready for you tomorrow, Ersilia, I promise!"

But the voice that answered belonged to a man. It was layered, as it often was, with a note of amusement. "I've been called many things," it said, "but very rarely Ersilia."

Faustina stared at the door in profound surprise. "Giacomo?"

"In person," answered the voice. "Are you going to let me in?"

"Giacomo?" Chiara whispered, her eyes wide. "Is that your brother? I thought he was in Dresden."

"So did I." To the door, Faustina added: "Do I have a

choice?"

She knew it wasn't the kind of welcome he was used to getting, particularly from women. Giacomo Casanova was hardly Venice's only libertine, but it was widely felt that the others would have to get up very early in the morning to keep up with him. The effect he had on women was the talk of the city, everywhere from the brothels to the churches. Even Chiara had heard some of the stories, and Faustina wasn't sure her friend had ever so much as looked at a man without blushing.

Even through a couple of inches of solid wood, it was possible to detect a distinct pout. "Is that any way to greet a beloved brother, after all this time?"

She knew then that she'd annoyed him, which fulfilled a deep-seated sisterly urge. Feeling that she had made him wait long enough, Faustina opened the door. Giacomo swept into the room, seeming too big for the space. Like Faustina, he was taller than average, and his costume added at least another foot. It was the collar, mostly—an enormous cluster of peacock feathers centred somewhere near the back of his neck, fanning out around his head. Below that was the suit, blue-green and eye-stingingly bright, with a golden cravat at his neck and matching lace at his wrists. A cloak in a darker blue hung from his shoulders and, atop his head, a powdered white wig concealed brown hair a shade or two lighter than Faustina's own. The final touch was the mask, at the end of a golden stick which he held in his hand, and Giacomo had shown no restraint there either. It was a full-face mask, predominantly a glossy white but with an exquisitely-detailed painting of a peacock on it. The bird's head sat above the right eyebrow, the body around the eye and a magnificent tail swept across the cheek and up over the forehead. Giacomo held the mask over his face as she looked at him in order to give the full effect, his eyes—muddy brown, yet another Casanova feature—glittering as he watched for her reaction.

"So you're planning to keep a low profile this evening, then?" she hazarded, the corners of her mouth twitching. She closed the door.

"As always." Giacomo cast his gaze around the room. It landed instantly on Chiara, and he smiled widely. "*Buona sera,* signorina. I don't think I've had the pleasure."

"This is Chiara," Faustina said, "and you're to treat her kindly—"

"Of course. *Dio,* Faustina, what do you think of me?"

"—And not try to get her into bed."

Giacomo's feathers quivered. "I am sure this beauty is capable of speaking for herself, aren't you?" He addressed this question to Chiara, who turned bright pink and squeaked. Giacomo looked discombobulated for a moment, then shrugged. "No doubt we will have the opportunity to get to know one another some other time, *bella.*" He turned his attention to Faustina. "It's good to see you, little sister."

"You too."

She gave him a hug, which he returned cautiously before stepping away.

"Mind the feathers."

"Sorry." She turned to face a somewhat battered dressing table that was serving as a makeshift easel. A canvas, bearing another wretched horse—or, at least, half of one—was propped up on it. "I didn't know you were back in town. It's been, what, two years?"

"They don't call it the Grand Tour for nothing." Giacomo examined a threadbare armchair thoughtfully for a moment before removing his cloak and the collar of feathers and placing them carefully on the floor along with the mask. Then he sprawled himself languidly across the chair, rearranging the cushions so that they were more to his liking. "I've been back a week or two, actually. The money ran out, as money so often does, so here I am."

"A week or two?" Faustina fought to concentrate on her work, but couldn't quite keep the hurt from her voice.

"Yes." He gave a world-weary sigh. "I meant to send you a note, but you know how it is. So many dropped threads to pick up, and only so much time in the day."

"Well, what brings you here now?" She had her suspicions.

"I wanted to see you." He attempted to sound wounded. "Can't a man drop in to see a beloved sister—"

"—Dressed as a peacock—"

"—Wearing an excellent and extremely tasteful *Carnevale* costume, in order to pass the time of day with her?"

Faustina shook her head. "Not really. For one thing, Ersilia doesn't like us to have visitors, especially male ones. For another—" she broke off, glancing over at Chiara, who was still staring at Giacomo and flushing furiously "—you in particular, Giacomo, are *persona non grata* here after what happened with Beatrice."

Giacomo's eyes glazed over in soft reminiscence. "Ah,

yes. Beatrice."

"And Agnese."

"Agnese." He was smiling now.

"And Serafina."

He finally had the grace to look a little sheepish. "I take your point."

"On the same night."

"Yes, I remember now. It was your Ersilia that chased me down the street with a broom, wasn't it? Charming woman. Puts on a surprising turn of speed."

"Exactly." Faustina put her brush to the canvas, delicately smoothing a thin line of hair over a hoof.

The chair creaked as Giacomo straightened up. "All right," he said, "since you asked, there was something else. I wondered if you might lend me a little money."

Faustina snorted. "I thought so. I'm afraid I haven't got any."

He looked dismayed. "You're sure you haven't got a little something squirrelled away? I'm desperate."

"You're always desperate for money."

"Yes, but I'm really desperate today. I've been asked to join a card game this rich eccentric's running. It's going to be a very wealthy table and I stand to make a good profit, but I need a bit to take with me to make sure I stay in the game."

She sighed, reaching into her pocket. She loved Giacomo, despite his faults, but she couldn't pull money from thin air. She withdrew a small handful of coins. "This is it," she said. "This is all I've got." Last *Carnevale*'s jewellery haul seemed a long time ago now.

"That's it?" Giacomo sagged. "Oh, well. No, keep your

paltry little pile of change." He folded his arms. "You've lost the thieving touch, I suppose?"

"No." She suppressed a flash of irritation. "I'm having a run of bad luck, that's all." This was a sensitive subject. Giacomo had often teased her about her work, and it had become more and more insufferable as the gulf between them had widened.

In spite of their age difference—six years—Faustina and Giacomo had been close as children. Inseparable, even. But life had taken them in very different directions since then. With their father dead and their mother, an actress, touring Europe, Giacomo had gone to live with a doctor and then on to university in Padua, where he had studied both law and several of the more popular forms of debauchery. Faustina, meanwhile, had found her home and education in Venice: first with her grandmother and then, after the old lady died, on the streets. Thieving was only the first of many skills she had learned to stay afloat.

But she couldn't hate Giacomo for being favoured, or for being a man. After all, even with those advantages, Giacomo was still like her: doing whatever it took to live a comfortable life on limited resources. Of course, in Giacomo's case, that meant a wealthy patron and plenty of ill-spent leisure time, while she languished in this alleged boarding house, scraping together the money—and horses—to fend off Ersilia. But Giacomo was her brother, and she loved him. That was what stopped her from attacking him with a palette knife.

"Well, keep your bad luck away from me," he said. "If all goes well tonight, I'll be well on my way to making my fortune." He rose. "Again," he added, after a moment's thought. "I hope you ladies have a pleasant evening."

Faustina bristled. "And I hope your card game goes well. I'd hate for you to suffer some kind of humiliating loss."

He gave an infuriatingly charming grin—a speciality of his. "Oh, there's no fear of that. I left Venice an excellent card player, and I've returned an even better one. I'll get what's coming to me."

"Not if you haven't got anything to bet with."

Giacomo reached into his jacket, producing a bulging leather purse. It clinked heavily as he tossed it up in the air. "I expect I'll manage."

Faustina stared at him. "I thought you were desperate for money."

"You said it yourself: I'm always desperate for money. I managed to borrow this off a few acquaintances earlier today. But it's always worth asking, isn't it?"

Faustina stood still, silenced by outrage. She was still trying to find the words to respond when there was a noise downstairs. She groaned. This time there could be no mistake. The stride was distinctive.

"It's Ersilia."

Giacomo paled. "Time for me to leave, I think."

"What are you going to do, just breeze past her and hope she thinks you're a real peacock?"

Giacomo wasn't looking at her. Having quickly gathered his things, he had turned his attention to the open window. "Well, it's been good to catch up. God speed, good Faustina."

"Giacomo—" But she knew she couldn't stop him. It was in the blood.

"*Ciao!*" he said. And, pausing only to secure his wig and bow to Chiara, he leapt from the window.

Faustina threw down her brush. "Come on," she said. "We're going out."

Two

The evening was not progressing quite as Giacomo had anticipated. He wouldn't have gone so far as to say that it had been a mistake to go out to Ca'Bellini, if only because he had never admitted to making a mistake before and wasn't familiar with the procedure, but he was beginning to think that there might have been ways in which he could have spent the time more profitably. He didn't like this island, miles outside the city and painfully devoid of amusement. He didn't like this palazzo, empty, echoing and, now that night had fallen, rather chilly. And, as for its owner... Well, Giacomo didn't know quite what to make of Benedetto Bellini, but he wouldn't have been sorry to see the back of him, either.

This was a very large, very grand room, unlit except for the candlesticks around the table, and it made Giacomo feel as if he and the other four men were sitting in the middle of a dark and infinite abyss. This, he decided, was hell.

Keep a low profile, he thought bitterly to himself, his patron's voice echoing in his head. Bragadin had been watching him closely since he had returned to the city: the price of his protection and a modest allowance. *You can't afford to draw too much attention to yourself,* the old man had said. Well, if it came to that, he couldn't afford much of anything, now. He hadn't had a lucky hand all night. Signor Bellini, on the other hand, had been quietly amassing a small fortune in winnings—a fortune which, to judge by the size and style of his sumptuous home, he scarcely needed.

The man to Giacomo's left—Maestri, he thought the name was—shuffled the deck. "Same rules as last time?" he asked. There was murmured assent around the table.

Giacomo put a hand in his pocket and drew out his last few coins. He held them tightly, allowing the warm metal to make grooves in his skin, and glowered across the table. The men weren't all strangers to him. Alonso Sartore—a wiry man with watery blue eyes and a thin moustache—he knew well, having shared numerous misadventures with him over the last decade or so. He had encountered Vico from time to time in the city and knew him to be a decent drinking companion. Maestri had travelled with them on the boat and, from what Giacomo had gleaned from his conversation before becoming bored and changing the subject, was a trader of some kind. The one thing they all had in common was that they had been approached by a stranger in a tavern and asked if they would be interested in a private card game, and they had all said yes.

At that moment, Giacomo hated them all, but it was at Benedetto that he was directing the better part of his silent ire. Giacomo had asked around and, according to popular speculation, Benedetto Bellini was an eccentric. A year ago, apparently, he had been the toast of Venice, at least in commercial circles. An immensely successful investor, he had lived in a richly-appointed apartment in the city and apparently spent his days routinely turning things into gold by his merest touch—metaphorically speaking, of course. Some sources even claimed that there had been a good marriage on the horizon. Then, seemingly without warning, Benedetto had taken it into his head one day to decamp to this island, and hadn't returned to the city since.

And he was never seen without a mask. No one knew why. Perhaps it was an affectation, or perhaps he had some other identity to hide. Giacomo didn't care about that. Some of his favourite people were eccentrics, affected, in possession of secret identities or some delightful combination of all three. But, for all that *Carnevale* permitted, it was forbidden in Venice to wear a mask while gambling. With each passing minute, Giacomo was becoming more and more convinced that Benedetto's wilful flouting of this rule was the reason for his extraordinary good luck. What else could it be? Giacomo was a good gambler, a master of the art. He had brought lords and viscounts down to their last few *soldi*. But tonight had been abysmal. He couldn't remember having lost this badly since learning the rudiments while at school.

It couldn't be a coincidence. Any gambler worth his

salt knew that the ability to read people, to watch their faces and find the chinks in their armour, was half the battle. And impossible, of course, if one's opponent wore a mask.

Giacomo sucked thoughtfully at his teeth for a moment, then decided to give his host the opportunity to do the right thing. He cleared his throat, reaching for the cards he had been dealt. "Signor Bellini, I wonder—"

Benedetto reached for a bottle. "Another drink?"

"Thank you, no. I'd like to make an observation, if I may."

Grey eyes gleamed behind the plain leather mask that covered the upper half of Benedetto's face. "Yes?"

"You know, of course, that you are among friends here?"

Around him, the men exchanged glances. It wasn't, Giacomo suspected, the word they would have chosen. "Acquaintances" was closer to the mark. Maybe "associates". But "friends"? Even Alonso appeared mildly taken aback, and he was probably one of the closest *acquaintances* Giacomo had.

Benedetto's response was cordial but lacked enthusiasm. "Of course."

"Good." Giacomo leaned in, coiled to strike. "Perhaps, then, in the spirit of friendship, I could invite you to remove your mask?"

Benedetto put a gloved hand to the beard that covered what the mask did not. His lips thinned. "I'm sorry?"

"The mask. It's hardly sporting, is it, covering your face while playing at cards?" He looked around at the others. "Don't you agree?"

Alonso shifted uncomfortably in his seat. "I suppose it's a little unorthodox."

Giacomo scowled at him. *Coward.*

Benedetto lowered his gaze and appeared to study his hand of cards for a moment, absently tapping the backs of them with one finger. Then he looked up and shook his head, slowly. "I'm afraid I'm going to have to decline that invitation—Casanova, was it? I am perfectly comfortable in the mask and intend to keep it on."

Giacomo huffed. That was another thing he didn't like about this Bellini character. Who in Venice didn't know the name Giacomo Casanova? True, he'd been gone a while, but surely he couldn't have been forgotten so quickly. No, Benedetto *had* heard of him, he was sure of it. He was just playing dumb to irritate Giacomo. It was working.

Well, Giacomo thought, *if that's the way he wants it...*

He forced a smile. "Fair enough." He glanced at the bottle of wine. "You know, I think I will take that drink."

"Very well." Benedetto picked up the bottle, topping off Giacomo's glass without looking at him. The others held theirs out for refills and he obliged before emptying what was left—barely a dribble—into his own glass.

Giacomo watched him closely. "Go on," he said, wheedling, "open another. It's a day of celebration, isn't it—the first night of *Carnevale*? Hardly an occasion to skimp on the libations."

He saw Benedetto's jaw clench a little. Nonetheless, the masked man eased the cork out of another bottle—the third or fourth of the evening—and poured some more.

Giacomo smiled and lifted his glass. "To friendship,"

he said. The others lifted their glasses and drank deeply. That was good. He didn't want anyone too alert for this next game. He had a few tricks up his sleeve—literally—and he intended to use them.

Since she had sold her finer clothes to pay her debts, and Chiara had never had any to begin with, Faustina had decided it would be best if they set their sights relatively low as far as the evening's entertainment was concerned. This party, already spilling out of both the house and the control of the moderately-successful cheesemonger who was hosting it, seemed to fit the bill.

"Well," Faustina said, as the pair of them smiled their way past the dairy dealer in question. "Here we are. Is this the sort of thing you had in mind?"

Chiara lowered her mask to take it in. The eyes that emerged from behind the starry crescent moon were wide with delight. "Oh, Faustina!" she exclaimed, breathlessly. "It's beautiful!"

"I'm glad you think so." For her own part, Faustina felt she might like it better once she'd found the refreshments.

"Look at all these people. And the masks! And the dresses!" Chiara's happiness was radiant and irresistible.

Faustina looked around. Across the room, a small orchestra played a sedate tune, to which a lace-drenched, gilt-edged crowd marched and twirled. If she tried, Faustina could see it the way Chiara did. A *Carnevale* ball—even a second-rate one—was a remarkable thing to behold. Among the masks, she saw demons and angels, fairies and centaurs—even one brave woman dancing with Death.

Faustina sighed. She really did love *Carnevale.*

"You're right," she said, returning Chiara's smile. "It's not bad, is it?"

Chiara was giving her a surprisingly wry look. "It's a shame, though," she said. "That we couldn't have gone to one of the big society balls, I mean. You're probably disappointed."

Faustina shook her head. "Oh, no—honestly, Chiara, this one's fine. It's just—" She sagged. "I'm annoyed about Giacomo. I mean, he was gone two years, and he couldn't even find the time to write me a note to say he was back. 'Dear Faustina, hope this finds you well, just thought you'd like to know I'm back in Venice. Your affectionate brother…' I mean, it wouldn't have taken him long, would it?" She was prepared to develop this theme, but she had noticed that Chiara was giving her a strange look. "Wait—what did *you* mean?"

Chiara looked discomfited. "Never mind."

"No, go on, what were you thinking of?"

"Well, I was only going to say—" Chiara smiled again. "Wasn't it the first night of last *Carnevale* that you met that man?"

Faustina affected a sudden interest in the ceiling. "What man?" she asked, but she knew even as the sounds came out that she wasn't being very convincing.

Chiara rolled her eyes. "The man in the goat mask. The one who thought you were going to get married."

"Oh. That man." Faustina didn't always tell Chiara

about her escapades with the opposite sex. Chiara was regrettably given to asking questions like *"What was his name?"* and *"Do you think you'll see him again?"* But the story of the man in the goat mask had been too good for Faustina to keep it to herself.

"Yes, that man." Chiara lowered her mask to grin impishly. "If we'd gone to one of the grand balls, we might have run into him."

"All the more reason not to," Faustina returned. Her irritation had faded completely, to be replaced by embarrassment. "What makes you think I'd want that?"

"Well, there's this." Chiara reached out and tugged Faustina's sleeve up her arm, revealing two strings of pearls clasping a painted rose.

"Ah." She had to admit that her friend had her there.

She shouldn't have worn the bracelet. In fact, she should have disposed of it as soon as she'd had the chance. She didn't know why she hadn't. At least, she didn't *understand* why she hadn't. She had been about to many times, but something always stopped her. It was ridiculous: her memories of that night were far fonder than they ought to have been. What she ought to have remembered was that she had spent it with a man who had nearly got her arrested and who apparently didn't know the difference between his fiancée and a total stranger. But what she remembered instead were soft lips and a dance that hadn't gone on long enough. Against all reason and logic, the bracelet made her smile when she looked at it, so she had kept it.

"Maybe," Chiara went on, "he immediately broke things off with his fiancée and has been searching the city for you ever since. But he can't find you, because he doesn't know what you look like without a mask."

"Or maybe he married the fiancée and has forgotten the whole thing?" It was the most likely option. The night probably held no significance whatsoever for her stranger—just as it should have for her.

Chiara shook her head vigorously, so that her golden ringlets bounced around her ears. "Not possible. I'm sure no one could forget you."

Faustina squinted at her, then smiled. If anyone else had said it, she'd have taken it as sarcasm—or an outright insult. After all, being memorable wasn't exactly an asset in her line of work. But Chiara was earnest to a fault, and cutting personal remarks were not exactly her stock in trade.

"Thank you," Faustina said. "But, even if you're right, I don't think any good would come of our meeting again."

"No," Chiara said, "I suppose not." But then she gave a wistful sigh. "You never know, though, do you? Perhaps, if it's meant to be..." She trailed off, her eyes misting.

Faustina cleared her throat. "Are you talking about...?" But she let Chiara be the one to say it out loud.

"Magic. Yes."

Faustina restrained herself. Of course, Chiara was far from being the only person in Venice to believe in magic. Faustina knew for a fact that there were dozens of charlatans and con artists in the city who made good money out of perpetuating and exploiting that belief. Some claimed to see the future, others to be able to produce healing potions of supernatural potency or to know incantations that would do anything from blessing the purchaser with good luck to raising the dead. For all the mystery that surrounded these practitioners of magic, there were two things that could be said about all of them with absolute certainty. First, that their services would be ruinously expensive and, second, that said practitioners would be impossible to track down once their "magic" was revealed as a sham. Even to Faustina, for whom today's ill-attended jewellery was tomorrow's lunch, it seemed a grubby way to make a living.

Chiara continued. "I know you don't believe in it. But, well… there was obviously something there, between the two of you. And if you belong together, maybe something will make that happen. I'm just saying… nothing's impossible."

Faustina nodded, slowly. She often—as now—had to bite her tongue to stop herself from warning Chiara that her belief in magic was a weakness. But it would do no good. For one thing, Chiara had nothing worth stealing. And, for another, her belief that there was some fantastic force at play in the world, above the drudgery of daily existence, was so sweet and so pure that arguing with her felt cruel. Sometimes, Faustina even envied that belief.

Still, to actually agree with her was a step further than Faustina was prepared to go, so she settled for a friendly shoulder-squeeze, followed by a change of subject.

"Come on." She pulled her sleeve back down to cover the bracelet, then slipped her arm through Chiara's. "Did we come here to talk about men in goat masks or to enjoy ourselves? Let's dance."

Chiara beamed, already making for the centre of the room. "All right," she said, "let's dance."

Back at the island palazzo, things were turning around for Giacomo. That was one of the advantages of flagrant cheating.

It was his turn to deal and he was shuffling the cards deftly without looking at them—so deftly, in fact, that none of the cards were actually changing position within the pack. That would have been a shame after all the trouble he had taken to arrange them. As he tossed them out to each of the players in a seemingly-slapdash fashion, he caught Alonso watching him closely. Their eyes met for a moment, though neither of them altered their facial expressions. He knew what that meant, and he wasn't surprised. Alonso knew what he was doing. Most likely he would want his money back later, along with a little something extra for not bringing it up at the table. Giacomo didn't mind that. With all this money in front of him, he felt almost generous.

Benedetto wasn't watching. He was examining the sleeve of his jacket, brushing off invisible specks of dust. That suited Giacomo. Not that he was worried. If their host's powers of observation hadn't caught anything already, they weren't likely to start now. His wine cellar had been depleted by several more bottles over the last couple of hours. Admittedly, much of it had been soaked up by Vico and Maestri, who were swaying and nudging one another and looked as though they might start singing sea shanties at any moment. Benedetto hadn't been indulging in the stuff to quite the extent that Giacomo would have liked but, nonetheless, he had lost some of the sharpness he had exhibited earlier in the evening and was becoming slightly clumsier in his movements. More importantly, he had been slow to realise that his lucky streak had ended, and a good deal of cash had made its way across the table from him to Giacomo.

Giacomo wasn't sure how much he himself had been drinking. Not enough to dull his sensibilities, of course, but it was good, well-aged wine and there was no sense in letting it go to waste.

This hand played out exactly as he had anticipated, which was hardly surprising. Alonso folded early, of course. So did Vico, with the air of one who considered all this messing about with cards to be a distraction from the free drinks. Maestri dropped out later than he ought and with bad grace. Bellini held on until the bitter end. There was nothing wrong with that: Giacomo had given him excellent cards. But the ones he had kept for himself were better.

Benedetto pushed the money towards him. "I see your luck has turned, Casanova."

Giacomo flashed him a beatific smile. He couldn't read the expression on Benedetto's face, of course, but now he didn't care anymore. "Luck is a fickle mistress, Bellini. Even a man of your background must know that."

Benedetto lifted his glass but didn't drink from it immediately. "Yes. I suppose he must." He spoke in a low voice, one that attempted to feign lightness and failed.

The polite thing to do would have been to let the matter drop. As far as Giacomo was concerned, however, this had ceased to be a polite gathering when their host had declined to remove his mask. He licked his lips, gathering the cards back into the pack, then met Benedetto's gaze squarely.

"What was it, then? Some kind of accident?"

"I beg your pardon?"

"Your face." Giacomo didn't blink. "Were you disfigured in some kind of accident?"

Benedetto paused for a moment. "What a question. I suppose no one has ever accused you of being excessively tactful?"

Giacomo waved a hand, breezily. "On the contrary, there are those who think me almost obsequious when in the company of those I wish to impress. But I find that it's the tactless questions that get the most interesting responses."

"I see." Benedetto sighed. "Well, you're half-right."

"Which half?"

Benedetto's gaze drifted upwards, so that he was focusing intently on the darkness behind Giacomo's head when he said "It wasn't an accident."

"How wonderfully melodramatic," Giacomo sneered. "It surely can't be that bad. Alonso here goes about with that ridiculous moustache on his face all the time without fear or shame."

Alonso raised his eyebrows. "What a pleasure it is to be your friend, Casanova."

Benedetto glanced between them, his lips twisted into a taut smile. "I suppose we can't all share Signor Sartore's courage."

Several silent seconds passed, then Alonso pushed back his chair.

"Well," he said, "I think it's time for us to be going. We have trespassed on Bellini's hospitality long enough, and some of us have businesses to run."

Benedetto put up a finger. "What about one more hand? I'd like one last chance to win my money back from Casanova."

Alonso glanced briefly, almost imperceptibly, at Giacomo. "I'm sure Casanova knows to quit while he is ahead."

Vico yawned. "I think I'm ready to call it a night. Once I've finished this, anyway." He drained his glass.

Benedetto remained placid. "All right, I won't keep you long. Casanova, how about this? We'll split the pack. Highest card wins. If you win, I'll double your little cache there. If I win, I take it all. What do you say?"

Giacomo smiled. He could feel Alonso looking at him. He ignored it. It was Benedetto who didn't know when to give up, not him. After all, there was no risk that he, Giacomo, would lose, was there? And Benedetto didn't need the money. This was pocket change to him.

If he wants to give the stuff away, let him.

"Anything to oblige a gracious host," Giacomo said, and he reached for the cards. He shuffled them quickly, only glancing down once. Once was enough. Then he put it on the table.

"After you," said Benedetto.

Giacomo shrugged, then reached out to cut the deck. "King," he said. He didn't grin. There was no need to gloat.

Benedetto reached out, drawing a stack of cards. He looked at it briefly before showing it around the table. "King." He didn't grin either.

"Again?" Giacomo felt his heart rate increase.

"I'll shuffle it this time."

"Of course." Giacomo's tone was even, though his throat was suddenly dry.

The pack flickered in Benedetto's hands. He placed it on the table before cutting it. "Ten." Nothing showed behind the mask.

Giacomo twitched but remained silent. He cut the deck.

The face of the card almost seemed to ripple in front of him. He couldn't focus on it properly. A cold sensation was spreading through his body.

Alonso leaned over. "What is it?"

Giacomo flashed the card around the table.

Vico whistled. "A three. You did say luck was fickle, Casanova."

"I did." Giacomo tossed the cards in his hand back in the direction of the pack, looking down at his pile of coins. It was a small fortune but a fortune nonetheless. There was a lot he could have done with that money.

Benedetto stood up and leaned across the table, raking his winnings towards him. When the money was in the middle of the table, he stopped. "Sartore," he said, quietly, "how much would you say Casanova has won from you this evening? I seem to remember that you were betting quite lavishly at one point."

Alonso frowned. "I don't know. Fifty, sixty maybe?

Why?"

Benedetto counted out some of the coins and pushed them across to him. "There's seventy. Vico, what about you?"

The chair beneath Giacomo felt unsteady. "What's this about? What are you doing?"

Benedetto ignored him. "Vico?"

Vico concentrated. "I think… a hundred, or thereabouts."

"And I'd say maybe eighty for you, Maestri, is that right?"

"Ninety." Maestri spoke up quickly. "Ninety at least."

"Just as you say," Benedetto responded, smoothly. He started counting.

Giacomo stood up. "Well, this has been diverting," he said, careful to keep his voice from shaking. "But I do think it's time to go."

"Not so fast, Casanova," said Maestri. "Bellini, what's all this about?"

Benedetto finished counting and pushed the last pile of money over to Maestri. Then he lifted his head and briefly regarded Giacomo before looking around at the others.

"Casanova has been cheating," he said. "I am redressing the balance." He smiled. "Do have a safe journey home, gentlemen."

Benedetto watched the boat leave from an upper-storey window. He lingered there for some time, staring at the dark water even after the lantern Alonso had carried out with him faded into the distance.

I don't know why I did that.

He had come up against swindlers before, of course. Men who would travel to a secluded island at unsociable hours in order to play at cards tended not to be the sort of people who were welcome in polite society. But at least they would come. He tried not to think about what that said about the depths of his loneliness. He couldn't leave the island, and the only people who would come to him were the kind of people who would follow the smell of money anywhere. But at least they came.

It had been an expensive hobby for him, at first. He'd learned most of the rules from books and most of the actual technique the hard way, by copying the people that beat him. He knew how to win now, mostly because he'd been able to afford to lose enough times to find out. As for cheats, he seldom noticed them. That meant either that Rambaldo, his agent, was digging up the most honest lowlifes in Venice to come and play with him—unlikely—or that Benedetto simply didn't know how to catch them. But he had never come up against anything quite as brazen as Giacomo Casanova. Benedetto didn't know if Giacomo had been drunk or arrogant or, perhaps, some potent combination of the two, but his technique had been appalling. A child could have caught him in the act.

Still, now that the adrenaline and alcohol were beginning to wear off, Benedetto wondered if he could have handled it better. A quiet word in Giacomo's ear, perhaps, or simply ending the game early. Indeed, these possibilities had crossed his mind when he had first noticed what his guest was up to, but something had stopped him. Perhaps it was curiosity about how far Giacomo would go. Perhaps it was that Benedetto's own pride had been wounded, and he was trying to think of the best way to even the score.

Yes, that's probably it.

He had expected Giacomo to become angry, even a little violent, upon being exposed. Instead, he had fallen completely silent, his face dark and still. Perhaps it was a lucky escape, but Benedetto didn't feel lucky. He felt… uneasy. Though possibly not as uneasy as Giacomo would be, sitting in that boat with the rest of the people he'd conned.

Benedetto made his way back downstairs. His precise footsteps on the marble steps echoed around the empty stairwell. It was a sad, sinister noise, one he could usually block out. On reaching the floor below he crossed quickly to the door that led into the drawing room and surveyed the mess. It was, it had to be said, mostly bottles. The pack of cards lay as Giacomo had left it, sprawled across the table. Benedetto swept them all together, squaring the corners. Tomorrow he would go through and count them. For now, though, he gathered up the bottles and carried them to the kitchen, where he set about rinsing them out.

There was probably nothing to worry about. What was the worst that could happen?

Or, to put it another way, what could Casanova possibly do that would be worse than what's already happened?

He got a kind of grim satisfaction from thinking like that.

He set the last bottle down on the counter. It was too

late now, but first thing in the morning he would go and deadhead something in the garden. That usually provided solace in times like this.

Giacomo had almost certainly had worse journeys than the one he was having now, but none that came readily to mind.

The boat was a *burchiello*, a luxurious passenger vessel featuring plush seats and rich upholstery, but Giacomo found himself distinctly uncomfortable aboard it. There was a sense of simmering hostility in the air. He kept catching Vico and Maestri glowering at him from the opposite end of the cabin, and none of his attempts at making airy conversation had met with success. Even Alonso had shown him little pity, apart from sitting next to him. Alonso was a decent sort, in his own way, but he could sense which way the wind was blowing and, at the moment, it was blowing in a distinctly anti-Giacomo direction.

The only blessing, though it was a small one, was that no one was speaking. That was likely owing to the presence of the two rowers, who steered the grand craft silently and steadily back across the lagoon, towards the light of the city. It was bright tonight. That was *Carnevale*. That was what Giacomo had been missing out on for this night of humiliation. The thought made him sick.

It made sense that Bellini had to hire opulent boats for his guests. It had seemed generous at first, but Giacomo was coming to realise now that mere transport was poor compensation for an evening in that man's company.

They were nearing the city now. The boat turned, gliding up a quiet canal that Giacomo thought he recognised. Relief washed over him. In about twenty minutes, he could be at Bragadin's, close to a warm fire and with a glass of something soothing in his hand. Bragadin might even be sitting up in his study, in which case Giacomo could be assured a sympathetic ear for his story—provided he told it right, of course. Bragadin might have some passing comment to make about whether or not Giacomo ought really to have been gambling, especially with strangers, but he was sure to grasp soon enough that a terrible injustice had been perpetrated.

The boat bumped lightly into the wall of the canal and one of the rowers stepped off to moor it. Giacomo didn't wait: he leapt nimbly onto the pavement as soon as it was in reach.

"Well, gentlemen, it's been a pleasure. No doubt we shall meet again." *In hell,* he added, silently.

Alonso was next to rise. "Yes, I should be on my way. *Alla prossima,* Casanova." He swept a quick bow to the others. "*Arrivederci.*"

It was too dark to be sure, but Giacomo couldn't help but feel that Maestri and Vico still had their eyes fixed on him, even as they bid Alonso good night. Unsettled, Giacomo started to walk away.

By the next canal, he was feeling a little better. The ordeal was over now. While it was regrettable that he hadn't thought to use a fake name, the city was already crawling with worms in human shape that felt they had grievances against Giacomo Casanova. What did a couple more really matter?

His attention now was on Benedetto Bellini. What had been mere dislike for the man when he had refused to take off his mask now became seething hatred. Benedetto had embarrassed him. Made a spectacle of him. That could not stand. It wouldn't stand. Giacomo wasn't sure how, but he was going to pay Benedetto back for what he had done to him—with interest.

He was still consoling himself with this thought when he became aware of footsteps, racing up behind him. A moment later, someone punched him in the back of the head. He reeled, staggering into a wall, and grasped at it for support. He turned around, and had just enough time to recognise Vico before receiving a blow to the right eye. Beside him, Maestri re-introduced himself with a swift punch to the gut.

"We don't like cheats," hissed Vico.

Giacomo would have liked to assure him that the feeling was mutual, but passed out instead.

When he came to, a blurry, roughly-humanoid shape was standing over him. He stared back at it, woozily, for a second or two, then scrambled to his feet.

"Bellini?" The word came out slurred, but he hoped the venom was clear.

"Guess again." The voice was female, tinged with disdain—and horribly familiar.

Leandra. Remarkably, the only person he wanted to see less than Benedetto Bellini.

Giacomo clasped his forehead, peeking out at the apparition from between cold fingers. He seemed to see her in pieces, disparate and disconnected: a crown of ink-black braided hair here, a tiny, corset-cinched waist there. These and all her other features, however, were quickly eclipsed by the dainty, delicate hand that was moving rapidly towards his throat.

"Oh," he said. "It's you." It wasn't up to his usual standards of loquaciousness.

"Yes," she said. "It's me." The hand made contact and squeezed a little. "You didn't tell me you were back in Venice."

"You know how it is." His neck was starting to sweat beneath her hand. "So many dropped threads to pick up, and—" But the stare Leandra gave him—fierce, hard and terrifyingly *close*—withered the words on his lips.

She leaned in, so that he could feel her breath on the side of his face when she whispered through scarlet lips: "Do you know what I think, Giacomo? I think you didn't tell me you were back in Venice because you hoped I wouldn't find out."

"Yes, well." Giacomo swallowed. "There's some truth in that. Not that it isn't a pleasure to renew our acquaintance, of course…" It was all coming back to him now, in raw, explicit detail. He'd known Leandra *very well*, on several occasions. "It's merely that we parted on, well, rather poor terms."

"Did we?"

"Yes." Giacomo was acutely aware of the movement of his Adam's apple against her palm. "You tried to take something that belongs to me."

She'd very nearly succeeded, too.

"So I did." Leandra lifted her other hand, the one not

threatening to close his windpipe, and put it behind his head. She worked her fingers beneath his wig, up the back of his neck to his scalp. A hot, tingling shiver rolled down his spine. She seemed about to kiss him, but released him instead, withdrawing both hands with an expressive sigh. "And I might as well warn you, I'm going to try again."

Giacomo smiled, raggedly, a little of his natural bravado returning now her hand was off his neck. "Then I might as well warn *you* that I won't make it easy."

She gathered her skirts, and started to walk away—so that she was looking artfully over her shoulder at him when she said, "Yes, you will."

THREE

Arriving in Santa Marina a few days later, Faustina found herself unexpectedly absorbed into a large and restless crowd. They were a mixed group: craftsmen and traders from all over the city, unified by the expressions of extreme displeasure on their faces. Faustina knew creditors when she saw them. And, given that the house they had assembled in front of belonged to Giacomo's patron, she thought she could make a fairly good guess at why they were here.

She checked her mask to make sure it was secure. Not many people knew Giacomo had a sister but, in a situation like this, one person who recognised her was one too many.

Senator Bragadin's palazzo was a large one and had been quite striking, when first built, but it was now easing gracefully into a dignified old age. The same, more or less, could be said of its owner. Once feared and loved in equal measure by Venice's many purveyors of wine and spirits, Matteo Bragadin now spent his time giving eloquent speeches to distinguished people—and affecting a look of wan ignorance when any reference was made to taverns, dancing or women named Elena. In fact, these days, as far as Faustina could make out, the one blemish on Bragadin's record was that he inexplicably allowed Giacomo to live with him. It was bewildering to think that any respectable person—even a politician—would knowingly allow someone with Giacomo's reputation within a mile of his home, never mind provide him with a suite of private rooms there. The presence of this crowd, however, made it seem even more inexplicable than usual.

Bragadin was standing on the palazzo's front steps, flanked by servants, staring out over the seething assemblage and looking alarmed.

"I say," he said, "what's the meaning of this? Haven't you all got homes to go to?"

Faustina took a moment to survey the people around her in a little more detail. Most of them looked harmless, if severely peeved. However, one cluster of particularly sinister-looking individuals gave her pause. They were large, muscular men, one with a spectacularly bushy moustache, who looked as though they held strong opinions and liked to express them through the medium of punching. Looking at them, she began to see why Giacomo had taken such a sudden interest in touring Europe two years earlier.

"Casanova!" yelled a voice from somewhere in the human ocean between her and the house. "We want

Casanova!"

"Well, you shan't have him here," replied Bragadin, in a measured tone. "I don't know any Casanova."

"Everyone knows Casanova!"

The anonymous voice had a point. Even Bragadin was forced to concede it.

"Well, naturally, I know *of* Casanova," he amended. "But I am not personally acquainted with him, nor am I aware of his whereabouts. *Buon giorno,* gentlemen." And, turning smartly on his heel, he retreated into the house. The servants, somewhat nervously, closed ranks.

This is a problem.

Even if the servants wanted to admit her—and it was probably not, she had to concede, in their interest to admit a woman presenting herself as the sister of a man allegedly not known at this address—they would find it very difficult to do so without admitting any unwelcome guests along with her. Even at this distance, she could tell that the mood at the front of the crowd was turning ugly, and the sinister individuals had started cracking their knuckles in a businesslike fashion.

She peered down again at the crumpled note in her hand. Written in Giacomo's distinctively-flourished script, it read simply:

Faustina. Need you urgently. Bragadin's, noon. Giacomo.

It wouldn't have killed him, she felt, to include a word or two of warning.

Someone tapped her on the shoulder. "Signorina Casanova?" whispered a voice.

Faustina turned to face a woman in a plain, clean dress, with a white apron tied around her waist. She looked to be around thirty, and she was the fierce sort of pretty that Faustina had often admired from a safe distance.

"Who wants to know?" Faustina demanded, surprise rendering her a little combative.

"I am a maid in the senator's house, signorina. Your brother sent me to fetch you. I can get you inside, if you'll follow me?"

"Oh." Faustina cleared her throat, waiting for her heartbeat to slow. "I'm sorry, I wasn't expecting—I mean, of course. Lead the way." She felt guilty, now, for thinking Giacomo had left her to battle her way into the house unaided.

The maid gave a bobbed curtsey, without breaking eye contact—respectful, but not *too* respectful. She was probably unsure exactly what status ought to be afforded to the poor relatives of a noted degenerate mysteriously adopted by a gentleman. Understandable, in Faustina's opinion.

"I'm afraid," the maid noted, "that we shall have to take a fairly indirect route to avoid attracting attention."

Faustina shrugged. "That works for me." She followed her new companion out of the little *campo* at the front of Bragadin's house and along a narrow side-street that ran parallel to the canal. From there, they veered off in a direction that Faustina was sure would lead them irrevocably away from the house, but a sudden dodge down an alley brought it back into view.

She sensed that the maid would have been happy to walk in silence, but she couldn't stand it herself for more than a few minutes.

"So," she said, once reassured that she wasn't being led astray, "what's it like working for my brother?"

The maid glanced over her shoulder. "I don't understand the question."

"Well, I don't see a lot of him. I wondered what he's like, you know, at home."

"I see." Her companion seemed to consider this for a moment. Then she said, "He's made quite an impression on the staff."

Faustina shuddered. "Especially the women, I imagine?"

The maid slowed to a halt beside a well-used door. "No, not just the women. Many people are afraid of him."

"Afraid?" Faustina almost tripped over her own feet. She hadn't been expecting that. Giacomo was many things, but he wasn't *dangerous*. She felt an overwhelming urge to defend him, but forced herself to wait to hear the charge. "What are they afraid of?"

"The influence he has over Senator Bragadin. Some of them call it unnatural."

"Oh!" Relief quashed the growing flames of sisterly alarm. "Well, that's nothing. Giacomo's just charming. He gets what he wants out of everybody."

Superstition again. It was everywhere! While she certainly wouldn't have put it past her brother to claim to be some kind of magician if the whim took him, that was hardly an excuse for anyone to take him seriously.

The maid shrugged, then reached for the door. She looked as though the conversation were boring her. Faustina, however, wanted to pursue it.

"Are *you* afraid of him?" she asked.

"Of Signor Casanova?" A note of amusement crept into the woman's voice. "Certainly not."

"Do you, um—" Faustina realised too late that she didn't know what she was asking. "Do you know him very well?"

"We are useful to one another, for the moment." Her expression was inscrutable. "I'm prepared to run any errands that he doesn't want the senator to know about—for a price, of course." She unlatched the door, then turned back with a slightly artificial smile. "That reminds me—"

Faustina had a sudden sinking feeling. "Yes?"

"He said you'd be able to cover my fee this time."

She gave a hollow laugh. "Did he. Well, I've got five *soldi*, will that do?"

"If that's what you have."

Faustina gave her a sidelong look as she dug into her own pocket. She was starting to feel a certain kinship with this woman, though it didn't ease the pain of handing over the coins. "Here."

The hand that accepted the coins snapped shut and withdrew. "The stairs are to your right. Keep going until you reach the top."

Faustina flashed her striking companion a smile. "It was nice meeting you."

She didn't get a response.

The door at the top of the stairs was locked. She knocked on it, but no answer came. She cleared her throat.

"Giacomo, I know you're in there. It's Faustina."

She heard movement inside. A moment later, the door

opened. A hand reached out and grabbed her by the wrist, pulling her into an unlit room. The door closed behind her and she pulled away, indignant.

"Giacomo, what are you doing?"

There was movement in the shadows. "You're late."

Faustina blinked, still waiting for her eyes to adjust to the darkness. She waved the note at him. "You said noon."

"Yes," Giacomo said, "and it's a quarter past already."

"You can thank your visitors for that. The maid you sent had to take me the long way round."

The floor creaked as Giacomo halted abruptly. "What maid?"

Faustina frowned. "Black hair, very pretty, gives the impression that if circumstances ever obliged her to murder one in cold blood she wouldn't lose any sleep over it afterwards?"

Giacomo resumed his journey across the room. "Oh," he said. "That maid. Listen, she didn't happen to say anything—" he hesitated "—anything unusual about me, did she?"

Faustina took a step forward into the darkness and collided with an armchair, so she sat on it. "Just that the servants here apparently think you're some kind of magician."

"Really? A magician?" He gave a brief, coughing laugh. "What a wonderful notion." He sounded tired. This was not, Faustina began to suspect, the jaunty, carefree Giacomo who had presented himself at the boarding house some days earlier.

She cleared her throat. "I suppose you could do with

some magical powers at the moment, with that crowd outside."

He wrinkled his nose. "They're still waiting, then?"

"In their droves. How long have they been there?"

He considered. "Is the gentleman with the impressive moustache still there?"

"He is."

"Well," Giacomo began, with the air of one embarking on an epic narrative, "I made that particular gentleman's acquaintance last night, when he presented himself to me as an emissary for a tailor in Padua, whom I have favoured with my custom on several occasions and who persists in the belief that I owe him money."

"Yes, it's funny how tailors seem to get these ideas." Faustina was quite familiar with her brother's habits. She was not nearly as surprised that he was in debt to a tailor as she was shocked that he had found one willing to serve him in the first place. That, presumably, was why he'd had to go as far as Padua.

Giacomo ignored her. "Well, I'm facing some rather trying circumstances at present—I'll tell you all about it in a moment—so I told the moustache-bearer that I was in no mood to discuss his employer's delusions. He was extremely persistent. I managed to give him the slip at one point and hoofed it back here, but he resurfaced with half a dozen friends. After that, I suppose, word must have got around that I was back at Bragadin's. They've been coming and going all morning.

Faustina arched an eyebrow. "Who are the others?"

"Oh, an assortment of life's little inconveniences. Mostly creditors, a couple of angry husbands. No one I care to invite in for a drink and a cosy chat. Speaking of drinks…?"

"No, thank you."

"Please yourself."

She heard him pour a glass of something.

"So, what are you going to do?" she asked. "Just sit here in the dark and wait for them to give up and go home?"

"That's what usually happens. Dear old Bragadin is a master of stout denial. You'd be amazed how often that works."

"It hasn't this time."

"No," he admitted.

Faustina folded her arms. "Well, I can see you've got everything in hand," she said, though without conviction. "What do you want me for?"

In lieu of a response, Giacomo crossed the room to join her, taking up the seat opposite hers. He had lit a candle and, as he sat, he held it level with his eyes, casting shadows across his face for maximum dramatic effect. When Faustina saw it, she gasped. What he was attempting to draw her attention to was no ordinary, common-or-garden black eye. This was a masterpiece. Centred on the outer corner of his right eye, the bruise spread as far as his hairline, displaying a spectrum of reds and purples and highlighted in some of the more obscure shades of yellow. Several assorted cuts and scrapes—not fresh, but not exactly healed, either—on the rest of his face completed the look.

She put a hand to her mouth. "What happened?"

He smiled crookedly—Giacomo was always pleased to

get a reaction—and sipped his drink. "Tell me, is the name Benedetto Bellini familiar to you?"

Faustina shook her head. "Should it be?"

"Certainly not. I am very glad that no one has ever discussed him with you. To speak his name too often probably runs the risk of summoning him, as is the risk with so many of these creatures of darkness and depravity. But he figures rather heavily in the tale of woe I am about to tell you, and so I am forced to include him among the *dramatis personae*."

Faustina was starting to feel a little dizzy, which happened to people quite frequently in Giacomo's presence. "Why don't you just tell me what happened?"

"Very well." He related the events of the first night of *Carnevale* to her in detail, lingering particularly over his description of Benedetto Bellini as the lowliest scrap of human waste material ever to cross a decent man's path.

"So, he beat you at cards?" was Faustina's summary, when she managed to get a word in.

"No. He cheated me." He held up a hand. "I suspect, Faustina, that you are about to accuse me of hypocrisy. But there is a distinct difference between the techniques I use, which require skill and dedication to perfect, and simply refusing to show one's face. Our faces were all uncovered and Bellini could read us all like open books, while keeping his own covers firmly sealed. It's cowardice, nothing more, and shows a profound disrespect not only for the art of gambling but also for the art of proper cheating, which is every bit as old and noble."

"I see." Faustina knew better than to attempt any sort

of debate with Giacomo when he was in full flow. Of course, she could hardly censure him for cheating, not with a stockpile of fake horse paintings in her bedroom back at the boarding house, but it sounded to her as though Benedetto Bellini had simply beaten Giacomo at his own game. Cheating at cards certainly adjusted the odds of a good hand in one's favour, but it was hardly without risk. "And what happened to you afterwards?" She gestured at his face. "Did Bellini do this to you?"

"Not personally. He exposed me to the others. They were… less than pleased." He took another sip.

"I suppose they would have been." She kept looking at his eye, even though the sight of it was making her feel a little queasy.

"Anyway," Giacomo went on, "I suppose you're wondering what all this has to do with you?"

"The question had crossed my mind."

He grinned at her over the top of his glass. "We're going to get my money back."

"You mean rob the place?" This was beginning to make a little sense now.

"I mean liberate assets to cover what Bellini owes me—plus our own expenses, of course." He drained his drink. "'Rob the place'. It sounds so vulgar when you put it like that."

Faustina rolled her eyes.

"So," said Giacomo, leaping back to his feet, "are you interested? I'm prepared to make it worth your while—and it seems as though you could use the money."

She didn't rise to the bait. "Well, I'm listening," she replied. "What's the plan?"

He shook his head. "Not here." He crossed to a rear window and opened the shutters. Peering out, he muttered: "Good. They never think to surround the place. They all want to be first in line when I walk out of the front door." He turned back to collect a plain black mask from the top of a chest of drawers. "Come on. Let's take a walk."

They took the staircase that led back down to the side door. Faustina checked the coast was clear before beckoning her brother out into the alley. Crossing half-a-dozen canals was enough for them to melt, unnoticed, into the masked throng of Venetians going about their daily business.

"You never did tell me how you got Bragadin to invite you to live with him," Faustina observed as they walked.

Giacomo turned back to grin at her. "No," he agreed, "I didn't."

"Well, how did you do it?"

"Magic!"

She could tell from the twinkle in his eyes that he was laughing at her.

"No, seriously."

Giacomo shrugged and turned away. "Seriously, then: I think the senator finds me good company, enjoys the little anecdotes I am able to amuse him with and—" he hesitated for a fraction of a second "—perhaps he sees something in me that others don't."

He sped up his pace, and Faustina hurried to keep up. She didn't push the matter any further. It was closer to a straight answer than she'd expected to get.

They made for Fondamenta di Cannaregio, in the

north-east of the city. The street was busy, thronging with merchants making deliveries and locals with somewhere to be. Next to it, the broad Cannaregio canal was just as crowded, lined with moored boats that bobbed a little every time a larger craft went past.

"Where are we going?" Faustina asked, but Giacomo wasn't listening.

"Alonso!" he called. "You've outdone yourself!"

Faustina looked up. They were approaching a *sanpierota*—a large fishing boat, rather different to the gondolas Faustina was used to. A man Faustina vaguely recognised was standing beside it, waving to them.

"Where on earth did you get hold of that?" she asked Giacomo.

"We've got connections," he said, which was about the same as not answering at all. "Are you ready to make some money?"

Faustina was stunned. "You don't mean now?"

"There's no time like the present."

"Giacomo, that's impossible. We'll need time to prepare. I haven't even seen this place—"

"I have. And I've got a plan."

"Well, I've got a plan for the rest of the day, and it relies heavily on my not getting arrested."

"That's hardly the comradely spirit I was hoping for, little sister." He looked reproachful. "Where's your sense of adventure?"

"Where it belongs," she replied. "Held securely under the thumb of my sense of self-preservation." She wasn't sure she'd ever been this firm with Giacomo before. There was something about him, something that worked its way into the mind and twisted thoughts into the shape he wanted them to be. But she had seen quite enough of prison for the time being.

Giacomo tightened his lips for a moment, looking thoughtful, then put a hand on Faustina's shoulder. "I'm sorry," he said. "I haven't been very fair to you." His eyes softened as they met hers and held her gaze for a moment. Then he turned and called to Alonso: "Excuse us a moment."

Alonso inclined his head by way of response. Giacomo took Faustina by the arm and steered her a few steps down the street.

"Listen," he said, in a quiet, earnest voice. "You know I don't like to admit when I need help but…" He sighed. "I'm in a lot of trouble. The money Bellini took from me was sorely needed. You saw all those vultures circling the palazzo but it's more than that. I've got enemies all over Venice. Senator Bragadin is a wonderful gentleman—if a little, shall we say, easily-swayed—but some of his friends are starting to put pressure on him. They think having me under his roof is bad for the old man's reputation."

Faustina snorted. "Imagine that."

Giacomo gave a weak smile. "I know, I know—who's to say they're wrong? But we're good friends, and I think Bragadin values my company. In any case, if he does dismiss me, I'll have nothing. I'll have nowhere to go. The way things are with my creditors at the moment, I could be run out of Venice for good. If I can pay the worst of them off, perhaps that will reverse some of the damage with Bragadin. And, if it doesn't, at least I'll be ready for when the worst happens."

Giacomo's was a powerful, penetrating gaze. It was easy to see how he got what he wanted from so many people. But Faustina wasn't ready to give in just yet.

"Giacomo, it's broad daylight, and these big houses are always overrun with servants—"

"Not this one. I didn't see a single servant in the entire place. I told you, this Bellini's an eccentric. He's got an unholy amount of money—some of which, as I mentioned, is rightfully mine—and just rattles around in the family palazzo instead of feeding it back into the economy where it belongs. He answered the door to us himself, if you can believe such a thing, took our coats, served us drinks." Giacomo shuddered. "It was quite embarrassing."

"Maybe he's not that rich."

"You wouldn't say that if you'd seen the way he was betting."

She gave him a sharp look. "I'm given to understand that people sometimes bet beyond their means."

If he caught her meaning—and she was pretty sure he had—he ignored it. "No. I've made enquiries. He's got investments all over the city, most of them doing very well. He could hire half the servants in Venice if he wanted them."

"If you say so." Reluctantly, she could feel herself beginning to relent. "So it's just him in the house?"

"It's just him. This will be the easiest money you've ever made. All I'm asking is a small investment of your time, and we'll all walk away from this a little richer." He clasped her hand. "Faustina, please. I'm begging you. I haven't been a particularly good brother, I know that. I've been away from Venice too long, and I haven't been good at showing how much you mean to me. But I'd like that to change. If you do this for me, if you help to free me from my debtors, things will be different. I'll have much more time, and it would be an honour to spend it with you."

Faustina groaned weakly, looking into her brother's pleading eyes. She had a soft spot for Giacomo a mile wide, and they both knew it. Even his heavy-handed attempts at manipulation couldn't change that.

"All right," she said. "I'll do it."

Giacomo's face broke into a smile, and he held out his arms, folding her into an embrace. "Thank you!" he said, suddenly as ebullient as ever. "I shall see that you are richly rewarded." He planted a kiss on her cheek, then led her back towards the boat. "You won't regret this."

Alonso watched them return with his arms folded. "Casanova, are you going to get on board this thing or not? It's a two-man craft, you know, and there's the sail to get up yet."

Faustina raised her eyebrows. "Sail? Are you sure you know what you're doing?"

Giacomo rolled up his sleeves. "Of course. We had to get the *sanpierota*. We're heading out into the lagoon, remember? I don't know about you but I don't fancy going up against ships in a rowing boat."

Faustina nodded slightly, conceding the point. At this time of day, the *Laguna Veneta* would be bristling with activity, thick with ships carrying vital supplies to the island city, or exporting Murano glass and other products of Venice to far-flung lands. A relatively small, narrow boat like a gondola would have been at the mercy of much larger vessels. Privately, she wasn't convinced that they were much better off in the *sanpierota,* but pointing this out would only delay the inevitable.

Giacomo peered round the mast at her. "All aboard!"

She stepped off the street and into the craft with an air of resignation. There was no backing out now.

"Where do you want me?" she asked.

Alonso indicated the stern. "We thought you might man the rudder."

Faustina climbed into the boat, eyeing the rudder with scepticism. "I'm not sure about this."

Giacomo waved a hand. "Nonsense," he said. "We'll be fine."

It took a few false starts but they made it to the end of the canal in one piece, having angered the occupants of only half a dozen or so other crafts by crashing into them. Given her lack of nautical experience, Faustina considered this a success. The pressure eased off a little out in the lagoon, where the traffic was on a grander scale: larger vessels, but more spaced out. As Venice began to shrink behind them, she found that she was starting to get the hang of it.

With the sail under control—Alonso, it had to be said, appeared to be doing most of the work—Giacomo ducked beneath it and came to join her. The wind caught his hair, pulling it free of its loose binding, and flapped the collar of his open shirt. The look of a dignified captain at rest on his ship was marred slightly by the black eye, which somehow looked even worse in the daylight.

"Well," he said, "I think this is actually rather pleasant."

"I suppose so." Faustina looked around. The broad, flat expanse of the *Laguna Veneta* was shimmering in the afternoon light. Between the merchant and passenger ships that clustered round the city, she could make out several ruggedly-shaped islands dotted throughout the lagoon, little green bumps in the water's glassy surface.

"Which one is it?" she asked.

Giacomo indicated one. "We're nearly there."

Faustina squinted. She could just about see a building: red-bricked and generously-proportioned. "So, what's the plan?" she asked Giacomo. "One of you keeps Bellini talking while I sneak round the back and look for a way in?"

"Nothing so prosaic." He sniffed. "Bellini thinks he's bested me. He needs to be sent a message. A simple smash-and-grab won't do."

Faustina scrutinised her brother, taking in the narrowed eyes and folded arms. "This isn't about the money, is it?"

Giacomo didn't answer. Before she could question him further, Alonso shouted from the front of the boat. He wasn't addressing either of the Casanovas.

"Hoy!"

Faustina noticed then that they had drifted very close to a cargo ship. She loosed an oath, making to turn the rudder, but Giacomo stopped her.

"Don't worry," he said. "All part of the plan."

A face appeared on the deck above them—a young man with a slightly rogueish grin. He returned Alonso's "Hoy!" then tossed one end of a long rope down to them. It landed on the deck of the *sanpierota,* and Alonso pulled it taut.

"These are Alonso's contacts," Giacomo explained. "Good, honest seafaring men who know people who know people. They'll give us a fair price for whatever you get. Right, Alonso?"

Alonso had started to climb the rope up to the ship. He made a grunt that sounded affirmative.

Faustina's thoughts had snagged on something. "You mean *we*, don't you?"

"I'm sorry?"

"You mean a fair price for whatever *we* get."

He wrinkled his nose in an apologetic grimace. "Not as such, no."

"Giacomo!" She felt suddenly nauseous, gripped by a potent mixture of anger and panic.

He shook his head. "I'm sorry, Faustina, it's the only way. Bellini will recognise Alonso and me, he's seen our faces—more than we can say for him, by the way. If we go back to that island, it'll create all sorts of trouble. I want a clean job, in and out without any unnecessary violence." He glanced up. Alonso had completed his ascent so Giacomo started to climb after him. "Look, it's very simple. You'll wash up on the island, tell him some story about how you got there and get him to invite you in and make you comfortable. One at a time, if you don't mind," he added, noticing Faustina reaching for the rope.

Shaking slightly, she withdrew her hand and he continued, still hanging from the side of the ship.

"You'll have to stop him sending you back to Venice or the mainland right away. I'm sure you'll come up with something. We'll come and get you just before dawn, so be ready." He had reached the top by now and clambered over the edge onto the deck of the ship before leaning over to look back down at her. "I have every confidence in you," he shouted.

Faustina reached for the rope, only to find it jerked out of her reach. She looked up again to see Alonso and the grinning sailor pulling it back up onto the deck. She felt her heart stop. "What are you doing?" she shouted.

Giacomo looked a little guilty. "Ah," he said. "Yes. Well, it has to look realistic." He produced an object. It took her a moment to realise it was a gun.

"Giacomo!" she shrieked.

"There's no need to panic," he called back, "but I do suggest you stay still."

After that, all Faustina could hear was noise: her own scream first, then the bang, and finally the ringing in her ears.

Four

It took Faustina several moments to be sure she wasn't hurt. Her body felt strange, rigid with shock and ice cold, but she couldn't see any blood. The boat, on the other hand, didn't look as healthy. Giacomo's shot had blown through the starboard side of the *sanpierota* from the inside, ripping a hole in the wood. Faustina stared at the water swirling through it. Hot fury ignited inside of her, only to be quenched by fear. There wasn't time to deal with Giacomo now.

Survive first, murder him later.

She counted her options. It didn't take long. The boat was essentially wrecked. Perhaps more pressingly, she was now caught in the slipstream of the ship with no way to free herself, meaning that she was liable to get swept hopelessly far out into the lagoon. There was also the small matter of her gun-wielding brother. She was reasonably sure that hitting the boat and not Faustina herself was what Giacomo had intended, but it was becoming clear that he did not mean to allow common sense or considerations of safety to influence his plan. Her priority now was to put as much space as possible between herself and the ship. One way or another, she was going in the water—and the sooner, the better.

She considered the frothing surface of the lagoon. It was not an inviting prospect.

There was a knife tucked into one of her boots. Faustina believed in taking precautions. She fumbled it out quickly, then worked the blade under the laces of her bodice and slashed through them. Having kicked off the boots, she wriggled out of her skirts as fast as she could, cutting them free when they got stuck. She knew from bitter experience—the botched getaway that had led to her incarceration, in fact—that a gown underwater was as good as an anchor. Finally, she took a deep breath and jumped.

The water claimed her. The cold seemed to plunge straight to her heart, ignoring the flimsy layers of underclothing and skin it encountered first. For a moment, she floated, stunned, then instinct kicked in and she started thrashing. A dark shape dominated her field of vision. The ship was almost on top of her.

She started to swim, though not with any elegance. A few haphazard strokes learned in childhood accounted for the sum total of her experience with swimming, and they had been poor preparation for battling against the current in the wake of the ship. She couldn't look behind her but the lack of shouting and frenzied activity confirmed her suspicion that no one was planning to rescue her. Then again, if the shot hadn't attracted attention from the crew, nothing would. Evidently, Alonso's friends aboard the ship were the kind to be infectiously unobservant.

She focused all her strength, lunging through the water with her arms and kicking furiously. Her muscles protested but she overrode them, barely remembering to breathe as she forced herself onward.

Something scraped across her foot. She gasped. Then it scraped the other foot. A stroke or two later, through the fog of panic, she concluded that she had most likely arrived at the shore. She struggled upright, eager to test this theory. The water clung to her, reluctant to let her go, but she got the best of it. Finally, and painfully slowly, she hauled herself up onto the beach and lay there, panting, as relief flooded through her. Her throat and lungs burned a little from the exertion and her tongue was coated unpleasantly in saltwater but she was all right—or would be, soon enough. She turned to study the water. The *sanpierota* was disappearing fast—only the mast was still visible. The ship had turned away and was making for the mainland. She couldn't see the figures on the deck but she could imagine Giacomo's smirk of satisfaction. Anger rushed to fill the void left by her fading panic.

"Giacomo!" she spluttered, clawing wet hair out of her face. She swore violently and profusely for several seconds, until the supply of adjectives ran out.

Now she knew why he hadn't revealed the whole plan back in the city. She felt foolish. It wasn't as though she didn't know what he was like.

What kind of an idiot gets on a boat with Giacomo Casanova without finding out exactly what's in store?

But he'd never done anything this bad before.

She wrapped goose-pimpled arms around herself, a light gust of wind easily penetrating her sodden underclothes. Looking down, she noticed that her bracelet was gone—lost, presumably, to the churning lagoon. It was the final straw. Hot tears began to mingle with the drops of water leaking from her hair.

I'm still going to have to do it.

The thought bubbled up inside her like foul air from a swamp. Giacomo had lied to her, manipulated her and nearly drowned her, and she was still going to have to go through with his plan. He was her only way off the island—unless this Bellini could be prevailed upon to help get her back to the city, and the picture Giacomo had painted of his character was not encouraging.

And what if he did? Giacomo would never speak to her again. He might not be able to—supposing he came back at dawn and went looking for her when she didn't turn up? It would be two against one, with him and Alonso versus Bellini, but this was Bellini's house—and the way Giacomo told it, he was a man with a grudge. Who knew what awful surprises might be waiting for them? And that was supposing that Giacomo had been right, and Bellini was alone here…

Oh, hell.

No, there really wasn't a way out of it—not when, against all reason, she still cared about both Giacomo and his opinion of her. She would have to do as he'd told her and think of a lie to explain her presence. The truth was hardly likely to inspire a warm welcome. After that? She didn't know. But she couldn't stay here. She was shivering violently already, and it would do no one any good if she froze to death. She picked herself up, fighting against the drag of her filthy underskirt. This wasn't going to be the best first impression she had ever made.

The palazzo was less appealing from this angle. While the front of the house had been visible from the water, the rear was enclosed by a high and somewhat unfriendly wall. There was a gate in it, though it did not look much used, presumably because there was nothing on this side of it but a narrow strip of patchy grass between the wall and the slope that led down to the water.

Up close, the gate was of a solid wooden construction, with a heavy iron latch. This was stiff with disuse and for a moment she was afraid it wouldn't open, but a ferocious jiggle seemed to loosen it. The gate swung open. Faustina picked up her underskirt again, taking a moment to muster what little dignity she had left before squelching into a stranger's garden.

It seemed a little warmer on the other side of the gate, perhaps because the walls protected it from the worst of the wind. That was the sort of thing that mattered to someone who had just taken a dip in the lagoon before lunch.

Lunch. Her stomach gurgled. She shouldn't have thought about lunch. *What kind of idiot gets on a boat with Giacomo Casanova without knowing what's in store and without having lunch first?*

She let the gate swing closed behind her and took a moment to absorb her surroundings. Despite her undesirable personal circumstances, she couldn't help but be impressed. She was in a little square of garden—part of a much larger whole, if the scale of the wall from the other side was any indication, but a compact slice of perfection all by itself. A neat flowerbed ran along each of the four walls, each one holding a row of truculent, spiky plants. Faustina barely spared them a glance. She couldn't. The garden was dominated, overwhelmed by a single focal point.

She approached it slowly, struggling to understand what she was looking at. In broad terms, it was a rose tree, but the words hardly did it justice. It was stunning: a slender stem stretching so high that she had to tilt her head back to see it give way to branches. These were long and graceful, arcing up to gleam in the white light of an overcast sky before trailing almost to the ground, and every weeping frond was heavy with petals, packed densely into fresh red blooms. In short, it would have brought a sensitive horticulturist to tears. Even Faustina, who generally viewed flowers with insouciance, was frozen by it for a moment, unable to move or look away.

She was still staring when the clouds broke, allowing a brief sliver of bright sunlight to fully illuminate the tree. The effect was startling. Catching this ray of light on their contours, the leaves glittered brightly—too brightly, as though they had been polished to an artificial sheen. The flowers, meanwhile, seemed to allow too much light through, detaining it only long enough to imbue it with a crimson glow. It almost looked as though the entire plant were made of glass.

But that's impossible.

Or just highly improbable. A moment later, a tiny breeze disturbed the sweeping leaves and she heard the sound: a light tinkling, like hundreds of tiny bells. It was the sound of countless delicate glass leaves brushing into one another.

Faustina blinked hard several times, trying to clear the mirage from her retinas. But she was still looking at a glass rose tree. Kneeling down, she cupped a palm and swept up a handful of the leaves from the very tip of a branch. They collapsed into one another and she realised that the branches were made up of delicate glass tubes, threaded together like beads to give them a little flexibility. Each one was embellished with tiny thorns, narrowing to a pin-sharp point. She stared at them, equally amazed and confused. Someone had gone to an awful lot of trouble over this.

Why?

Straightening up, she circled the tree, staring at it from all angles. The slim trunk was solid glass, the leaves and branches tiny elements strung together. As for the roses—she supposed for a moment that they were moulded, which would explain why they were all so alike, but closer inspection revealed that they were far too intricate. Perhaps they were individual petals, cast one-by-one and then linked together? Hesitantly, she reached out for one. As her fingertips grazed the cool surface of one of the petals, she barely noticed the hot, sharp sensation of one of the exquisite glass thorns catching her skin. In that moment, she had forgotten everything—Giacomo, the boat, the clammy sensation of wet underclothes against wind-bitten skin. There was only sunlight, and one perfect glass bloom.

Then a deep, harsh voice behind her shouted, "What are you doing? Stop!" And the moment was over.

She turned and found a man slowing from a jog to a halt beside her. He was dressed in an elegant but understated olive-green tailcoat, with a cream-coloured waistcoat and breeches. His dark hair was tied back and he wore a black mask that covered everything above his mouth. He didn't seem happy.

Signor Bellini, I presume.

"I'm—" She hesitated, waiting for her head to stop spinning. She wasn't ready for this. "I'm Faustina," was about all she could manage for the time being.

He shook his head, visibly agitated. "Never mind your name! What are you doing?" His tone was more alarmed than angry, but she didn't care much for his approach.

"I'm… sorry?" It should have been a statement rather than a question but she wasn't sure what sort of an explanation he was looking for. "I wanted to see how it was made. I didn't do any harm."

"What's that on your hand?"

Faustina looked down. There was a thin scarlet line on her right palm. A quick inspection revealed the offending thorn on the tree—a particularly vicious specimen sporting a smear of blood. She wiped it off with a wet fingertip. "It's nothing," she said. "Only a scratch."

This did not appear to comfort her companion. He put a hand to his head, digging his fingers into his hair. "Oh no." Through the mask, she could see that his eyes were wide and panicked. His gaze flickered from her to the tree and back again and he repeated his "Oh no" a few more times.

Faustina swallowed growing unease. It wasn't as though she'd had high expectations about the reception she would receive here, but she had dared to hope for a grudging welcome and perhaps a supply of blankets and hot food. This man was falling considerably short of her ideal.

"It's all right," she said, cautiously. "It barely hurts."

The man continued to clutch his head, apparently unconsoled by this thought.

Seconds passed. In an effort to distract herself from the mounting feeling of discomfort, Faustina took the opportunity to study her horrified host. He was perhaps half-a-head taller than her, fairly broad, and his clothes were immaculate—far more modish than she would have expected to find on a hermit. The mask obscured most of his face, yielding only to his hairline at the top and a high collar and carefully-managed beard at the bottom, and he wore gloves, so that almost every inch of his skin was covered. Whatever he was hiding, he was hiding it well.

Growing bored with this examination, Faustina remembered that she was still wet, cold, underdressed and too far from home. She decided to see if anything could be done to move things along a little.

"Excuse me," she said, having cleared her throat. "I wonder if I could trouble you for a towel?"

"A towel?" He lowered his hand slowly, seeming to come out of a trance. "Oh. Oh, yes, of course." His shoulders dropped. "Come with me," he said. "I'll get you some food and dry clothes."

In spite of her confusion, Faustina couldn't help but

smile. Those were the words she had been waiting for. "Thank you," she said.

He led her through a series of gates into a number of other small gardens. She did not pay these any particular attention. The words "food" and "dry clothes" were doing somersaults in her mind.

They reached the back of the house and he held a small, unassuming door open for her. Passing through, she found herself in a kitchen large enough to cater for a sizable banquet. Copper pots and pans of all descriptions hung on the walls around her. Most of them looked too pristine to have seen much use, though some of the smaller ones were a little worn. There was a fire just turning to embers in the grate. Faustina made for it immediately, crouching down to warm her hands and face.

The man closed the door behind them. "Wait here," he said.

Faustina barely acknowledged him. With the delicious warmth of the fire starting to seep through her skin, the room could have contained a hundred eccentrics or none at all for all she cared.

He left, returning a few minutes later. "Here."

He placed a towel and a pile of clothes on the table, then retreated a few paces as she got up to claim them. They were a man's clothes, good quality ones. She picked them up, then looked meaningfully at her host. He remained impassive.

She cleared her aching throat. "Are you just going to watch, or…?"

A moment of silence passed, then his eyes widened.

"Oh. No, of course not. Excuse me."

He left the room again. Faustina closed the door behind him, relieved, then set about peeling off her wet underthings and hanging them over the back of a chair beside the fire to dry. She dressed quickly, savouring the utter joy of warm, dry clothes against damp skin. The fit was adequate, though the shirt reached her knees before she tucked it in. She pulled the jacket tight around herself and slipped her feet into a smart pair of slippers. She had to shuffle when she walked to keep them on but it was better than the feel of cold flagstones. Finally decent, she approached the door again and heaved it open.

There was a corridor on the other side of it leading, on the left, to a small, narrow staircase. The palazzo's proprietor was sitting on it, staring at the ground. He looked up as she stepped out into the corridor.

"This is much better, thank you," she said, feeling much more inclined to be polite now that her extremities were reaching a more reasonable temperature.

He touched the mask. "Good."

Neither of them, it seemed, really knew what to do next. Faustina tucked a dripping strand of hair behind her ear, trying to think of pleasantries. She supposed it wouldn't hurt to check that he was who she thought he was.

"I'm sorry, signor," she said, in her most cordial tone of voice, "I'm afraid I didn't catch your name."

"Bellini," he answered. "Benedetto Bellini." He stood up. "I don't think you gave your surname."

She stopped herself from telling the truth just in time. The Casanova name often didn't carry much goodwill in places where Giacomo had been, and it sounded like that would be truer here than anywhere else. Besides, right now she didn't particularly want to admit to being related to him.

"Farussi," she said. It was her mother's name.

Benedetto nodded, though he seemed reluctant to look at her. "I'll get you something to eat. I've got a little bread and cheese; will that be all right for now?"

"That sounds wonderful," she said, completely truthful.

Back in the kitchen, Faustina took a seat at a large wooden table—as close to the fire as she could get. She watched as Benedetto cut neat wedges of bread and cheese and put them on a plate, which he brought over to her.

"Here."

She accepted it gratefully. The bread was soft and tasted fresh, and the cheese was strong. Such was her focus on the food that she didn't notice Benedetto watching her intently until she had almost finished.

"What are you looking at?" she asked, in as neutral a tone as she could manage.

Benedetto looked away quickly. "I'm sorry," he said. "I hope I'm not making you uncomfortable."

Faustina considered this for a moment. Under normal circumstances, she would have been happy to confirm that he was, in fact, making her uncomfortable. Just at the moment, however, it seemed prudent to indulge her strange host a little. She decided to change the subject. It was odd—very odd—that he hadn't yet asked what she was doing there. Perhaps he was simply surprised.

"I must thank you for your hospitality. I'd been having a terrible time until you showed up." That much, at least, was true. "I was travelling to the mainland with some friends and somehow I fell off the ship. I suppose no one saw me, and they didn't hear me shouting." It wasn't a great story, but it was the best she could come up with under these conditions. "I was lucky to wash up on an island, especially one with such a kind—" She stopped herself again. She wasn't supposed to know the island was his. "—Resident," she finished.

From the dark recesses of the mask, his grey eyes met hers. They were painfully sad, and Faustina was taken aback.

"I'm sorry," he said. "Really, truly sorry."

Faustina struggled to process this. "It's all right," she said, bemused. "I'm fine, just—" she looked down "—damp. I'm sure I'll be reunited with my friends soon enough."

He stood, abruptly. "I'll go and prepare a room for you," he said.

Benedetto crossed quickly to the kitchen door and closed it behind him. The dark, cool corridor beyond seemed so quiet that his own heartbeat was almost deafening. He stood there for a moment, his back to the wall, and put his face in his hands. The velvet mask was soft against his palms. His thoughts seemed to swarm around him, thickening the air. He forced down a couple of deep breaths.

This was terrible. Living with the curse all this time, he'd assumed that the worst had happened. For it to have claimed a woman on a passing vessel, someone with no connection to him, someone he'd been unable to protect—that was an unprecedented horror.

And yet…

It was that *"and yet"* that was concerning him most of all. If he closed his eyes, he could still see the impression of her face seared inside his mind. Months of loneliness and desolation seemed to hang along the darkened hallway around him.

She can't leave.

She was stuck here, like him. *With* him.

He shook his head and started to move down the corridor, towards the servants' staircase. He was disgusted with himself. This—this hollow shell of a house, full of dust and misery—this was something he wouldn't wish on anyone.

And yet…

He slammed his feet into the stairs, as though leather boots on stone would make enough noise to drown out his thoughts. He emerged on the second floor: the guest suites. He had almost forgotten they were there.

The plain, dark staircase opened onto a grand corridor, with intricate parquet flooring and large windows overlooking the front lawn. It was punctuated now and then by alcoves containing various busts and other artefacts on marble plinths. He barely glanced at them. Instead, he opened one ornately-carved door, then another, subjecting the rooms beyond to a brief examination. The third one was the largest, so he settled on that. He could afford to be generous, especially under the circumstances.

Will she hate me?

The question stopped him in his tracks for a moment. He imagined having someone besides himself to blame for his own situation, and found his hands curling into fists.

Hmm.

Still, perhaps even being hated would be better than being alone. At the very least, it would make a nice change. He sighed. His was a fairly pathetic existence, but it wasn't as though that was news to him.

Remembering what he was doing, he walked over to one of the large windows and thrust the curtains apart. The afternoon had brightened a little and the room welcomed the sunlight gladly, allowing it to slowly permeate long-forgotten corners. Clouds of newly-risen dust seemed to sparkle for a moment before floating back to the ground. Benedetto coughed as he circumvented the bed, making for the doors that led out onto a small balcony. Opening these allowed a light, pleasant breeze to disturb the cobwebs. He turned to see what he was dealing with.

It wasn't as though he had completely neglected the house. There were simply more rooms here than one person could clean—or use, for that matter. He cared for those parts he lived in. The rest of the house was dead, in a way. It had never seemed to matter before now.

Someone had had the foresight to put dust sheets over the furniture. He set about peeling them off, folding the corners inward so that the dust wouldn't spread. He didn't recognise the items underneath. There was no particular reason why he would. These rooms were relics of a time when the house had regularly hosted guests, and preparing for those guests had been the work of servants. It seemed like ancient history now. Still, the furniture he unearthed was in good condition, so at least there was that.

He left the room briefly to retrieve a spare set of fresh bedding and a broom. With the room swept, he spread the sheets out carefully on the mattress, smoothing wrinkles and perfecting folds, then added plump goose-feather pillows. The drapes for the bed—thick cotton, dyed red and embroidered with yellow-gold wool—had been pressed and carefully packed away in a wardrobe, so he hung those up too, balancing carefully on the chair belonging to the dressing table. All in all, as he stepped back to admire his handiwork, he found he was pleasantly surprised.

A perfectly good place to be incarcerated.

He rather doubted that she would see it that way.

After a slow, deliberate walk back to the kitchen, he found his guest snuggled close to the fire. She looked up at him expectantly as he came in, her sharp brown eyes meeting his.

It took him a moment to find his voice. "Your room is ready," he managed, eventually.

She looked faintly puzzled. "Oh. Thank you."

There was something appealing about the way she looked in his clothes. Of course, she had looked like a drowned rat when she had arrived, so anything would have been an improvement. But now, with her dark hair tousled and semi-dried and the soft folds of the shirt skimming her curves, she looked… different.

He forced himself to turn away. "This way," he said.

The servants' staircase was windowless and narrow. He knew it too well to notice the darkness but when he heard her stumble behind him he realised he should have brought a candle. It was cold, too, with its bare walls and stone steps. He regretted not taking her via the main staircase. That was much more impressive. Then again, she was going to be anything but impressed when he told her his secret.

She drew a purposeful breath behind him. "It's very kind of you to take in a stranger like this," she said. "Of course, I hope I won't have to trespass on your kindness for very long, but it's a relief to know I'll have somewhere safe to wait until my friends can arrange to come back for me."

Benedetto felt his stomach twist. *Tell her*, he thought. *Tell her now, and get it over with*. But his mouth wouldn't open.

They reached the second floor. He pushed open the door and light flooded the staircase. He moved into the corridor, holding the door open for Faustina to follow him.

She smiled in acknowledgement, then continued, "I think a night or two should be plenty, if that suits you?"

He frowned. "They'll come here to collect you?" He hadn't considered that.

Faustina hesitated for a moment, glancing out of a window at the cloud-streaked sky before looking back at him with a sudden smile. "Yes—well, I hope so. I suppose they'll have to search the lagoon for me, but I hope it won't take them long to think of checking these islands."

"Oh." His head felt a little fuzzy. There was something a little peculiar about his guest, something he couldn't quite put his finger on, but he couldn't bring himself to concentrate on it. Not when there was so much to think about already. If what she said was true, he didn't have long to tell her about the rose tree. Her friends might arrive at any time to retrieve her and if she tried to leave with them…

No. It was too awful to think about.

She was peering at him closely. "Are you all right?"

He paused, collecting himself. "Yes," he said. "Forgive me." He set off again, leading her back to the grand corridor and along it to her room. Glancing over his shoulder, he saw her examining the elaborate decorations with interest.

I hope you like them, because you'll be looking at them for a very long time.

But he couldn't say that out loud.

"Here it is," he said, pushing open the door to the room he had prepared for her. "I hope you'll find it to your liking."

She walked in ahead of him and looked around. In spite of the situation, he couldn't help but be a little pleased to note the smile on her face as she took it all in. He wondered what sort of a home she had come from. She spoke like a woman of some breeding, but he couldn't quite take her for a society lady. It was hard to picture a woman used only to the finer things in life tearing into a meal of bread and cheese with quite such vibrant enthusiasm.

She turned to face him. "This is beautiful," she said. "A lady could get very comfortable in a room like this."

He dropped his gaze to the floor. "Make yourself at home," he said. He reached for the door. "Excuse me."

Alone in a corridor once again, he clenched his fists in frustration. Waiting wasn't going to make it any easier. He had to tell her, tonight.

Dinner, he thought. *I'll tell her over dinner.*

Faustina chewed her lip as she watched the door close behind her host. Benedetto Bellini was not quite what she had been expecting. The eccentricity was there by the bucketload, of course, but she'd imagined someone louder, brasher, with a false smile and a razor-sharp edge about him. It was hard to imagine this quiet, solemn creature beating Giacomo at his own game. She would have thought that a person who could do that would be… well, more like Giacomo.

She wasn't afraid of her host, not exactly. His actions so far had been gentlemanly, if a little odd. While she knew from Giacomo's account that he wasn't above a little deception, it would have been quite a leap from cheating at cards to causing her any serious harm. But, on the other hand, the short time she had spent on the island so far had thrown up an awful lot of questions for which she was desperately short of answers.

The mask, for instance. He wasn't gambling now, so why was he so keen to keep his face covered? Had he spotted her in the garden and rushed to put it on before coming to challenge her? Or, as she was beginning to suspect, did he keep the thing on all the time, even when he was alone?

And what was all that business with the rose tree? She recalled the strain—even anguish—in his voice when he had discovered her. She could understand a recluse being distressed to find a stranger in his garden but the fact that she had been trespassing hadn't seemed to trouble him at all—just her proximity to the tree. And the scratch on her hand.

She held her palm up to the light, taking another look at it. It really was only a scratch. It had stopped bleeding almost immediately, and was now nothing more than a thin line made up of broken skin and puckering red dots. She couldn't even begin to understand why her host was so upset about it. But maybe there was nothing *to* understand. This was a man who shut himself away on a small island and, perhaps, wore a mask when there was no one to see him. In context, losing any semblance of composure over an utterly negligible wound wasn't *that* remarkable.

Growing bored with examining her hand, she began to absorb more of the details of her surroundings. This was, indisputably, a magnificent room. The overwhelming impression was of light and plenty of it, thanks to a large, arched window that stretched from the floor to the high ceiling. It was framed by heavy velvet curtains, and she could make out a balcony beyond it, ideally placed to soak up the morning sun. Against the wall to her right loomed an elegant, if outsized, four-poster bed: dark wood with a spiral design carved into the posts. Equally ornate were the wardrobe, dressing table and washstand that accounted for most of the rest of the room's contents, though the bed was clearly intended to dominate the room.

It was dominating her thoughts, too. It was hard to believe that she had woken up at the boarding house only a few short hours ago. She could almost hear that big, beautiful bed calling to her, inviting her to take the best nap of her life. She turned her back on it. She had work to do. If she was going to rob this house later, a certain amount of exploration was called for.

Signor Bellini did say to make myself at home…

FIVE

Giacomo parted ways with Alonso and his seafarers at the docks and made for home. Many of the creditors were still there, but he got past them without much difficulty. Giacomo had a knack for avoiding people he didn't want to talk to—with one notable exception.

"*Buon giorno,* Giacomo." It was the exception in question. She was draped languorously over a chaise longue in his private sitting room, a vision in black silk. "Bragadin's made you very comfortable here, hasn't he? I'd forgotten."

Giacomo cleared his throat. Their last interaction hadn't gone terribly well for him: a fact he put down to surprise and the recent pummelling he'd received. This time would be different.

"Leandra, my dear, if you're intending to maintain this maid masquerade as a means of getting close to me, you ought to at least pretend to dust something now and then."

She laughed. "I don't need a masquerade to get close to you. That was for your sister's benefit—and you should be thanking me, by the way. The poor thing wouldn't have made it in here without my help." She examined her nails for a moment. "Mind you, I made five *soldi* out of it."

"Yes, I heard you'd been making certain suggestions to Faustina." Giacomo took a seat himself, making a deliberate effort to emulate her relaxed posture. "And I'll reserve my thanks, if you don't mind."

Leandra's lips tightened. "She really has no idea what you are, does she?"

"That's none of your concern."

She sat up straight, swinging her feet round and lowering them onto the floor so that she could lean forward and give him the full benefit of a wide-eyed pout. "Poor Giacomo," she crooned, her voice suddenly full of artificial sweetness. "You're having a difficult time at the moment, aren't you? Creditors outside, me inside. And this unpleasantness with Benedetto Bellini, of course."

Giacomo stood up again, this time making for the decanter. She'd summed up the situation very well. The creditors he'd expected. Leandra, too, though he had hoped that two years might have been long enough for her to find another target—especially when he'd spent those years taking measures to protect the thing she wanted to steal from him.

But Bellini…

Even now, with his plan underway, the man's name was enough to boil Giacomo's blood.

"What do you know about Benedetto Bellini?" he

asked her.

"Only what you told Faustina." She smiled again in response to his confusion. "Please. I don't need *your* abilities to listen at a keyhole."

"Oh." Giacomo poured himself a drink. It was a matter of urgency.

She got up and walked over to him, standing fractionally closer than he would have liked. Without taking her eyes off him, she lifted his glass from the sideboard to her own lips and took a sip. "It must have been very tempting," she said, her voice almost a whisper, "to do something you shouldn't."

Giacomo poured a second drink. For several moments, the silence in the room was disturbed only by the clinking of glass and the soft *slosh* of pouring liquid. Then he resumed his seat. "I'm dealing with Bellini," he said. It was a very careful answer.

She cocked an eyebrow. "By having your sister rob him? Is that really enough to satisfy you?"

He shrugged. "For now."

"But you could inflict such suffering on him. You could make him spend the rest of his life ruing the day he crossed you."

Giacomo swallowed. He knew what she was doing: appealing to his dark side, to the basest elements of his soul. It was working.

He shook it off. "I could," he said. "But it wouldn't be worth it."

"Look at you, Giacomo." She took a step towards him. "Look at the state of your face."

Giacomo put a hand to his eye, then winced. The

bruising was still tender, and the sight of it kept taking him by surprise when he checked his reflection.

"He did this to you," Leandra went on. "He *humiliated* you. And you're going to be satisfied with a few stolen trinkets?"

Giacomo drained his glass, then glowered for a moment as the fiery liquid coursed down his throat. Then he put down the glass and stood up again. "You ought to stop antagonising me," he said, quietly, allowing a note of menace to enter his tone. "Anything I could do to Bellini I could do to you, remember?"

She smiled. "Yes. But you won't. For the same reason you won't do it to him. Because it would leave you vulnerable."

She was right. Although there was still one possibility she wasn't taking into account.

"Not if I killed you," he said.

But he didn't mean it—and it showed.

"Oh, Giacomo," she said. She'd lowered her voice, so that it sounded like the soft growl of some graceful predator right before it disembowelled something. "You'd miss me if you did." She pulled away, making for the door. "*Ciao, bello.*"

He waited for her to go, then flicked his wrist. Across the room, and well out of his reach, the door slammed. Giacomo threw himself moodily back into a chair. Some days, magic was only barely worth the trouble it caused.

Reasoning that at least one of the people involved in this

burglary might as well behave like a professional, Faustina decided to make her search a thorough one, and returned to the ground floor to conduct it from bottom to top. She allowed herself, however, to give the kitchen a wide berth. She could hear signs of occupation there and feared that another bizarre exchange of views with the man she was trying to rob might break her concentration.

The footprint of the house, she discovered, was a rectangle, centred around a huge, winding marble staircase, the bottom of which faced the imposing double doors at the main entrance. On the upper floors, the accommodation in both wings was linked by galleries that overlooked this grand entrance hall on all sides, so that guests might be observed as they entered without knowing it. It was difficult to imagine this cold, empty house hosting huge, sparkling parties, but it was certainly equipped for them. To the right of the staircase, an ornately-carved polished-stone archway led to an enormous reception room. The ceilings on the ground floor were almost impossibly high and every inch of this wall space dripped with sumptuous detail, from candle sconces just above eye level to sculpted angels endeavouring to hold up the ceiling. The expansive floor space, meanwhile, was broken up with clusters of sofas and armchairs and lined with bookshelves, while a grand piano dominated one end. Faustina's keen eye noted plenty of valuables, all too big to steal.

She found the dining room a much more promising prospect. A cluster of silver candlesticks occupied one end of the huge table, while more silverware—most of which she couldn't even identify—was on display in a cabinet. The room otherwise failed to hold her interest, being cavernous and rather generously draped with dark, heavy curtains that seemed to absorb all the light from the windows. Back through the entrance hall, the other side of the ground floor was almost entirely given over to an immense ballroom. This room was overwhelming, with wood panelling on the walls up to about eight feet and a mural, depicting a view of Venice and the lagoon, covering the rest. But for a few rather isolated chairs, it was completely empty. Faustina left it quickly.

The rooms on the other floors held her attention for longer, mostly because there were more of them. Along the same corridor as her room she found several other rooms that were very similar, each containing a selection of grand furniture and little else. Perhaps someone had concluded that guests were not to be trusted with expensive trinkets, a point Faustina was prepared to concede, though there seemed to be precious few of them anywhere else, either. On the same floor in the other wing she found more reception rooms, including a drawing room with a card table, which was presumably where Giacomo and Benedetto had cheated one another. It was one of the few rooms not swaddled in dust sheets.

She found her enthusiasm for the task at hand waning. Having unfettered access to a whole house took a lot of the fun out of burglary, as it turned out. Besides, while there was plenty of evidence of wealth and status on display here, it wasn't quite the Croesian treasure trove Giacomo had promised, and it was becoming less and less likely that she would suddenly stumble upon a chest of jewels or some other easily-pocketed spoils. This was going to require some lateral thinking.

She returned to the main staircase, meaning to proceed to the top floor, but she had taken only four or five steps up it when she heard a shout.

"Signorina Farussi?"

She didn't respond immediately, unwilling to highlight the fact that she had been snooping in parts of the house in which she had no business. Instead, she padded quietly back down, and waited for him to shout again.

"Signorina Farussi!"

She put her head over the marble balustrade. "*Buona sera.*"

He looked up. "Ah," he said. "Your dinner is ready."

She studied him as she descended. He had changed his mask. This one was a sparkling yellow-gold, with a v-shaped beak that hooked over his nose. Studying it, she discovered that it was in the shape of a phoenix, with wings that swept over his cheeks, delicately ornamented with tiny golden feathers. The bird's head rested on the bridge of his nose, with two tiny black eyes glittering between his own, and a long spray of tail feathers made a sort of crown over his forehead. As with the other mask, only his mouth and bearded jawline were left visible.

Benedetto turned his face away from her, which made her realise that she had been staring. "I thought we might eat in the dining room," he said.

Faustina felt her face fall. After her extensive exploration of the large, chilly house, she had been looking forward to returning to the relatively unassuming kitchen and—more specifically—its cosy fire. The cavernous dining room, which could have contained the house where she had grown up a dozen times over, failed to appeal. Dinner, on the other hand, appealed immensely, and she was reluctant to antagonise the hand that intended to feed her.

"That sounds wonderful," she said. "Can I help you with anything?"

He shook his head. "I'm just going to fetch something to drink. I'll join you there."

She trailed obediently through to the dining room. At the end of the table closest to the door, two places had been set, complete with multiple knives and forks and silver cloches over the plates. That reminded her: she looked around quickly to check that the candlesticks and other silverware she had located earlier were still in place, since it looked as if they were the richest prize the palazzo had to offer. They were. Satisfied, she lifted one of the domes to take a peek at the plate beneath. It contained fresh seafood pasta, blackened with squid ink. A Venetian speciality—not one of her favourites, but certainly better than anything she had eaten for some time. It was all she could do to replace the cover and await her host.

He reappeared with a bottle of wine—a bright, clear white. "Are you ready to eat?" he asked her. His manner was as courteous and odd as ever, but he seemed—if it were possible—even more distant. His mood appeared to have darkened. It was unnerving, but there was a lot Faustina could overlook when faced with a free meal.

"Absolutely," she replied.

They sat down. Benedetto poured two large glasses of wine. Faustina examined the cutlery thoughtfully for a fraction of a second, then picked a knife and fork at random. She started to eat, uncomfortably aware of the sound of her cutlery on the plate and, worse, her own chewing in the huge, echoing space. Benedetto sipped from his glass, not making to touch his food.

It didn't take long for discomfort to get the better of her. "This is very good," she said, to break the silence.

He stared deeply into his drink. "Good." His tone was flat.

She persevered. "I see you've dressed for the occasion."

"What do you mean?"

"The mask." She pointed at it.

"Oh. Yes."

"You must take *Carnevale* very seriously."

He gave her a brief glance before returning his attention to the liquid abyss in his hand. "I'm sorry?"

This was exhausting. "The masks. You're obviously an enthusiast."

He slumped a little deeper into his chair. "No, not really."

Faustina lowered her knife and reached for her own drink. She almost wanted to give up, but she couldn't stand the deafening quiet. "Are you… all right?"

He looked over at her and then quickly away, as though unable to hold her gaze. "There's something I need to tell you."

She took a long drink, trying not to invent possibilities. "What?"

"It's about the rose tree. I don't want to alarm you…" He hesitated.

"Go on," Faustina said, encouragingly, though it seemed to her that there could be very little more likely to cause panic and dismay than a man who did not wish to alarm her.

"I mean to say, it's not a death sentence or anything. I think." He ran his hand through his hair, obviously a nervous habit. "As long as you stay on the island."

An unpleasant tingling sensation began to radiate from the base of Faustina's skull—confusion, coupled with the sense that someone was trying to pull the comfortable rug of reality out from under her. "I beg your pardon?"

He rubbed his beard, shifting uncomfortably in his seat. "The rose tree is cursed. If it leaves a mark on you, like the one on your hand, you can't leave the island."

"Oh." There didn't seem to be much else to say to that.

Magic again? She was sick of hearing about magic.

"I'm so sorry," he said, excruciatingly earnest. "I didn't know how to tell you before."

She tapped the table thoughtfully a couple of times, trying to process this. "But how… What do… I mean…" She swallowed, attempting to collect her thoughts, then tried again. "What are you talking about?"

"The scratch on your hand," he repeated. "It means that you're under the curse. If you leave the island, you'll get this awful, searing pain in your hand. It's sort of a warning, as I understand it. It gets worse the farther you go and, if you go too far, or are gone too long, the curse will prove fatal."

Oh, for goodness' sake.

Faustina remembered her intention to indulge him. It

was probably still the safe choice. This was none of her business. She would be out of here first thing tomorrow—and far more easily if she could avoid upsetting him.

In the end, though, curiosity overwhelmed her.

"Surely you don't mean… that is, surely you aren't saying that the rose tree is under some kind of—" she felt silly even saying it "—magic spell?"

He nodded. "That's exactly what I mean, yes. Although 'spell' hardly seems to cover it. I call it a curse because that's what it is, a malignant enchantment that has blighted my life." He broke off. "And now yours." His mouth was downturned and his eyes wretched.

Faustina's features had twisted so tightly into an expression of incredulity that her face was starting to ache. "But that's, you know… *impossible*."

He laughed. It was a brief, mirthless laugh that echoed sharply around the empty room. "I wish I shared your conviction," he said.

Through heroic effort, Faustina managed to force her face back into a neutral expression. "Is that why you—" She broke off. She had been about to ask if that was why he never left the island himself, but that was something else she wasn't supposed to know. She tried again. "So you're under this curse too?"

"Yes." He sighed. "You will have noticed that I am the only person on this island. I have done my best to keep others away, for the most part. The guests I do have, I watch carefully to keep them safe. I can only apologise that I wasn't able to do the same for you."

Faustina drained her glass. She didn't know what to think. He seemed so solemn, and what he was saying was so ridiculous. Did he really believe this? The thought that he did made her sad. He was a prisoner of this delusion, confined to a small, lonely life on this small, lonely island by a false belief.

And if he doesn't believe it…

That was an alarming idea. She could conceive of several reasons that a lone man who never left his island might concoct a bizarre lie to keep a young woman there with him, and none of them were good.

Either way, there was no sense in pursuing the matter with him. Giacomo and Alonso were coming back for her in only a matter of hours. After that, she intended to do her absolute best to forget that this whole sorry episode had ever happened. To question her host would be to let him know that she didn't believe him, and it would do her no good to antagonise him now.

She turned to find him looking at her again. He leaned towards her a little.

"Is there anything I can do for you? I realise that this must be quite a shock."

She pushed back her chair. "I think I'd like to be alone for the rest of the evening, if that's all right."

He stood up as she did and held the door open for her. "Of course," he said. "Let me know if you need anything."

She made an affirmative noise, without looking back at him. She was crossing the grand hallway to the staircase when he called after her.

"Signorina Farussi?"

She turned, reluctantly. "Yes?"

"I know what I've told you must seem quite

incredible. You will promise me that you won't attempt to leave this place, won't you?"

Faustina swallowed. "Of course," she said.

She took the stairs two at a time to get back to her room and locked the door behind her once she was there. Her overriding feeling was of intense uneasiness, not helped by the fact that the sun had disappeared behind the horizon, leaving her unfamiliar surroundings in murky darkness. She sat on the bed, looking out of the window at a cloud-streaked sky. The weather had deteriorated over the last hour or so.

Giacomo had better know what he's doing, she thought, but it was a forlorn hope, and she knew it.

It occurred to her then to wonder what she was going to do with herself for the next few hours. She would have to wait until she could be sure that her host had gone to bed before helping herself to his valuables. It was a strange and unfamiliar sensation, to be looking for something to do. Life at Ersilia's had brought her many other troubles but never boredom.

She was still pondering this when exhaustion—held at bay until then by confusion, anger, fear and hunger in various combinations—suddenly claimed her. She sat down on the bed, contemplating the pillows.

She knew she shouldn't. It was irresponsible, even dangerous.

But I won't fall asleep. I'll just shut my eyes for a moment…

Benedetto paced up and down the library, listening to the

storm that was in full flow outside, his measured tread wearing a long impression into the floor. It was nearing dawn, but he hadn't slept. Now and then, he ran his fingers along carefully-aligned spines on a crowded bookshelf and snatched up a volume, riffling through the pages before snapping it shut, exasperated, and returning it to its proper place. In short, he was behaving much as he had done on any number of previous nights, but now his thoughts were very different.

Signorina Farussi…

She hadn't believed a word he'd told her; he was quite certain of that. That was reasonable, probably. Frustrating, but reasonable. After all, she hadn't had the dubious benefit of being present at the curse's inception. The memory wasn't exactly a fond one for him—indeed, it chilled him to the core every time he thought about it—but, after what he had seen, there had been no denying the truth.

Sometimes he could still see it: a flash of white light, the first sight of the glass roses in all their surreal, awful beauty. But nothing haunted him like that first glimpse of his own flesh, altered beyond all recognition.

He pulled the glove from his right hand, turning it over in flickering candlelight. He should have been used to it by now: the thick fur, the dark, curved lines of his claws. It was true that the sight no longer made him nauseous, but there was still a cold, prickly sensation that radiated out from his spine whenever he looked at his own body.

He parted the fur around the heel of his hand. The slash the rose tree had left was still there, identical to the mark on Faustina's hand. He looked at it for a moment, then touched the pads of his fingers to his face. He had changed back into the plain mask, returning the phoenix to storage. Even without the feathers, though, his face felt uncomfortably warm. He told himself, for the thousandth time, that he ought to take the thing off. He knew he wouldn't—and not just because he had company. The masks had become a habit, a part of him, and now he felt naked without one.

He hadn't told Faustina everything. He had meant to: walking into that dining room, he had absolutely intended to present her with a full account of the detestable situation in which she had become entangled. But her disbelief had shaken him. Better, he had decided, to let her come to terms with the fact that she was trapped here before introducing the curse's other element. It would be kinder to her. Less overwhelming.

Either that, or he was the most abominable coward in the Veneto. He wasn't sure which.

Still, there was some good news. In struggling to figure out how to tell her about the curse, he had almost forgotten how attractive she was. Those brown, teasing eyes had barely affected him at all over dinner. That was just as well. It was too much, far too much, to expect her to feel anything better than a resigned, dull loathing for him once she had come to terms with the curse. To allow himself to develop anything more serious than a passing fancy for her would amount to self-torture.

He replaced the glove, taking care to work the claws into the specially-reinforced fingertips he'd had custom-designed. Then he crossed to the window, intending to glare moodily out over the beauty of nature, as was his usual habit. Aside from the weather and the waxing and waning of the moon, the view of the front garden from this window had changed very little over the last year: the same shadows and silhouettes, the same distant shimmer in the lagoon that marked the proximity of Venice. But tonight, something was different: a hint of movement on the front lawn, inching slowly towards the beach.

Puzzled, he pressed his masked face against the window, using his hands to block out the reflected light from the candles behind him. Gradually, his eyes adjusted well enough to pick out shapes, then details. A flash of lightning illuminated the shape of Faustina, who was dragging something behind her that looked like a sack. He regarded this at first with pure bemusement but, as he followed her progress towards the water, it soured into something else.

She was going to try to escape.

Six

Faustina had awoken slowly at first, then with a sudden, sick start.

Panicked, she threw off the blanket that she had somehow become entangled in and launched herself out of the bed and towards the window. Dark clouds had knitted together across the sky and rain and wind lashed at the lead-edged diamonds of glass as she peered out. Despite the gloom, though, the faint orange rays of dawn were just visible on the horizon.

She swore, violently. *What have I done?*

But self-recrimination would have to wait for later. She grabbed a sheet from the bed, tugging at it roughly until it came free and then bundled it up in her arms. Then she made for the door, realising only as she began to race down the stairs that bare feet and solid, ice-cold marble were an undesirable combination.

The dining room had been cleared since she had left

Benedetto there, all evidence of their uncomfortable meal taken away. Fortunately, the cluster of abandoned candlesticks was still in place. She spread the sheet out on the floor and placed them on top of it, wincing at every *clink* of silver against silver. Next, she opened the cabinet and helped herself to platters, tea caddies, goblets, whatever she could lay her hands on. The resulting bundle, once she gathered the corners of the sheet in her hands, was far too heavy to carry. Barely breathing, she hoisted the corners as high as she could and then started to drag it towards the door. Now, finally, the polished marble worked in her favour. Her load slid across it smoothly, though not easily.

The grand double doors at the front of the house were bolted from inside the entrance hall. She fumbled the bolt across. To her horror, this produced a loud, squeaking sound—followed, a moment later, by an even louder *creak* as the doors swung open. She stood completely still for a moment, paralysed by fear, but there was no sound of anyone approaching the stairs. Still not sure how much time she had, she quickly dragged her haul out onto the top of what turned out to be a small flight of steps leading down to the path outside the door. She whimpered softly to herself before lowering the bundle, achingly slowly, from one to the next. From the path, she dragged it quickly onto an expanse of lawn. It was tough going out here. The raindrops were so thick and close that they seemed like one continuous sheet of water and the grass turned to mud under her feet. Thunder roared overhead, followed swiftly by a flash of lightning.

This small front garden was outside the bounds of the

huge wall that encompassed the small courtyard gardens to the rear. Faustina found the wall and followed it. She had realised, too late, that she didn't know where Giacomo and Alonso intended to meet her, but she guessed that it would be the same side of the island that they had left her on. Arriving there now, though, she could see no sign of them.

She swore again. Temporarily abandoning the loot, she jogged around the wall, scanning the horizon from the other side of the island. There was nothing to see there, either. She trudged back, feeling strained. Now that her fear of being late herself had subsided, her anger at Giacomo for not being here was growing to fill the vacuum. Every minute that went past was a minute she risked Benedetto wandering out for a late-night stroll and catching her in the act.

Something caught her eye as she reunited with her treasure trove: a light on the water, visible only for a moment before it winked out. A signal. She stared hard at the place where it had been and made out a dark shape that seemed to be moving towards her.

Finally.

She dragged the silverware down to the beach. As the shape drew closer, it became a rowing boat, occupied by a single figure. The figure waved at her. A minute or two later, the boat nosed onto the shore. Giacomo was smiling even though his shirt was soaked through and his hair plastered to his face.

"Where's Alonso?" she hissed.

Giacomo looked hurt. "You wound me, Faustina," he said, "Aren't you pleased to see me?"

Faustina bit her tongue. It was tempting, *so tempting*, to unleash the anger she had been nursing since she'd last seen him, but this wasn't the time. Right now, getting off this island was all she cared about.

"Of course I'm pleased to see you," she muttered. "I just want to get this over with."

Mollified, Giacomo clambered out of the boat. "Well, then, to answer your question," he said, "Alonso is on the mainland awaiting our return, since we were only able to secure this modest vessel for the return journey."

"Hmm." Faustina was looking at the boat—more carefully, this time—and she didn't like what she was seeing. It was a tiny rowing boat, suitable for carrying two people from one place to another but not much else. By the look of it, it did not allow for much in the way of personal space. "We're escaping in *that*?" she asked, somewhat redundantly.

"You needn't look so perturbed. I got here in it, didn't I?"

"What happened to 'I don't fancy going up against ships in a rowing boat'?"

"Who said that?"

"You did."

"Did I?"

Faustina rubbed her forehead. This wasn't getting them anywhere. "Never mind," she said. "Let's just load it up and go."

Giacomo leaned over, pulling back a corner of the sheet to look inside the bundle. "Not bad," he said. "Though it's a shame you couldn't have brought a bit more. Couldn't you have made a few trips and stashed some stuff in the gardens?"

The time to have made that suggestion, Faustina thought, *would have been before you pointed a gun at me and left me to drown.*

Out loud, she said, "Sorry, this was all I could find."

Giacomo gathered the corners of the sheet in his hand. "Let's not let the matter detain us for now. Give me a hand with this, will you?"

Between them they hoisted the loot into the boat, letting it rest in the middle. Giacomo held the little vessel steady for Faustina to climb in before getting in himself. The boat seemed to be sitting alarmingly low in the water.

"Are you sure this is safe?" she asked him.

"Of course it is."

Faustina wished she could find this more reassuring.

Giacomo rummaged around in the bottom of the boat, then got hold of the oars and lifted them into the rowlocks. He used one of them to push away from the beach and the water parted around them with a soft swishing sound. Faustina watched him concentrate and get into a rhythm, then turned back to look at the island over her shoulder. There wasn't much to see, just the black silhouette of the house against the grey-pink sky.

Goodbye, Benedetto Bellini, she thought. She was surprised to find that she was a little sad. Not much—certainly not enough to not go—but a little. Benedetto had been kind to her, if rather strange. There were, at the very least, people who deserved to be trapped on an island by an imaginary curse more than he did.

She turned back to face Giacomo. He looked nervous, which worried her. There wasn't much that made

Giacomo nervous.

"What's wrong?" she asked him, though she knew the answer. Now that they were properly out on the water, the feeling that this boat was not fit for purpose was intensifying. The wind was nothing short of dramatic, pushing hard into the side of the boat and whipping up choppy waves in the usually calm water, and the rain was still coming down with a vengeance. No one in their right mind would set out on the water in weather like this, not in such an utterly unsuitable boat and with no idea what they were doing. But she had never been quite sure that Giacomo *had* a right mind.

Giacomo took a couple of laboured strokes with the oars before answering. "Nothing," he said, unconvincingly. "It's just a little more like hard work with you and the cargo on board, that's all."

Well, if you hadn't wrecked a perfectly good sanpierota…

"Oh," she said. "Can I do anything to help?"

Giacomo huffed, his composure slipping. "That depends. Have you got another pair of oars secreted in that marvellous pair of trousers you're wearing?"

"Giacomo…"

He raised an eyebrow. "No? Then you can keep quiet and let me concentrate."

She folded her arms, looking at the dark, churning water. "Don't talk to me like that."

"What?" Giacomo thrust the oars into the water with a splash. The boat rocked perilously.

"I said 'don't talk to me like that'. This is your scheme, remember?"

"Oh, and I suppose you think I can plan the weather,

do you?"

"You could have planned a better boat." Her composure had frayed, along with her intention to keep her anger bottled up until they were on dry land. "What did you do, make this tub yourself?"

"We'll be lucky to make back the cost of hiring this 'tub' from the miserable little pile of silver you brought out." He sniffed. "I wish I hadn't asked for your help now."

"So do I."

They were still glowering at each other when a huge gust of wind hurled a wave at the side of the boat. It splattered over them, getting at parts of Faustina's clothing that the rain had missed. The boat rocked furiously. Faustina threw her weight against the movement, fighting to steady it. Water swept in over the sides as they dipped below the surface but eventually the rocking subsided.

"Get the water out!" Giacomo barked at her. She did her best, cupping her hands and bailing furiously as Giacomo attempted to push the water out with one of the oars. A moment later another wave launched itself at them, this one landing squarely in their laps. Giacomo yelped.

"What now?" Faustina demanded. Water was swirling around her thighs.

He was staring over the side of the boat. "One of the oars has gone."

"What do you mean, gone? You let go of it?"

"I didn't let go of it, the water took it clean out of my hand."

"So you let go of it."

"Faustina—" Giacomo stopped short. Presumably the thought that had struck him was the same one that had just struck her.

We're sinking.

Faustina felt panic bloom inside her. "We have to go back."

"No we don't."

"The boat is sinking, Giacomo. The only bit of land we have a chance of getting to is the island. We have to go back."

He was staring gloomily after the departed oar. "No, there's got to be a better way out of this. Let's think for a moment."

"I'm not drowning while you think of a better idea." She grabbed for the oar they still had. "Give me that."

He yanked it out of her reach. "Faustina!"

"Fine." She took hold of the bundle of metal in the bottom of the boat. "Then I'm throwing this overboard."

"No you're not." He knocked her hand away. "You get out of the boat and grab the other oar. I'll stay on board and keep bailing out."

She stared at him incredulously. "You want me to get out of the boat?"

"Yes." He adjusted his grip on the oar so that he was pointing the end of it at her. Viewed from a distance it would probably have looked ridiculous but, from where Faustina was sitting, it registered as a threat. "Now," he added.

She gritted her teeth, feeling fury boil her insides. She hated to do as Giacomo told her, but it looked as though she was going to drown either way—and they might as well try *something*.

The boat was too unsteady for her to stand up. After thinking about it for a moment or two, she leaned over the edge and let herself flop out of the boat and into the water. When she surfaced, Giacomo was shouting at her.

"That way!"

She snorted salt water, turning to look at him. "What?"

He pointed. "Over there!"

She couldn't see the oar but she started to swim in the direction he had indicated. She didn't get far. A moment later, another wave hit the boat. This time the craft didn't right itself. Giacomo crashed on top of her, pushing her underwater before she had a chance to breathe. She heard a gargling scream that might have come from her own throat. Everything hurt. She felt Giacomo thrashing uselessly above and behind her and kicked hard two, three times, trying to get some distance between them. The water lurched around her, and suddenly her head was above the surface. She coughed, trying to fill her aching lungs, and looked around. She couldn't see the boat, or Giacomo. A fog of cold, sick horror closed around her.

This is it. I'm going to die.

She felt rather cheated. She had always pictured her own demise as something a little more romantic than a poorly-planned robbery gone predictably awry. Still, she didn't have long to lament it. A moment later, her head was back below the surface. An involuntary gasp took in more water. She tried to swim, though she didn't know which was the right direction.

Then something pulled at her. She tried to scream in surprise but didn't have the air to spare. Strong arms were hooked under her shoulders and she was lifted and dragged bodily over the side of a boat. Salvation—of a sort.

She lay, spluttering, on the floor of the vessel. A firm hand nudged her onto her back.

"Are you all right?" It was more of a bark than a concerned enquiry—and it wasn't Giacomo.

She coughed up a lungful of water before answering. "Yes. I think so." She clawed sodden hair out of her face, then stared up at her rescuer. A mask stared back, black and impenetrable. She was surprised. "You!"

"Of course it's me." Benedetto's grey eyes blazed through the mask holes. "What the hell were you thinking?"

But he didn't wait for an answer. Instead, he reached back into the water and hauled Giacomo out, dropping him on the deck. He landed with a conspicuous *clang* and Faustina noticed that he was still grasping a silver serving tray. Relief suppressed her anger for a moment. At least he was alive.

Benedetto knelt over Giacomo, who was lying face down. "Signor? Are you all right?"

Giacomo spat onto the deck, which Benedetto seemed to take as an affirmative.

He turned his mask-shadowed gaze back on Faustina. "You could have been killed! We have to get back to the island, this is..." He trailed off, suddenly staring at Giacomo once again. "Casanova?"

"Bellini." Giacomo smiled faintly, starting to sit up.

"What an unexpected delight."

Faustina watched Benedetto's gaze flick between her and her brother. "Signor Bellini—" she began.

"What's Casanova doing here? And what—" Benedetto bent to examine the platter. "What is he doing with my silverware?"

Giacomo seemed to make a sudden recovery. "I'm collecting what you owe me."

It was amazing how much emotion could be read on Benedetto's mostly-covered face in such dim light. His jaw was taut, his eyes all but glowing. Faustina felt as if the rain ought to turn to steam when it landed on him.

"What I… owe you?" he repeated, with slow menace.

Giacomo continued blithely. "Yes. I didn't much care for that stunt of yours when we last met. Most ungentlemanly. And I'm afraid I can't afford to lose that sort of money at the moment, so I've come to square things up, so to speak."

"By moving the Bellini family silver from my house to the lagoon?"

"Yes, well…" Giacomo faltered a little. "I will admit that events have deviated slightly from the original plan."

"I see." Benedetto looked at Faustina. His tone was cold. "And what's your connection to all of this?"

Faustina stared down at the bottom of the boat. She had been hoping they would continue to leave her out of this exchange. "He's my brother," she muttered. She managed to meet Benedetto's gaze just long enough to see his eyes darken.

"Oh," he said. He packed a lot of sentiment into the syllable, none of it good.

Giacomo gave Faustina a playful punch. "Don't say it like that," he said. "Say 'I'm lucky enough to call one of the greatest men of our generation my brother'. People will think you're ashamed to be related to me."

Faustina's lip curled. "Oh? Did you want me to keep that a secret?"

Giacomo looked confused. "What?"

"Well, this isn't exactly a proud moment for the Casanova family, is it?"

"You weren't so reluctant to be associated with me yesterday when I offered to put some easy money your way."

"Oh, *yes*." She spread her hands. "This has been the opportunity of a lifetime. Thank you *so much*."

"Be quiet, both of you!" Benedetto snapped. "Casanova, get over there, in front of me. You—" he glowered at Faustina "—sit at the other end. And both of you—and I know this is going to be a challenge—both of you try to avoid doing anything stupid until we're back on the island."

Faustina and Giacomo exchanged glances. Faustina didn't feel like disobeying. She hoped her brother didn't either. Giacomo seemed to waver but, after a moment or two, he manoeuvred himself to the front of the boat. Benedetto rowed them back to the shore in silence. He was better at it than Giacomo—possibly, Faustina theorised, because he was powering through the waves with the sheer force of his righteous fury. She was reminded of the time she had attempted to run away from her grandmother's house with the vague notion of seeking her fortune. Giacomo, stumbling across her as she wandered a marketplace a couple of hours later, had been forced to explain that, while a couple of coins and a pocketful of *baicoli* might seem like riches to a child of seven or eight, it wasn't quite enough to pay for food, board and passage to one of the major European cities. Then he had taken her home, where she was hugged, kissed and threatened with extremely detailed consequences if she ever did it again. This time the hugging and kissing were, thankfully, in short supply, but she recognised the mixture of relief and anger radiating from their rescuer.

Perhaps he really did think we were going to die. She rubbed her cold, wet arms. *Then again, so did I.*

Benedetto took the boat around to the front of the island, where there was a jetty and a small boat shed, hidden from the view of the house by strategically-placed trees. He moored the boat in the shed, securing it with rope as the Casanovas sheepishly disembarked.

"Are either of you hurt?" Benedetto asked, finally breaking the silence. They both shook their heads. "Good. Casanova, you wait here. I want you off my property as soon as the weather calms. Take the boat. It'll be a small price to pay for getting rid of you. Signorina, I'd dismiss you if I could. As it is…" He sighed, heavily. "You'd better come with me."

Faustina wrapped her arms around her chest. "I think I'll stay here with Giacomo."

Benedetto rubbed his temples, then put a hand to the mask as though afraid he might have dislodged it. "You're soaking wet."

"So is he." It wasn't that she was particularly

desperate to freeze in a boat shed with her brother. She just didn't want to let him out of her sight—or, for that matter, spend any time alone with the man she had so recently tried to rob.

Benedetto eyed her for a moment. "Fine," he said, eventually. "You can both come in. But only as far as the kitchen."

They trailed after him, dripping profusely. The rain was letting up now, but the wind was still fierce. Benedetto led them through a gate and around the side of the house to the kitchen door. There was no fire in the grate this time and, although her welcome the previous day had not exactly been effusive, this one was markedly chillier.

Benedetto made straight for the door that led into the servants' passage. "Stay here. I'll get you some towels."

The door clicked closed behind him. Giacomo waited until his footsteps had faded, then nudged Faustina.

"What was that about? He can't get rid of you? What have you done, seduced the lunatic already?"

Faustina pulled out a chair and sank into it. "No. Nothing like that."

"Well?"

Faustina hesitated. She hadn't been planning to mention the alleged curse to Giacomo once they had left the island. While she didn't exactly consider Benedetto a friend, he had been kind to her since she had washed up on his doorstep and it seemed unfair to expose any more details about him—even imaginary ones—to someone who would spread them all around Venice the way Giacomo would. But being back on the island changed things. Whatever his intentions, Benedetto obviously didn't want her to leave—and he was likely to be rather less accommodating now that he knew she'd been trying to steal from him. Not telling what she knew could prove dangerous.

Besides, she and Giacomo would have to talk about something. Her brother hated sitting in silence even more than she did.

She exhaled slowly. "There's a rose tree in the garden, made of glass. He says it's cursed. He thinks that if it leaves a scratch on you—" she showed him her hand "—you're under the curse too. He says I'll die if I leave the island."

"A curse?" Giacomo took the seat beside her and grabbed her hand. He examined the scratch for a moment, then frowned and released her. "Interesting. Do you think he's serious?"

"I'm not sure." She swept her hair into her hands and squeezed some of the water out of it. "I mean, if he does believe it, it's as good an explanation for him being a hermit as any. But it's crossed my mind that he might have some—ah—*other* reason for not wanting me to leave. Still—" she threw her hair back over her shoulder "—it doesn't matter now, does it? We'll just go when he's not looking. He can't come after us if we've got his boat."

Giacomo was looking at her with uncharacteristic seriousness. "You're sure it's a good idea to leave?"

Faustina lowered her hands slowly, searching her brother's face. *What is he up to?*

"Do I think it's a good idea to leave the home of a man who wanted to keep me prisoner even *before* he knew I was trying to rob him? Yes. Yes, I do."

But Giacomo was shaking his head. "So you don't believe in the curse?"

Faustina blinked at him—very, very slowly. "You're asking me if I believe that I'm under an actual magical spell?"

"Yes."

She layered her voice heavily with sarcasm. "Oh, well, *yes, certainly*. Just look at this *grievous magical wound* on my hand." She gestured at the scratch. "Giacomo, since when do you take this sort of thing seriously?"

Giacomo hunched his shoulders, tilting his head forward to massage his eyelids. "There are more things in heaven and earth, Faustina, than are dreamt of in your philosophy."

"What?" She was starting to get that dizzy feeling again.

Giacomo looked up, his expression still startlingly sombre. "Has Bellini told you anything else about the curse? Who cast it, when, what words they used?"

"No. He only told me what I've just told you." She thought for a second. "Oh, and something about pain in your hand. The pain gets worse the further you get from the island until eventually it, I don't know, hurts you to death." She scowled. "I'm not clear on the details. I don't make a habit of taking notes when people are spouting nonsense at me."

Giacomo rubbed his chin. "And he's under the curse too? That's why he never leaves the island?" He straightened up, letting his hand drop back into his lap. "I don't know if we ought to dismiss this out of hand."

She was incredulous. "Giacomo, what is this? You really think I'm under a curse?"

"I don't know. But it might be best if you don't leave the island right away."

Aha. Now it made sense. She was relieved, in a way. Giacomo appearing to take the curse seriously had been starting to rattle her. Giacomo attempting to manipulate her, on the other hand, was so familiar as to be almost comforting.

"If you think for a moment that you can leave me here again—"

Giacomo stood up. "I'm only thinking of you, *sorella*. And besides—" a sudden smile crossed his lips "—there's still work to do, isn't there? I'm still up to my neck in debts and Bellini still has the money he took from me. His reluctance to dismiss you is a stroke of luck for us. It'll take a while for you to win his trust again, probably, but if you can do it you'll have another chance to get your hands on some really good loot, stash it away somewhere—"

I knew it.

"Forget it. The minute this storm blows over, I'm going home. This is the last time you'll get any help from me. You'll be lucky if I acknowledge you when we meet on the street after this."

Giacomo was prevented from responding by the sound of approaching footsteps. He scrambled to his feet and stepped forward as their host reappeared in the doorway. "Ah, Signor Bellini. We were just saying how much we missed you."

A brief, bitter smile flashed across Benedetto's lips for

a moment as he unceremoniously tossed each of them a towel. "Here."

Giacomo rubbed his hair dry, so that it stuck up at odd angles. "I don't suppose there's any chance of borrowing some dry clothes?"

Benedetto shook his head. "I don't think so. I'm afraid I shall have to start being a little more cautious with my possessions." He was looking at Faustina. She dried her face slowly so that she didn't have to meet his gaze.

Giacomo took this lightly. "All right. How about a drink?"

Benedetto gave a curt nod and started to move away from the door, then turned back and locked it, pocketing the key. "You'll forgive me if I don't want the two of you roaming the house unsupervised."

Giacomo raised his eyebrows. "No offence taken."

There was a half-empty bottle of wine on the kitchen counter—probably the one left over from the previous night. Benedetto poured a glass and handed it to Giacomo, then offered one to Faustina. She declined. She wasn't in the mood to drink, nor did she want to accept anything else from him. Something was churning her insides and she had to assume it was guilt. She had been perfectly ready to hate Benedetto Bellini, for Giacomo's sake, but her brother was making it difficult for her to rest her loyalties with him.

Giacomo drank deeply. "Ah. Good stuff, this."

"I'm glad you think so." Benedetto looked at him with disdain. "Perhaps you'd like to empty my wine cellar into the lagoon too?"

"My dear Bellini, you do keep harping on." Giacomo

put his glass down. "I'd like, if I may, to steer your attention to more important matters."

Benedetto didn't exactly sound enthralled. "Such as?"

Giacomo indicated the door to the garden. "Could we step outside for a moment?"

"It's raining."

"Not as much as it was." Giacomo shrugged. "Although I'd be happy to go into some other room in the house if you'd prefer that?"

Benedetto pursed his lips. "Outside it is." He went to open the door. Behind his back, Faustina caught Giacomo's eye.

"What are you doing?" she snarled, *sotto voce*.

He just shook his head and smiled. She got up to follow them out but Giacomo had prepared for that. As Benedetto passed through the door, Giacomo seized a chair from beside the table and shoved it into Faustina's path, so that it caught her abruptly and rather painfully in the knees. She stumbled, and Giacomo pulled the door closed behind him.

Faustina's stomach lurched. Pain, shock and growing panic brought prickling tears to her eyes. She had a very bad feeling about this.

Benedetto eyed Giacomo suspiciously as he closed the door. He could still feel his heart racing a little. This was exhilarating, in a way. Generally, the most excitement that life on the island had to offer was a gull landing a particularly large squid on the beach—or one of his little card games, of course. This was almost refreshing. Not that he planned to write the Casanovas a thank-you note for it.

He didn't know whom to be angriest with. It seemed very much as though Giacomo was the driving force behind this little operation. But Giacomo was a slimy, unpleasant piece of work through and through. There was a kind of honesty to his underhandedness. One expected that sort of thing from him.

But Faustina…

His cheeks burned under the mask, the fur there itchy against his skin. He had been a fool. His horror that the curse had claimed another victim—and, yes, her beauty—had distracted him from her flimsy story about falling overboard. He had given it barely a thought until now. She had seemed so guileless, so helpless. She had seemed to need him.

And he had been pleased at her misfortune. The more he thought about it, the more humiliated he felt by the memory of those thoughts. How naive, how repulsive, to think that she had arrived on the island by pure chance and to delight that the curse had bound her to him. It didn't even ease his guilt to know that the curse hadn't trapped a completely innocent soul, because he felt guilty for thinking that.

She still can't leave. It didn't seem like such a blessing now.

He glared at Giacomo. He was a tall man, but so was Benedetto. They squared up to each other, each barely concealing his extreme distaste for the other.

"What do you want, Casanova?"

The easy amiability that Giacomo had displayed in the kitchen faded quickly, replaced by a look of dangerous seriousness. "I must say, I don't like the recklessness with which you've been handling my sister's safety."

Benedetto bristled. "I beg your pardon?"

"Faustina has just been telling me about this curse. How you could let her waltz out of the house and onto my boat like that, knowing the danger she would be putting herself in..." He shook his head. "It's disgraceful."

Benedetto felt his hands clench into fists. He took a deep breath, exhaling hard. "I was not aware that Signorina Farussi—"

"Casanova," Giacomo interjected.

"—That Signorina *Casanova* intended to leave the island this morning. Particularly, as I think you are probably aware, in possession of a large quantity of my personal property."

"That's hardly the point. The thrust of what I am saying, Bellini, is that it was down to you to keep her safe. Faustina doesn't know you well, she has no particular reason to trust you. I must take some responsibility for that: I'm afraid the account I have given her of you is not a flattering one. She doesn't know you're telling the truth. But *you* do." Giacomo didn't blink. "Don't you?"

"Yes." The word felt heavy.

"And yet," Giacomo continued, "knowing that, and surely suspecting that the situation might easily frighten a young woman into some rash action, you went to your bed and slept soundly, making no attempt to stop her from trying to leave?"

Benedetto felt a surge of some unidentifiable emotion. It was more than anger. Giacomo's accusation deeply wounded a sense of honour that Benedetto had long thought to be in tatters. He reacted defensively. "What would you have had me do, Casanova? Physically restrain her?"

Giacomo glanced into the kitchen through the window, keeping his voice low. "That possibility had occurred to me, yes."

Benedetto was incredulous. "Are you serious? I don't how you and your delinquent sister were brought up but I feel bound to inform you that decent people don't make a habit out of tying up their house guests."

"So they just let them get killed?" Giacomo arched an eyebrow. "I'm not so sure that I want to be one of your 'decent' people, if that's how they behave. What's more important? Good manners, or saving the life of an innocent…" He trailed off, seeming suddenly amused. "Well, a woman, anyway."

Benedetto scowled. "What's your point?"

Giacomo beckoned for him to lean closer. He did, but only barely.

"My point, Bellini, is that this is an opportunity for you to make things right. The storm has eased off. I'm sure I could make my way home now, particularly since I am not, ah…" He showed his empty palms. "… *Overburdened.*"

Benedetto felt uneasy. He hadn't liked Casanova drunk and he liked him almost-sober even less. "Go on, then."

Giacomo pointed at the door, which he was still

holding closed with one hand. "Lock it."

"Lock it?"

"Yes. She'll follow me otherwise."

Benedetto put a hand in his pocket, feeling the keys there. "You want me, someone you evidently have very little respect for, to lock your sister in my house?"

"Yes." Giacomo attempted an innocent expression that did not suit him. "That's how much I love her."

Benedetto extracted the keys. He looked at them for a moment, then over at Giacomo, who nodded encouragingly. Benedetto furrowed his brow under the mask.

Am I going to be dictated to by a man who's tried to both cheat and rob me?

But he couldn't deny that Giacomo had a point. Faustina was his responsibility now, and her disbelief in the curse made her reckless. Perhaps that was understandable. But Benedetto knew the awful truth—and that meant that it was up to him to look out for the safety of his felonious house guest, whether he liked it or not.

Giacomo let go of the door and Benedetto reached for it instead, just as it opened. Faustina had pulled it from the other side. Reacting quickly, he grabbed it and slammed it closed. Still holding the handle, he felt the force intensify from the other side.

"What are you doing?" Faustina yelled. "Let me out!"

"Signorina Farussi—Casanova—" Benedetto began, falteringly.

Giacomo interrupted. "Now, Faustina, don't panic. Signor Bellini here is doing what's necessary to keep you safe. I'm sure you understand."

The wood creaked as Faustina thumped it. "Open this door, or I'll..." She trailed off, evidently unable to condense what she was feeling into a convenient threat.

Benedetto cleared his throat. "I'm sorry, Signorina Casanova. Your brother is about to leave, and I'm afraid I can't risk you attempting to go with him." Still holding the door fast, he put the key in the lock and turned it. A second later, a crash, judder and slight whimper from the other side of the door indicated that Faustina had thrown herself at it.

"Giacomo!" she screamed. "Let me out! You can't let him do this to me. I—I'm sorry that the plan didn't work out the way you had in mind. But you're my brother! You can't leave me here."

Giacomo leaned towards the door, finally starting to look a little uneasy. "Hush, little sister. Don't make a scene in front of Signor Bellini. Just—" He shot Benedetto a sideways look. "Just trust me."

Faustina's voice was thick with emotion, cracking under her strength of feeling. "Giacomo, please. I don't want to stay here. I just want this to be over."

Benedetto felt a sudden ache inside him. She might have been on the other side of both the door and the argument but her words struck a chord with him. She was echoing his own feelings, the ones he pushed deep, deep down. But he didn't have a choice, and neither did she.

And now they were going to be stuck together for the rest of their lives.

Giacomo put a patronising hand on his shoulder. "Cheer up, old man," he said. "You're doing the right thing."

Benedetto shook him off. He didn't want to talk to Casanova. He didn't want to talk to anyone. For someone who had spent much of the last year desperately missing human companionship, that was a bit of a shock.

"Just go," he growled.

Giacomo touched his forehead in a mockery of respect. "With pleasure."

Faustina slumped against the door. It wasn't going to move. Not with the strength she had to throw at it. Even if she did break through it, Benedetto was waiting on the other side. Whether his belief in the curse was real or an elaborate pretence, he obviously didn't intend to let her go. Not now, not ever. Looking out of the window through tear-blurred eyes, she saw Giacomo make his way past the beds of herbs in the kitchen garden and open the first gate. She turned and ran for the other door, the one that led to the rest of the house. That one was just as solid as the outer one, with a lock just as sturdy. Benedetto was, presumably, worried about burglars getting in. The irony of the situation was not lost on her.

She crossed back to the window in time to see the gate swing closed behind Giacomo.

This can't be it, she thought. *He can't just leave me like this.*

She examined the window. It was comprised of tiny lead-edged squares, each with a thick piece of glass in it. The glass would smash but the lead wouldn't. She pushed on it, hard, but there was no movement. It was embedded firmly in the wall. Tears of rage and frustration and disappointment spilled out over her cheeks and splashed onto her chest.

"Bellini!" she screamed. She could see him out of the edge of the window, still standing by the door.

He didn't leave his post or answer but she saw him lift a hand to his head.

She kept trying. "Please, I'm begging you. Let me go with him."

He was silent. A moment later, she saw him walk away too.

There was no clock in the kitchen so she didn't know how long she was waiting there, except that it was too long. She used the time to cry, hurl the bottle of wine at the floor and, in an ill-fated venture, attempt to escape by climbing up the chimney. The fireplace was broad enough but the chimney quickly narrowed and she was forced to withdraw, aching and covered in soot.

After that, she got angry. Angry with Giacomo for leaving her here. Angry with Benedetto for keeping her. Angry with herself for not bolting through that door when she'd had the chance. By the time she heard a key turn in the door to the servants' corridor, she was sitting on a chair with her elbows on the table, her face buried in her hands.

She looked up sharply as Benedetto entered. He had changed and now wore a smart velvet ensemble in dark sapphire, with a mask to match. He might have been an ordinary gentleman going about his business in the city during *Carnevale,* but Faustina knew now that there was nothing ordinary about him. He was delusional and dangerous, and he was going to keep her here forever. She glared at him as he entered, almost feeling the force of her dislike for him pulsing out through her eye muscles.

He moved towards the centre of the room. "Signorina Casanova, I..." He seemed to suddenly register his surroundings and looked around, his mouth hanging open slightly beneath the impassive mask. "What happened in here?"

Faustina looked around at the mixture of glass, wine and soot strewn over the floor and shrugged. "I don't know."

Benedetto's eyes narrowed. He slowly pulled his gloved hand down over his chin, stroking his beard. "All right," he said. "Then here's another question for you. Just how far did you expect to get in that ridiculous little boat?"

Faustina set her jaw. "Don't ask me, that boat was all Giacomo."

"You got in it."

She scowled. "Yes, well, at that point it was that or swim, wasn't it? I wasn't exactly front and centre at the planning stages of Giacomo's little heist, in case that isn't obvious."

The silver serving tray was on the table. Giacomo must have left it there. Benedetto brandished it at her.

"And was it worth the risk? For this?"

She rolled her eyes. "Not *just* that."

"I know. I looked in the dining room. You've cleaned it out very neatly, I must say." He fixed her with a harsh stare. "Was that silver really worth your life?"

"I didn't know my life was going to be in danger until I saw Giacomo's ridiculous little boat, did I?"

"This isn't about the boat!" His teeth were bared in fury. "It's the curse. This island is the only safe place for you now. You were lucky that the weather and your brother's stupidity stopped you from getting any further. It could have been much worse. Don't you understand?"

"Understand?" Faustina stood up. "I understand that you're keeping me a prisoner, that's what I understand!"

Benedetto let the tray *clang* back onto the table. "You think I want this? You think I'm going to enjoy sharing my home with a thief?"

Faustina was starting to lose control now. The words slipped out before she knew they were coming. "I don't know what you might enjoy. I don't know what you want with me. You didn't know I was a thief when I got here. And at least you're in your home! All I know is that there's three miles of water between me and every friend I have, and the only person who knows I'm here is my swine of a brother!"

His stare was intense. "I see. So, I catch you and your brother with a boat filled to the brim with my property and I'm the one fielding accusations of impropriety?"

Faustina clenched her fists. Between the exhaustion-induced dizziness and fearful trembling, she began to feel as though anger was all that was keeping her upright. "You should have let me go," she said, through gritted teeth.

"Oh, really?" His eyes blazed behind the mask. "I should have let you die? Try to rob me again, perhaps I'll be tempted."

She could feel the tears coming now. She didn't want to cry in front of him. "I'm going to my room." She stared at him as she moved towards the door, daring him to try and stop her. "Is that a problem?"

Benedetto's lip curled as he held open the door. "Be my guest."

Seven

"Signorina Casanova?"

The voice, and the knock at the door that accompanied it, shook Faustina from a reverie. She had been sitting on the edge of the grand bed for what seemed like hours, swinging her feet and attempting to bore a hole in the wall with her gaze. She blinked, but otherwise didn't move. What would be the point? She was a prisoner—and, it seemed, would be a prisoner no matter what she did or didn't do. She might as well stay here in her own tiny fortress of fury as get up and interact with Benedetto Bellini, which was surely to be avoided if at all possible.

"Signorina Casanova!" Benedetto sounded worried now. "Look, if you don't answer me, I'm going to have to come in to check you're all right. I'm sure there's a spare key for this room somewhere."

That changed things. Faustina snapped out of her frozen posture and seized a cushion from the bed beside her, which she hurled at the door. "Go away."

"Always a pleasure talking to you," he growled. "There's food out here if you want it." His footsteps faded down the corridor.

Faustina flopped back onto the taut sheets, so that she was staring up at the four-poster's canopy, and carefully began to examine her own feelings. Her fear had faded a little—and so, despite her best efforts, had her anger. At the very least, some of her wilder conjectures were starting to seem less likely. If Benedetto intended to do her some unspeakable harm while she was here, he was taking his time about it. Her security in this room had been an illusion even before this "spare key" motif had been introduced. Her host looked easily strong enough to break down a door, especially with unlimited time and no witnesses. Moreover, his dismay at having to keep her here had seemed genuine—as it would be, if he didn't have any unthinkable *use* for her.

He had gone away when she asked him to. She appreciated that.

She turned the matter over in her mind a few times, but she still didn't know what to make of it. Realising that she was hungry, she gave up and crossed the room to the door. She lingered there long enough to be absolutely sure that there was no one outside it, then unlocked it and stepped outside.

There was a silver tray on the floor—suspiciously similar, she thought, to the one that had survived the attempted burglary. Perhaps Benedetto was trying to make a point. She placed a similar interpretation on the small pile of books on it which, upon closer examination, turned out to be rather dry tomes about virtue rewarded. But there was a steaming plate of rice and fish in the centre of the tray, and her stomach was growling again, so she snatched up this lightly-barbed offering and took it back into the bedroom.

The only table in the room was the dressing table, so she endured the faintly disorientating experience of eating a meal while trying to avoid eye contact with her own reflection in the mirror. This, more than anything else she had been through so far, drove home the loneliness of her situation. She was used to busy meals at the boarding house, to squabbling with her fellow residents over meagre portions of what had always been rather loose and free-form riffs, on Ersilia's part, around the theme of food. Here, the meals were infinitely more edible, but she was very surprised to find herself missing the company.

She wondered what Ersilia would be making of her disappearance so far. Not much, probably. Ersilia usually heard when one of her residents had gone to prison—after all, she knew almost every criminal, vagabond and ne'er-do-well in the city—and put their things into storage for them. For a price, of course. But this wouldn't be the first time someone had disappeared without a trace. Most likely she would wait a week or two, increasing Faustina's rent debt as the whim took her, then re-let the room and sell anything she found in it. The thought sent a twinge down Faustina's spine, but she had to admit that it wasn't much of a loss. Most of what she had was stolen anyway. The sale of their family home had parted the Casanova children from any mementos they might have liked to keep and, since then, she had more or less given up on sentimental attachments. The bracelet had been an exception.

And look how that turned out.

It had been a silly thing to keep. She hated that she was mourning it.

Having finished her meal, Faustina got up and crossed to the balcony, throwing open the doors. A light sound of bird song fluttered up to meet her as she stepped outside. In spite of everything, she couldn't help but love this bedroom—which was just as well, since she was never leaving it again.

Having left the food outside the guest room, Benedetto strode back up the corridor towards the servants' staircase, fixing the marble busts he encountered along the way with the most venomous glares he could muster. This did little to soothe his frustration.

The woman's gall was unparalleled—except, perhaps, by that of her brother. But even Giacomo had received the hospitality that he had utterly failed to deserve with something resembling politeness. Benedetto grimaced. The thought that he was waiting hand and foot on someone who had tried to rob him—indeed, who had very nearly succeeded in doing so—was almost too much to bear.

Then again, what was the alternative? He couldn't leave her to starve to death, any more than he could send her away to be at the mercy of the curse. And he couldn't be completely sorry that she was staying so comprehensively out of his way. After all, it wasn't as though they had very much to say to one another.

There were dishes waiting to be washed in the kitchen, a matter he ordinarily couldn't have put from his mind until it had been dealt with. At the moment, however, his mind felt so crowded and full that the odd spoon here or there hardly seemed to make a difference, so he took a book out into the garden instead. But, of course, he couldn't concentrate. His mind kept drifting.

Mostly, he thought about the curse. He had become so used to agonising over it over the last year that the mixture of anger and self-loathing it engendered in him were now no more than the background hum of existence, but Faustina's presence had introduced a new twist. Now the plot had thickened still further, and he could add to his list of woes a sense of deep regret over what had happened with Giacomo. He had noticed Giacomo's black eye, and hadn't been able to escape a stab of guilt, even as some dark part of him had yearned to blacken the other to match. But, more importantly, if he hadn't gambled with Giacomo, if he hadn't pointed out his cheating—hell, if he had even done so in a way that would have allowed Giacomo to withdraw with a little dignity, Faustina would never have come here.

And that would have been better, wouldn't it?

He shook himself.

Of course it would.

The effect Faustina was having on him—that she'd been having on him ever since she arrived—was ridiculous. Even now that he knew her for the thief she was, knew that she had come here with the express intention of deceiving and robbing him, it never seemed to take long for his thoughts to circle back to her. He wanted to blame it on the fact that she was the only woman he had seen in a year. Under this sort of confinement, it was certainly true that just about any change in the local scenery was enough to arouse his interest. But it was more than that.

In actual fact, he hadn't seen an awful lot of women even back in Venice. There had been plenty of them in his peripheral vision, of course, dancing around him at balls and so on, and he'd been aware that at some point he would marry one. But it had been clear to him from an early age—his aunt had been the sort of woman who could make things *very* clear—that he was to have no hand in choosing this wife himself, and so he had never given the matter any particular thought. Frankly, it had suited him. While he appreciated them from a distance, the idea of approaching a woman he didn't know had always filled him with a deep sense of horror. It was fitting, therefore, that the one time he had done it had been by accident.

He had thought a lot about the woman he'd met last *Carnevale*. How beautiful she had looked in the moonlight, how meeting her had ruined his life—the usual fond reminiscences. And now, just as those thoughts had begun to dwindle, Faustina was picking up where that woman had left off, on both counts. Even in the depths of his anger, guilt and confusion, his subconscious persisted in reminding him at the most inconvenient moments how attractive his larcenous guest was.

In fact, the only comfort to be drawn from all of this was that she had been there long enough that he was now reasonably sure that she couldn't possibly be a hallucination—though perhaps that would have been preferable. After all, how bad could a slow slide into insanity really be?

A day or two later, Faustina had made herself surprisingly comfortable—considering the circumstances. Each evening, Benedetto brought her a candle, a meal and a few more books, followed by breakfast, a change of clothes and some water for her washstand in the morning. Each time, he knocked until she acknowledged him, then left his offering and went away. While it would still have been all right with her if he'd gone and boiled his head, she was pleasantly surprised at this thoughtfulness.

Maybe he just didn't want her to leave the room. If that was it, she could certainly see his point, since their recent exchanges hadn't exactly been amicable. She had managed to avoid seeing him again so far, on the few excursions she had taken in order to relieve herself. But she was bored now, painfully bored. She couldn't remember when she had gone this long without doing something or talking to somebody. If she'd only had her paints, that would have been something.

When she had no longer been able to stomach the books—they were every bit as dire as they had looked—she had been spending a lot of time on the balcony, staring out over the garden. Whatever her views on Benedetto Bellini, there wasn't much that could be said against his garden. Faustina had never seen one like it. What Venice made up in canals it lost in open spaces so many of the city's private gardens were of the compact, walled variety. This garden was a variation on that theme but on a grand scale, with a dozen individual courtyards linked together to create an impressive whole. From up here, it looked like part of a fantastic chessboard, a riot of greenery organised into neat, regimented squares. She longed to explore it. Finally, when her frustration had reached an intolerable peak, she decided to do it—even if it meant risking an encounter with her host.

She didn't see or hear any sign of him on the main staircase, nor in the servants' wing or the kitchen. Passing through the kitchen door, she found herself able to appreciate the details of the petite kitchen garden that had gone unnoticed the first time she passed through it. A precisely-defined flowerbed ran around the edge and she quickly identified this as the source of the fragrant aroma of herbs that greeted her as she stepped out into the sunshine. The square of space in the centre, meanwhile, was given over to neat rows of nondescript greenery. Faustina was forced to confront her own ignorance at this juncture. She knew nothing about plants, and was familiar with vegetables only as they had appeared on her plate or arranged on market stalls, but she guessed that that was what these were.

The space was enclosed by walls, built from the same reddish-gold brick as the house. Proceeding, she had the choice of two elegant, curled-iron gates, one to her left and one straight ahead. She went ahead, lingering at the gate for a moment to peek between the bars before opening it. The next garden was larger than this one, though just as neat. The gate swung easily closed behind her: recently oiled. Her host was nothing if not meticulous.

This garden had been planted for flowers rather than food and smelled gloriously sweet. Only some of the plants were in bloom, but these were spaced carefully throughout the beds, so that the bright colours of the petals shone from every angle. More unassuming plants budded between them—ready, she guessed, to burst into flower as their companions faded away.

A light, clear sound caught her attention, and she realised that she was within earshot of the gently-tinkling rose tree. She followed the sound to another gate and peered through. It really was a remarkable sight. It was easy to see how someone with superstitious leanings and a good imagination could have ascribed magical properties to it. Of course, she had no doubt that any Murano glassmaker worth his salt could have explained how the thing was made, but she still shivered a little as she turned her back on it.

She would have denied it if questioned, but she was genuinely enjoying the garden. Each gate she opened seemed like a portal to another quiet, perfect little world, as beautifully-designed and as carefully-ordered as anyone could wish for. Several contained flowers, though her favourite was one that contained a large pond. Various aquatic plants provided food and shelter for an elegant collection of glistening, brightly-coloured fish, and stone benches were arranged around the water so that one could sit and contemplate it.

She didn't find the next gate immediately. The wall furthest from the house was overgrown with rambling greenery, which seemed at odds with the rest of what she had seen. It had been clipped back to allow the gate to open but still managed to obscure it from some angles. This gate was solid wood, so that she couldn't see what lay beyond. She pushed it open.

Sunlight and a brisk breeze surrounded her. She had reached the edge of the garden and very nearly the edge of the island itself. The *Laguna Veneta* stretched out in her peripheral vision. She stood for a moment, enjoying the fresh, clean air, then allowed her more immediate surroundings to come into focus. She was standing on grass. While it was by no means untidy, this final stretch of the garden seemed to be missing the attention that had obviously been lavished on the rest of it. It was just grass, turning raggedly to muddy beach as it sloped down to the water. She must have run round here the night Giacomo had come, looking for him, but it was much less odious in the sunshine.

There was a spade stuck in the ground by the wall. It filled Faustina with a sudden sense of dread, though she couldn't work out why until, a moment later, she heard footsteps. Unwilling to spoil a pleasant morning in this magnificent garden by spending any time with the owner, she started to move quietly back through the gate, but it was too late.

"Oh," said Benedetto. "There you are."

Faustina would never have claimed that people were

always pleased to see her, but they didn't usually react as though they would have preferred a sharp kick in the shins, either. She drew herself up.

"Should I be somewhere else?"

Benedetto looked away, apparently disinclined to answer. She took the opportunity to look him up and down. It was the first time she had seen him less than impeccably dressed. His shoes were scuffed and muddied and he was wearing a loose white shirt. The overall effect was difficult to reconcile with the austere, gentlemanly figure she had encountered previously. Still, he had taken as much care as ever to see that his skin was covered and, of course, he was wearing a mask. This one was cut from brown leather and, like the others, shaped to cover the face from forehead to cheeks. It was plain enough but, even so, it was a very strange thing to wear while gardening.

She decided to ask. It wasn't as though she had anything better to do.

"What's the mask for?"

Benedetto looked back at her for a moment, then rammed the large, pronged article he had been carrying into the ground, prongs first, so that it stood up by itself. "I believe," he replied, somewhat stonily, "that they're generally used for covering the face."

"Yes, but—"

"I don't want to talk about it." He planted a foot on the tool and forced it into the ground, churning up the earth. Then he changed the subject. "I've ordered you some clothes, so that you can stop ruining mine. I trust that meets with your approval."

She cocked her head, surprised. "You ordered me clothes? How did you do that?"

"It's not a particularly specialised process. One simply indicates to the vendor that one wishes to make a purchase and then supplies sufficient funds—"

"You know what I mean. We're the only ones on this miserable spit of land, and we can't leave. Who did you order clothes from?"

He attacked the ground again. "I have an agent," he said, "Rambaldo. He carries messages to and from the city for me and sees that I am supplied with food and other necessaries. He was here yesterday."

Faustina let this information percolate in her mind. *Another human being! With a boat!* She didn't want to get too excited. For all she knew, Rambaldo believed in curses and imprisoning young women too. But he was definitely a useful line of inquiry.

She coughed. "And when is he coming back? I'd like to know how long I have to endure these absurd garments." In truth, they were physically quite comfortable, but it troubled her to have something against her skin that had previously spent a lot of time against his.

"He'll be back tomorrow, but I doubt he'll be able to get the dresses right away."

She pushed her luck. "What time will he be here?"

Benedetto straightened, a clod of earth suspended on the prongs. "He comes early in the morning, usually." He gave her a searching look. It was Faustina's turn to look away.

Better change the subject, she thought.

"How did you know what size clothes to order?"

"I, er, took the liberty of measuring the article you were wearing when you arrived." He had the grace to look deeply uncomfortable about it.

She winced, not sure how to feel about the idea of Benedetto measuring her underwear. "That's very thoughtful," she said. "Although you could have just asked me."

"Could I?"

She saw his point. They hadn't exactly been engaging in lengthy discourse over the past few days. Something occurred to her. "What happens if Rambaldo can't get here? There must be times when the weather keeps him away."

He paused, wiping sweat from the edges of the mask. "Well," he replied, "there's the vegetable plot in the kitchen garden, and I try to keep a supply of dried meats and so on in the larder, but it does pose a challenge at times. And it's likely to get worse, of course, now that I have another mouth to feed."

Faustina was about to observe that both she and her mouth were more than happy to leave if that would ease the situation, but decided against it.

"That's why I'm digging up this grass," he continued. "I'm going to turn this part of the garden into an enclosure and have Rambaldo bring me a few pigs and chickens, so that I'm not forced to rely on regular food deliveries."

"I see." In spite of herself, Faustina found that she was a little impressed. It was the resourcefulness that struck her. There probably wasn't another man in Venice who had been born into the privilege that Benedetto had and yet was willing to roll up his sleeves and build a pig pen if that was what the situation required. "It's unusual, isn't it, for someone in your position to do this kind of work?"

"My 'position'?" He gave her a questioning look.

"Well, this huge house, all these gardens. I took you for a—well, I hesitate to say *gentleman*, of course, but a man of some wealth."

"Slightly less wealth, if you'd had your way."

"True." She couldn't argue with the facts. "But I've never known a house like this not to have at least a handful of servants about the place."

"My aunt took them to Paris with her," he replied, matter-of-factly. "She was the last person to live here. There weren't many of them left, in any case. I opted not to replace them."

"Why not?"

"I like the peace and quiet—and it saves exposing anyone else to the curse." He looked a little distant for a moment. "Besides, I don't need them, so it would be a waste."

"You've fallen on hard times by the standards of the palazzo set, then? Giacomo talked as though you were up to your eyeballs in riches. I was expecting this place to be built out of gold bricks."

He smiled, faintly. "I'm sorry to have disappointed you." After a moment or two, he seemed to decide that there was nothing to be lost by elaborating a little. "Actually, not that it should concern you, the family coffers are very healthy. My father saw to that, and I have tried to build on his success as an investor. But he didn't spend much time in the house, and nor did I, until—" he hesitated "—my circumstances changed. Since then, I've put a lot of work into the garden, but I'm afraid the house itself has been neglected. I expect to be able to live out my life in reasonable comfort here, after which the place can rot and fall into the lagoon for all I care."

Faustina was surprised by the sudden bitterness in his tone. "You're not expecting to produce any heirs, then? I thought that was all you nobles had to worry about." It didn't occur to her until she had finished speaking that the question might be an insensitive one.

He scoffed. "Yes, well, as you may have noticed, my social calendar is rather sparse, at present. Most opportunities to meet potential partners in the heir-producing business are somewhat inaccessible to a man confined to his island abode, and who—" He broke off for a moment, and looked down at his own gloved hands. Then he concluded, "Card games with criminals are about as far as I can stretch." He said this in a cool, detached sort of way but, when he met her gaze again, the look in his eyes didn't quite match it.

Faustina frowned. She almost wished she could believe in the curse. It might have made all of this easier to understand.

"I should get back to work," Benedetto said, eventually.

"Yes, I should—" She paused, squinting up at the sky for a moment. "Actually, what is there to do here? I'm bored out of my mind."

He smiled. It was unfamiliar, and she wasn't sure she liked it. "You could always give me a hand," he said. He indicated the spade.

She regarded the object with suspicion. "What do I have to do?"

"I'll show you."

It was with bemusement, mixed with mild horror, that she allowed him to make good on this threat. Pigs, she learned, liked to forage for their food in dirt. Dirt, meanwhile, was in plentiful supply underneath the grass. All they had to do was dig it up. This was all news to Faustina. She was dimly aware, as were all the residents of the floating metropolis, that Venice was sustained by a number of farms and fields on the surrounding islands and the mainland. If it had ever occurred to her to wonder exactly what the workers on these farms did with their time, however, there would probably have been no one to ask. In Venice, food came from the sea. Whether it arrived in a net or a crate was of minimal interest. What mattered was whether or not you could afford it.

Benedetto was holding out the spade. "Here," he said. "Can I trust you to use this without injuring yourself?"

She narrowed her eyes. "Yes." She waited until his back was turned before adding, "Though it's brave of you to trust me not to use it to injure you."

He gave a short, barking laugh. "You'll forgive me for not taking that threat particularly seriously."

Struggling to force the spade into the earth, Faustina was forced to concede—at least internally—that he probably had a point. The spade certainly didn't appear to be an ally of hers.

After watching her wrestling with the truculent item for what felt like an age, Benedetto said, "I could show you again if you like."

Faustina narrowed her eyes, scraping sweat-slicked strands of hair from her forehead. "I should be at home at the moment," she told him. "I had things to do there. Things I know how to do."

"I know." Something in Benedetto's tone showed her that her impression that he had been gloating was false.

He demonstrated the technique again and she copied him, this time managing to drive the spade into the ground through judicious application of her foot. It was still a fairly tentative movement but it allowed her to lever up a little of the rough grass, which restored some of her confidence. They worked in silence for several minutes, until Faustina caught him looking at her.

"What?" she demanded.

He blinked, then looked away. "I, ah…" His jaw tensed a couple of times. "Are you comfortable in your room?"

"Oh, yes." She held the spade firm in the ground and jumped on it, forcing it through the earth. "It's by far the nicest jail cell I've been in."

"You'd be the expert on that, of course. I expect you've seen quite a range."

Faustina scowled. "Just the one." She threw a spadeful of dirt in his general direction and was not altogether sorry when it landed on his shoes.

"I find that hard to believe. With the level of competence you showed in robbing me, one would think you'd be in and out of them all the time. Hardly worth keeping a bed of your own, I should have thought."

"I'm having a run of bad luck." She thought about that

evening at the boarding house, when she'd said the same thing to her brother. She thrust the spade into the ground again. "Followed by a run of Giacomo, which is worse."

Benedetto swallowed, looking serious. "You know I'm no great admirer of your brother," he said, "and I'm sure he deserves plenty of censure, but I don't think you can blame him for leaving you here. Not when the alternative was death."

"Hmm." It took a lot of effort not to correct him.

The conversation lapsed and Faustina began to concentrate on the task at hand. She got to grips with the technique eventually, turning the earth so that the bright blades of grass were lost beneath rich, dark soil. Despite the sweat and the discomfort and the fact that the spade seemed to be actively trying to sabotage her efforts, she felt quite proud of her little expanse of dirt—provided she didn't look over at the much larger one Benedetto had dug. She kept catching him glancing at her spade with an air of apprehension, but she decided to ignore it.

It was mid-afternoon before they finally paused for a break. Benedetto led the way back to the kitchen, stopping once or twice to examine a particular plant or to touch the soil in a flowerbed. It said something about him, she thought, that he kept the garden so tidy and organised when there was usually no one to see it.

What would she do, alone in a huge, beautiful house like this, with no one to answer to? Slide down the banisters? Dance around it naked? She wouldn't keep everything neat and pristine and tidy, she knew that for a fact. But that seemed to be important to him. He dressed smartly and kept things in their proper place, avoiding any disruptive influences. Until now, anyway.

A disruptive influence. It wasn't a bad description of her.

She noticed, when they passed it, that he was every bit as keen to avoid the rose tree as she was. His pace quickened as they walked through the adjacent garden.

"Why don't you guard it?" she asked him.

"What?"

"The rose tree. If it's so dangerous, why don't you do something to stop people going near it?"

He reached the next gate and started to push it open, not looking back to speak to her. "I do," he said, "when I'm expecting company. It's Rambaldo who arranges my card games, like the one that gave me the questionable opportunity of meeting your brother, and either Rambaldo or I will always make sure that my *invited* guests do not wander through the gardens unaccompanied." He gave her a pointed look. "As I'm sure you can appreciate, unexpected thieves are difficult to factor into one's plans."

"But surely, some sort of sign—"

"Would a sign that said 'please don't steal anything' have stopped you doing that?"

She followed him quietly after that.

Inside the kitchen, she flopped heavily into one of the chairs by the fireplace, unsure if the resultant squeak came from the furniture or her own joints. Benedetto remained outside, prising off mud-caked boots and replacing them with slippers.

She looked over at him. "So, do the staff get fed here or what?"

Benedetto's lips twitched. "I suppose something could

be arranged, since you asked so nicely. I haven't had a chance to find out what kind of food you like best. Do you even enjoy it if you haven't stolen it?"

She folded her arms. "Never let it be said, Signor Bellini, that you don't know how to hold a grudge."

"At least I know how to hold a spade." He crossed to the counter, where a basin of clean water was waiting for him, and set about washing his hands. "I'm almost afraid to give you cutlery now, since tools in general present such a challenge for you."

"Would it make you feel any better if I starved to death?"

"That would be one solution, yes, but I'm loath to waste valuable space in the garden on your burial."

Faustina snorted. "Charming."

Benedetto dried his hands carefully on a towel, then folded it. "It's been a very long time," he said, "since anyone has accused me of charm. Now, if you'll be good enough to remove your shoes and clean up the mud you've tracked into my kitchen, I'll see about some lunch."

She thought about disobeying. Her whole body ached like she'd been trampled on and the last thing she wanted to do was to get up and clean, but she was afraid of pushing him too far. He might actually refuse to provide her with food and, at that moment, she could think of almost nothing worse. Finally, slowly, she reached forward and untied her borrowed shoes. Some of the drying mud flaked off onto the floor and she noticed then the trail of footprints leading from the doorway to the chair. She couldn't recall ever leaving muddy footprints before.

She carried the shoes to the door, leaving them beside his. She noted, with mild interest, that he had lined them up neatly against the wall, perfectly parallel to one another. She put her own down untidily: a small act of rebellion. Turning around, she found Benedetto holding out a damp rag.

"Here. Use this." The eyes inside the mask were unblinking.

She took it from him wordlessly and set about wiping the floor.

He busied himself around her, constructing a generous platter of cold meats, cheese, bread and fruit. When he finally put the food on the table, it was all Faustina could do not to dive into it face-first. She helped herself with enthusiasm, inhaling the meal with an uninhibited joy that bordered on bliss. It wasn't until several bites in that she became aware of Benedetto's gaze on her.

She swallowed slowly, turning to look at him. "Sorry," she muttered, suitably cowed. "I didn't realise I was so hungry."

Benedetto reached for the cheese, cutting a neat slice with infuriating grace. "No need to apologise," he said. "I'm learning to view our interactions as a fascinating insight into the behaviour of the common criminal. It's like watching some exotic creature in the wild."

Faustina took a deep breath, exhaling slowly, then looked pointedly down at her fingers.

"What are you doing?" he asked.

"Counting. I'm working out how much more of this I'm going to have to suffer through if I live to be as old as my grandmother did. Longevity is starting to look like a serious burden."

He let out a brief, sharp laugh. "Very amusing. Keep going, I'm sure I'll crack and leave you to the mercy of the curse eventually."

"Any time suits me."

He gave her a look of irritation but said nothing.

"So," she said, resuming her meal, "what do you do when you're not digging?" She was becoming very curious about his life here, in a scientific sort of way. "For fun, I mean."

"Fun?"

"Yes, it's something that we lowly criminals have when we're not relieving the obscenely wealthy of a few coins in order to feed ourselves. Surely the upper classes have some equivalent?"

"This isn't all of my work," he said. "Obscene wealth, as you put it, takes management. I have to monitor my investments and my properties in the city. It takes a lot of paperwork and correspondence, especially now that I'm doing it from a distance. The rest of my time is spent tending to the garden—or on research."

"What are you researching?"

"Magic." He poured himself a glass of water from a jug in the middle of the table. "I believe—at least, I hope—that I may be able to find a means of breaking the curse."

"How's that going?"

"Brilliantly." He gestured around them. "As you can see, I'm now free of the curse and am living a completely normal life."

"Ha ha." *Zio*, but he was hard work. She pushed back her chair and decided to have one last go at civility. "That was delicious," she said, gesturing at her empty plate.

"Good." He stood up. "Thank you for your help in the garden this morning. I suppose you weren't entirely useless."

In spite of herself, Faustina smiled. "Thank you for not letting me and Giacomo drown. I suppose you're not a total monster."

He was looking at her strangely. For a brief moment, she found herself agreeing with Giacomo. It *was* infuriating that the mask made it so difficult to read her host's expressions.

"How kind of you to say so," he replied, eventually, in a mild tone. "Are you coming back outside?"

She nodded, surprised to find that she wanted to. It was amazing what boredom could do.

Eight

Later, as evening fell, Benedetto stood at the farthest reach of his island and surveyed the freshly-dug earth with a critical eye. It wasn't much to show for a day's work. He certainly could have got more done if not for the necessity of frequently abandoning his own efforts in order to stop the Casanova menace from putting a spade through her foot. The woman was a liability.

Still, he thought, as he walked back to the house, *at least she's doing something*. And her presence had, though he wouldn't have cared to admit it outside the privacy of his own mind, made the day go by rather faster. One hour spent bitterly contemplating the curse while tending his garden was very much like another. Responding to a barrage of sarcastic remarks, while not exactly calculated to fill one with a sense of blissful wellbeing, was at least something different to do.

There were candles lit in the drawing room and he

found Faustina among them, sitting cross-legged in the chair her brother had once occupied and building a house of cards.

"Glad to see you're using your time productively," he noted.

She didn't answer him, preferring to concentrate on a particularly fiddly manoeuvre involving a joker and the knight of clubs. Her hair was loose around her shoulders and a lock of it had fallen in front of her left eye, but she was ignoring it valiantly. The candlelight made her skin look almost golden, and he was suddenly uncomfortably aware of the great, dark shadow he was casting in it.

Still, he'd begun the approach now, so he finished it. "I never asked what you do with your spare time." He pulled out a chair. "Unless this is it, of course." He gestured carefully at the cards.

She withdrew her hands from the delicate structure, eyeing him through its triangular gaps. "Well, I don't have a lot of spare time. Earning money keeps me pretty busy—"

He couldn't help himself. "Earning?"

She narrowed her eyes. "All right, call it what you want. It might not be what it pleases gentlemen like you to think of as the honest toil that keeps you in palazzos and imported livestock, but we can't all inherit the family investments."

He sniffed. "I begin to sense, Signorina Casanova, that you have something of a grudge against the upper classes."

"You're sure it's not just a grudge against you?" she asked, but she was smiling a little. "No, you're right, I do.

I can't help it. People like you will never know what it's like to sit in a gutter with nothing, so you'll never really know what you've got.

He was surprised. "I had the impression, meeting your brother, that the Casanovas weren't so badly off."

Her cheeks coloured a little. "*That* Casanova isn't." She picked up another pair of cards. "I'm afraid he isn't representative of the breed. I suppose it's all luck, isn't it? That's what makes it seem so unfair."

Benedetto took a deep breath, raising his gaze to take in the distant, shadowy fresco on the ceiling of his ancestral home. "Wealth isn't necessarily synonymous with luck."

Even without looking, he could feel her eyes on him.

"No," she said, "I suppose it isn't. But each goes a long way towards creating the other. Some people work hard their whole lives without ever finding the luck they need to become rich."

"But the rich can't *buy* luck," he pointed out. He was thinking about St Mark's Square a year ago, and a case of mistaken identity.

"No, but they can buy opportunities, and that amounts to the same thing." She sighed, a little too hard. The house of cards wavered, then collapsed. Looking deflated, she started to gather up the wreckage. Benedetto spotted a three—the one that had undone Giacomo all those evenings ago.

"So, your brother chooses not to share his wealth?"

Faustina glanced up. "He's not exactly a miser. He spreads his money around freely, for as long as it lasts. And that's his right, I suppose. There were times I wished he'd spare a little for me, times I thought I needed his help, but I don't feel like that anymore." She fidgeted in her seat. "Actually, until the first night of *Carnevale,* I hadn't seen him for two years."

"Did that bother you?"

She looked thoughtful for a moment. "We used to be very close, but that was a long time ago. If I'd known what he was going to get me into, I might have wished he'd stay away longer."

Benedetto nodded. He saw her point.

"What about you?" she asked. "Do you have family?"

"Not in Venice. That is, not anymore. My parents died when I was young, and I don't have any brothers or sisters. I was raised here by my aunt, then moved to the city when I was old enough. Like I said, she's in Paris now."

She frowned at him. "How old are you?"

He had to pause to think about it. "Twenty-four."

"You seem older."

That didn't surprise him. He *felt* older.

Faustina picked up another couple of cards, propping them up against each other and beginning the enterprise again. After a moment or two had passed, she said: "Painting, to answer your question."

"I'm sorry?"

"It's what I do in my spare time. And in time that isn't spare, come to that. Ersilia's got me forging paintings of horses now."

He raised an eyebrow. "Ersilia?"

"My landlady. She owns the boarding house where I live—lived," she corrected herself. "I've been a bit short of cash lately so she's started accepting equine facsimiles in lieu of rent."

"That's generous of her."

Faustina looked doubtful. "I suppose so. The rate of exchange hasn't really been in my favour."

A thought struck Benedetto and he stood up, crossing to a sideboard. Opening one of the drawers, he retrieved a long, slender wooden box and a stack of paper, which he brought back and placed on the table. "Here," he said, sliding them across to her. "You can have this, if you like."

She looked puzzled for a moment, then opened the box. The item inside was a leadholder: a thin device made of wood and decorated elegantly with fine scrollwork. It looked like a pen, but without a nib. Instead, the end was hollow. In the box beneath it, cradled in a scrap of cotton, were a number of small, thin sticks of graphite. It was an artist's tool, used for sketching.

When she looked up, her brow was wrinkled in confusion. "How did you know?"

He shrugged. "I didn't. I ordered it a couple of months ago on a whim—I wondered if I might have latent artistic ability that hadn't had the opportunity to shine."

"And did you?"

"No." He gave her a rueful look. "Not even with limitless free time in which to look for it."

Faustina was absently stroking the leadholder. "It's beautiful. Thank you."

Her eyes were shining, which made her even harder to look at. He dropped his gaze.

"You're welcome."

She balanced another arch, then lay a card across it and its neighbour. "You can help me with this if you like."

Benedetto held up his hands. "I'm afraid the gloves make that sort of thing quite difficult." It was the claws underneath that were the real problem, of course, but this didn't seem the moment to mention that.

She looked at his velvet-covered fingers for a moment, then at his face. He felt the fur beneath his collar rise in apprehension. She hadn't pressed the matter of the mask in the garden, but he had known that the reprieve would be only temporary.

"You could take them off," she hazarded.

Benedetto swallowed, lowering his hands back to the table. "I would prefer not to."

The truth was that his resolution to reveal the curse's other element was wavering. He knew he ought to. It would go a long way towards convincing her that the curse was real. Whatever she believed about the rose tree, there could be no explanation for what lay under the mask that didn't involve magic, and she would probably be a lot easier to be around if she believed that he was keeping her here for good reason. But he couldn't bring himself to do it.

He knew it was stupid. Yes, it was painful to admit what he had become—to himself, never mind to anyone else. But what did that matter? Who cared what a thief thought of a… *A beast*?

He'd answered that question almost as soon as he'd asked it. *I do.*

He didn't know why. Because Faustina was beautiful,

probably. Not *remarkably* beautiful—he'd seen bright eyes and luscious hair and tempting lips before, and on women who didn't infuriate him every time they opened their mouths—but a little too beautiful to bear.

They sat in silence for a few more minutes, Faustina still concentrating on the cards. Finally, though, they fell again, and she gave up and settled back in her seat.

"How, um..." She hesitated, then tried again. "How do you know there's a curse on your rose tree? I mean, how did it happen?"

He was surprised. "Are you taking it seriously now?"

Her answer was diplomatic. "I'm open to further information."

"All right. I suppose I owe it to you." But he hesitated. "It's hard to know where to begin."

"Well, how did you come by the rose tree in the first place? Was it *cursed* when you got it?"

"No." He wished she wouldn't say 'cursed' like that—as though she were quoting an unreliable source. "Although I hadn't had it for long. It was a gift for my fiancée, in anticipation of our wedding."

"Fiancée? Wedding?" Faustina looked surprised and intensely curious, and Benedetto instantly regretted having introduced the topic.

"The engagement was terminated," he replied, praying that this would close the matter. He didn't hold out much hope—which was just as well.

"Why?"

He scowled. "Do you *want* to hear about the curse, or a broken engagement?" Of course, technically, they were the same story, but he wasn't ready to say so out loud.

"I think I could probably manage both. I've got some free time between now and—" she pulled a face, pretending to think about it "—oh, *eternity*."

It was his fault, Benedetto realised. He shouldn't have offered her the choice.

"One thing at a time, I think."

He leaned back in his seat, trying to relax. Closing his eyes for a moment, he could almost see it in front of him. The rose tree.

"About a year ago, I was still living in the city. I had an apartment there. It was convenient for managing the investments and, as I mentioned, my aunt was living here on the island. But, of course, the apartment wasn't suitable for a married man and, besides, as I understand it, my fiancée's family were quite keen that her residence at Ca'Bellini should form part of the marriage negotiations."

"Negotiations?" Faustina's tone was somewhere between amused and appalled. "You're making this sound like a business transaction."

Benedetto shrugged. "In a sense. But she and I were both amenable to it."

He thought he saw her mouth the word *'amenable'* to herself, but she didn't say anything. He considered mounting a more robust defence, but changed his mind. The truth was that he'd had his own misgivings about being married off to a woman who—though all reports of her beauty and personality were very favourable—had been a stranger to him. He'd never said so, of course.

I didn't have to.

He swallowed, then continued: "In the end, my aunt

agreed to move to Paris, in return for a stipend and whatever the servants could carry. She went almost immediately, though promising to come back for the wedding, and I divided my time between the city and the island, in order to prepare it for the arrival of my bride."

My bride. The words tasted strange and bitter now.

"I started in the garden," he continued. "I'd heard she liked roses, so I wanted to make her a rose garden." He remembered it vividly: the fluttering hope that she would like it, and him, and that they'd be happy together.

"Hence the rose tree?"

"Hence the rose tree." He'd envisioned it as the crowning glory: not only of the rose garden, but of the entire island. He'd had it imported at great expense from some far-flung land by a merchant who specialised in horticultural curiosities.

"So, wait—you 'heard' she liked roses?" Faustina repeated. "You didn't know?"

"No. I didn't know her. We'd only exchanged a few letters." He ran velvet-capped claw-tips over the surface of his mask. "Anyway, by the time the plant arrived, the engagement had been broken."

It was an abrupt summary of the consequences of the worst mistake he'd ever made. There'd been more to it than that, much more. Gossip, whispers, viciously-worded letters—most of them from his aunt—and damage to his reputation that had almost cost him most of the family investments. And that was before the curse had cost him everything else.

He remembered the first glimpse of the rose tree. The merchant had left it in the garden, since he hadn't been there to receive it. He'd hastened to the island as soon as he'd received word. He'd been glad of the excuse to get away from the city, to begin with, but seeing it had been much worse than he'd expected. Even with its branches trussed-up in string, it had been impressive: a great behemoth of a thing next to the ordinary roses in the border. And it was wasted—all that time, effort and expense, wasted because of what he'd done.

At the same time, though, he'd fallen in love with it. How could he not? The last few months had re-awoken his love of gardening: a part of himself that he had almost forgotten about in the long years since he had lived on the island as a boy. And this was the most beautiful rose specimen he had ever seen. Though he'd hated himself—and still did—for what he'd done, failing to take proper care of such a glorious rose tree would have made him truly irredeemable. So, he'd planted it.

"Wait," said Faustina, when he told her that, "You planted a *glass* tree?"

Benedetto let out a long, slow sigh. "It wasn't made of glass. That's what I'm telling you. When I bought it, it was an ordinary rose tree. Well, an extraordinary rose tree, actually, but a real one."

"I see. Go on."

She was laughing at him, he could tell. Faustina was the most irritating woman he'd ever met, which made his growing attraction to her confusing as well as doomed.

"It was difficult to get the tree into the hole, and to keep it that way while I buried the roots. To tell you the truth, I was surprised I only got scratched the once." He broke off here for a moment, looking down at the glove that concealed his scratched, malformed hand—then across the table at Faustina. As he watched her, she glanced down at her own scratched palm, then back up at him. He continued: "I was cutting the branches free when it happened. A flash of white light and a sound like a thunderclap, only closer at hand. For a moment, I couldn't see anything. When I could, I was looking at a glass rose tree."

It was the image that haunted him. The tree had been flawless, and now it was frozen that way, shimmering in the sunlight, beautiful and terrible at the same time.

Faustina cleared her throat, and he realised he'd been lost in thought.

"And then what? You looked at this glass rose tree and you thought to yourself: 'Ah. A cursed rose tree. I'd better never leave the island again'?"

Benedetto let his hand fall into the table with a *thump*. He could feel pressure building in his chest. "If you're going to treat this as a joke, then I'd just as soon not tell you, if you don't mind."

She dropped her gaze. "I'm sorry. Please continue."

He hesitated. She really didn't believe him, that much was clear. It made her a very difficult audience. But for now, just having her know everything was a start. He'd have to hope belief would come later.

"There was a figure behind the tree. A man—or a close approximation of one. He wore a cloak, hat, gloves, mask—so that every inch of him was concealed."

"I think I can picture it."

He glared at her but continued. "He knew my name. He asked if I was Benedetto Bellini. When I answered, and asked him who he was, he told me—" He broke off again, remembering the man's words.

I am one who would see you pay in suffering for the suffering you have caused to others.

The voice had echoed somehow. And Benedetto had known exactly what it was referring to.

"He told me he'd placed a curse on the rose, that anyone who touched it would get a scratch like the one on my hand. Anyone who got scratched would be unable to stray far from the tree. If they tried, the curse would kill them."

"Did he say why?"

Benedetto exhaled slowly. "He wanted to punish me."

"For what? That seems an extreme punishment."

He shook his head. When he spoke, his own voice sounded distant. "That wasn't the punishment. That was to keep me—and anyone who found out about the punishment—from leaving the island to tell the tale."

"So what was the punishment?" For someone who didn't believe a word of what she was hearing, Faustina sounded very interested now.

Benedetto clenched his jaw. He remembered asking the same question.

No answer had come—at least, not in words. The figure had extended an index finger, pointing at the thin red line of broken skin on his hand. A heartbeat passed, maybe two, and then he felt it: excruciating pain, radiating from his palm. It ripped through him, searing his veins and clinging, caustic, to every inch of his skin. He fell to his knees, letting out a scream that seemed to come from some deep, primal part of him. Then, as suddenly as it had started, the pain had stopped.

Now he looked down at his gloved hands, then up to meet Faustina's expectant gaze.

"Well?" she asked. "What happened?"

Benedetto stood abruptly. He took a few paces, in no particular direction, just to put some distance between himself and Faustina before answering. And he knew he would have to answer. He still couldn't show her, he wasn't ready for that, nor would he ever be. But he was going to have to tell her something. Her hunger for information was more than evident, and if he didn't give her something he was liable to wake in the night to find her standing over him with a candle and an expression of clinical curiosity.

"That's the part of the curse I haven't told you about," he said, at length. "When I looked down at that point I found that I had... changed. Physically. My hands..." He held them out for a moment, examining the backs of the gloves in the candlelight, then dropped them to his sides. "It's unpleasant," he concluded.

Faustina stood to face him. "Why didn't you tell me that before?"

"I didn't think it was relevant. That element of the curse has obviously not affected you. You're still—" He stopped himself. "I mean, you look the same as you did when you arrived."

"What about the man? Or magician, or whatever he was?"

"When I looked up again, he was gone."

They faced one another in silence for several moments. Then, slowly, Faustina resumed her seat. She was examining her hand, the scratch that mirrored his. She looked uneasy.

"That's quite… incredible," she said, hesitantly.

"I know. But it's true." He faced her, unblinking.

"Haven't you… I mean, have you at least considered that it might not be? That you could have imagined some of it?"

"I have the evidence of my eyes for what's beneath this." He pointed to the mask.

"But you won't share that."

"No." He could feel frustration starting to knot his innards.

"Then what about this?" She held up her hand. "All my eyes tell me is that I got scratched by a thorn."

"Signorina—" He forced himself to remain calm. After all, he'd felt at least some of the confusion she was feeling, even if his had been quickly crushed by the horror of realisation. "Look. I tried it. All right? As soon as I recovered, my first thought was to row back to Venice. I got about a mile out before the pain in my hand became a barely-manageable distraction. After two miles, it was unbearable." He closed his fist. "Of course, I don't know for certain that I would have died if I'd gone further, or if I hadn't come back, but I confess that I've never been sufficiently curious about the matter to find out. Only magic could have done *this* to me. I am certain that the magician was capable of putting a fatal curse on the rose tree, and I see no reason to doubt that he actually did."

Faustina's eyebrows were raised. "I see."

He felt a surge of annoyance. "Signorina Casanova, please. The curse is real. If I could prove it to you, I would, but I'm afraid it's not a cause I'm willing to die for. Or to see you die for."

She was like a little curse of her own. Just as he had had a decent life destroyed by the curse, now even the mediocre existence he had built up here was going to have to be given over to convincing Faustina not to take any fatal risks.

Faustina looked away, into the darkness. Her face was contorted slightly in thought, her brown eyes narrow and shaded by dark lashes. "You do understand, though, don't you, how frightening it would be if you were making this up?" Her voice was calm, though with a hint of strain.

"What do you mean?" But he thought he knew. He had been trying to forget about the implication she had made the day Giacomo left. *I don't know what you might enjoy. I don't know what you want with me.* So far, he hadn't been successful in doing so. "You still think you're in danger here?"

"I don't know." She chewed her lip. "I don't know how I *can* know. What you're asking me to believe is impossible."

He saw it then: how hopeless this all was. It was clear that nothing short of absolute proof was going to make her believe in the curse, and he didn't have any—apart from what was under the mask, and showing her that wasn't going to do much to lessen her fear of him. And even if she did believe in it, what then? Instead of being merely suspicious of his motives for keeping her here, she'd despise him for getting her caught up in a cruel enchantment. Either way, to her, he was a monster.

Sudden exhaustion overwhelmed him. "I should go," he said. He stood up again and lit a spare candle from one of those already burning.

"Oh." Her face, usually remarkably expressive, was suddenly inscrutable. "Well, I suppose I'll see you tomorrow, then."

"*Buona sera,* Signorina Casanova." He bowed, then started to make his exit.

"Wait!" She called him back.

"What is it?"

She looked uncomfortable, as though regretting having spoken, but forged ahead anyway. "You know," she said, quietly, and without looking at him, "I really don't want to believe that you're lying."

"I don't want that either."

Their eyes met and, for several moments, they looked at one another in silence. Then, in the absence of anything else to say, Benedetto excused himself and left the room.

The dark halls and corridors between the drawing room and his quarters seemed very cold after the flame-lit warmth of the drawing room. He walked through them as quickly as he could, shielding the little flame of his candle from the draft. The dancing spot of light was something to focus on, a welcome distraction—though not, regrettably, enough to stop the conversation he had just had from echoing in his ears.

A clean nightshirt, pressed and neatly folded, was waiting for him at the end of his bed, exactly as he had left it. He closed and locked his bedroom door behind him, then lifted the candle to lip-level to blow it out. He generally preferred to undress in the dark. Tonight, though, something made him lower the candle again and place it, still lit, on a sideboard.

He took off the gloves first. He had experimented, in the early days, with keeping them on while dressing and undressing, to eliminate the risk of tearing his clothes. That had worked well enough, as far as it went, but it had made buttons and other fastenings nearly impossible to handle. By now, he had learned simply to be careful: to use the very tips of his claws to ease the buttons through their holes, and the pads of his fingers to touch the actual fabric. He used the pads now: delicately pinching the cords that held his mask in place and pulling them slowly apart. When they were loose, he moved one hand to the front of his face, catching the mask as it fell away.

There were no mirrors in his bedroom—he used the one in his dressing room in the mornings, and only once he had put on a mask—but his ethereal reflection was just visible in the window against the dark sky. Against his better judgement, he looked at it.

It was as appalling as ever. The curse had warped the structure of his face beyond recognition, exaggerating his cheekbones, widening his eyes, so that the upper part of his face had a too-sharp, angular quality to it. Meanwhile, his cheeks were sunken and his mouth and lower jaw seemed to protrude, creating a sort of muzzle. And then there was the fur. He'd found, with practice, that the hair that grew around his jaw could be shaped and groomed sufficiently to look like a beard, and to hide what the masks didn't. The hair on the top and back of his head, too—though thicker than it had been before—still looked passably human, and could be arranged and tied so that it covered his pointed, furry ears. These little efforts, however, did nothing to soften the impact of seeing himself unmasked.

He turned away from the window and sat on the bed to remove his shoes and socks. The socks had the same reinforcement as his gloves, to secure the claws, but it wasn't enough. He had endured a lot of pain, trying not to pierce the leather, before learning to buy shoes a couple of sizes larger. Even so, his feet ached with the effort of walking carefully in them. It was the shoes he had been most tempted to give up on, but to stop dressing properly would have been to admit to losing his humanity.

He'd been lucky, in a way. At least it was possible to hide the curse's effects, even if it did involve keeping himself almost completely covered. If magic could do this to him, presumably it could have twisted his body, too, turning him into something so monstrous that no one would have mistaken him for human even in the most favourable lighting. Then even what little interaction he had with the outside world would have been impossible. Perhaps the masked sorcerer had been merciful.

It doesn't feel like mercy.

Growing increasingly desperate for the dark release of sleep, he turned his attention to his jacket, which he was able to wriggle out of. He employed the pinching method again on his shirt, working the bottom of it out of the waistband of his trousers before gathering it up and lifting it over his head. He didn't need to steel himself as much for this: he had seen the worst already. His torso looked relatively normal, aside from the thick coat of fur. He stood up as he peeled the sleeves off, preparing to hang the clothes up to air. But, in the process of freeing himself from the cuffs, he froze, staring down at his left arm.

"*Porca miseria,*" he breathed. He staggered, suddenly weak, as he tried to make sense of what he was seeing.

In truth, it wasn't much—a jagged break in the fur, an expanse of perhaps three inches on his inner forearm where the hair had disappeared. White skin, starved of sunlight, seemed almost to glow against the thick, dark hair above and below it. Isolated in that sea of fur, it looked strange and almost wrong, but it wasn't. It wasn't wrong at all.

It was human.

Nine

Faustina went out to the garden before breakfast the next morning. She had worried about encountering Benedetto, not having a good excuse for this early-morning activity, but he was nowhere to be seen. Having made her way to the jetty, she sat down on it, letting her feet dangle above the surface of the lagoon. The air was still and cool here, and the water was calm. It swirled lazily around the wooden legs of the jetty and sparkled in the early light. In the distance, Venice's misty skyline reached up to the sparse clouds, bridging the gap between sea and sky.

Her fingertips unconsciously brushed the raised line of the scratch on her palm and she looked down at it, yet again. She had never paid so much attention to such a minor wound before but, ever since Benedetto had related the full story of the curse the previous day, she hadn't been able to pull her attention from the scratch for long.

She was starting to believe that he really did think

there was a curse. There was no evidence that he wanted to hurt her, and he had had ample opportunity to do it.

And he's not exactly short on motive, either. If he was on the fence about brutally murdering me before, you'd think that the incident with his silverware would have pushed him over the edge.

In particular, it was the mention of his escape attempts that she had been turning over in her mind. Of course, escape was a theme close to her heart, right now, but it also added a little realism to his story: he hadn't believed in it himself, at first, either. He had answered all her questions confidently, and with neither so much nor so little emotion as to seem suspicious.

Then again, to believe that *he* believed what he was saying raised an awful lot of new questions. What had caused the pain in his hand—pain so bad he thought it would kill him? Who was the man who had appeared by the rose tree, and how had he managed to swap it for a glass one? And why? Any explanation she could imagine only seemed to make the whole thing more incredible.

Unless magic is real, and there really is a curse.

She shook off the thought.

Despite the early hour, there were quite a few vessels making their way to or from the city. Faustina watched them pass, noting that most of them gave the island a wide berth. Eventually, however, she thought she saw one detach itself from the traffic and move with purpose toward her. She watched it closely. It was a largish craft, rowed by four men. A fifth man was moving about on the deck, checking the crates stacked there. He seemed suddenly to notice her and straightened up, his cargo apparently forgotten. He wore a purple mask beneath a feathered hat. Ordinarily Faustina enjoyed the novelty, during *Carnevale,* of seeing so many masks, of guessing at identities and hiding her own. But here, on this strange, lonely island, she was starting to long for the sight of a human face.

She got to her feet, running a cool hand over her suddenly sweat-slicked forehead. Benedetto must have trusted Rambaldo, if he was his only link to the outside world, but that didn't mean Faustina could.

The boat was slowing now, coasting toward the shore. One of the rowers had lowered his oar and was doing something purposeful with a length of rope. The man at the front scrutinised her, pale eyes taking in first her face, then her clothing. He smiled.

"*Ciao,*" he said, as the boat bumped gently into the jetty. His tone was cheerful, though he was no doubt a little bemused. "This is a surprise."

Faustina reflected his cheeriness back, rather pathetically pleased to be greeted by someone who didn't obviously despise her. "*Ciao*!" she repeated. "You must be Signor Rambaldo?"

He bowed, sweeping off the hat to briefly reveal a head of thick grey hair. "At your service," he said. "And you must be Faustina Casanova."

Faustina was taken aback. She wasn't used to having her reputation precede her and, now that it had happened, she found she didn't like it very much. "How did you know that?"

"Signor Bellini told me about you. Besides, you look just like your brother—only, I'm pleased to say, rather prettier."

"Oh." She wasn't exactly thrilled to be reminded of Giacomo's existence. "You know my brother?"

"We've met. It was I who invited him to Signor Bellini's card game." He gave another smile, and she noticed this time that it didn't quite reach his eyes. "A misdemeanour," he added, "for which Signor Bellini has been good enough to forgive me."

"Ah." So *Giacomo's* reputation had preceded her. She tried to relax.

Rambaldo started to turn away. "Well," he said, "it's been delightful to make your acquaintance, but I'm afraid I'll have to ask you to excuse me now. I need to get this boat unloaded." He gestured to the men, who began to pick up some of the crates.

"Actually, signor—" she laid a hand on Rambaldo's arm "—I was hoping I could ask you something."

He seemed to consider this for a moment, then he crossed the jetty and stepped onto the grass, motioning for her to follow. She did so, and the men on the boat began to unload their cargo.

He leaned in and lowered his voice. "How can I help?"

"I need passage back to the city." She glanced towards the boat. "I won't be any trouble. I can sit where some of those crates are."

There was a moment of silence, during which she felt her heart sink.

"You'd be very uncomfortable," Rambaldo responded, at last. "Surely Bellini could arrange a proper *burchiello* for you?"

Faustina licked her lips. "Actually—"

"Bellini doesn't know about this, does he?" He had a way of seeming faintly amused while crushing her hopes beneath his heel that reminded her a little of Giacomo.

"Um—"

"And I'm guessing he doesn't know you're a thief, either."

Alarm rushed back up Faustina's spine. She tried for innocence: "What do you mean?"

"You don't have to admit to it, signorina. I know what you are. And, so long as you know that anyone who robs Signor Bellini will answer to me personally, I don't think we ought to have a problem."

"I don't want to rob him." She tried to sound confused, and a little offended—the way someone might have if they weren't guilty of everything they'd just been accused of. "I want to go home."

He scoffed. "Of course you don't want to rob him. I'm sure when your brother told you about a palazzo full of valuables, guarded by one lone eccentric, you weren't the least bit tempted to head over and help yourself. That's why you're not here right now." He looked her up and down, meaningfully.

Faustina dropped the pretence. "Are you serious? Rob a house on an island, sight unseen? I can think of better ways to risk my neck. And if I were going to do it, don't you think I'd plan a better means of escape than waiting for a kindly stranger to happen by?"

Rambaldo spread his hands. "So one would be disposed to imagine. And yet, here we are."

Faustina shook her head, thinking fast. "All right, cards on the table. I'm a thief. Signor Bellini knows that now and, apparently, you do too. But I'm not here to rob him—at least, not anymore. The whole thing was Giacomo's idea, and I'm no longer willing to participate."

"Giacomo's idea?" Rambaldo was looking at her with intense interest. "You're telling me you knew this would end in disaster but you went along with it anyway?"

"Well—" she folded her arms "—he wasn't completely honest with me about what I was letting myself in for."

"And that surprised you? He's your brother. You must know what he's like."

"I—" But she didn't have an answer to that. She'd thought the same thing herself.

"Your brother must be very persuasive."

"He is." She arched her shoulders. "Of course he is. That's what he does."

"Hmm." Rambaldo let his gaze roam to the sky, apparently giving this some deep consideration.

Faustina began to lose patience. "Please," she said, "take me back to Venice. If it's money you want, I can get some. Maybe not right away, but I'll get it for you, however much you want." It was a bold boast, given her recent form, but she was desperate.

"I don't want your stolen money." The note of amusement was back.

To her shame, Faustina found that she was swallowing frustrated tears. "Signor, please. I'm begging you…"

"I'm sorry." He turned away again. "If Bellini wants you on this island, then this is where I'm going to leave you."

"But he doesn't want me here, not really."

Something behind her had caught Rambaldo's

attention. "Then you can get him to tell me that himself," he said.

Faustina followed his gaze. Just visible between the trees, Benedetto was making his way down the path towards them. He was back in smart attire today, at least partially. His trousers, shoes and shirt would have been welcome at any high society gathering—though it would have been a shame if they insisted on bringing him with them. Today's mask was burgundy, and he'd left what Faustina assumed was a beautifully coordinating jacket inside.

Rambaldo touched the brim of his hat respectfully as the master of the house approached. "Signor."

Benedetto nodded. As usual, what was visible of his face gave little away. "*Buon giorno,* Rambaldo. I see you've met my guest."

"Yes, indeed."

Faustina looked between them, thinking. She *could* ask Benedetto to let her go. The worst he could do was say no.

But he *would* say no. She thought about how angry he'd been that she had ignored his warning by trying to escape with Giacomo—and that was before he had told her the whole unbelievable story. She didn't know what he would say if she asked if Rambaldo could take her back to the city, but she guessed it wouldn't be "Goodbye and good luck".

She had been silent for slightly too long. "Ah… *ciao,*" she mumbled.

He inclined his head slightly. "*Buon giorno.*" He spoke with an air of forced friendliness. Faustina was sure that if Rambaldo hadn't been there the greeting would have been served on the usual bed of sarcasm with a side of disdain and a light resentment dressing.

"I was about to go back inside—" she began, but Rambaldo had started talking at the same time.

"Signorina Casanova here says you'd like me to take her back to Venice." Rambaldo glanced from Benedetto to Faustina and back again. It was impossible to be sure, of course, but Faustina was certain that the face behind Rambaldo's mask was a picture of smugness. She could feel the colour rising in her cheeks.

Benedetto turned to look at her. "Is that so?"

Rambaldo was still talking. "I told her I'd just check with you, and then we can be on our way."

Benedetto waved a hand at him, not looking away from Faustina. "A moment, Rambaldo. Signorina Casanova, is this true?"

Faustina sagged. Her mind was racing for some explanation, some way to wriggle out of this, but what was the point? She had failed, once again, to extricate herself from the island, and now she was going to lose even the modicum of respect with which he had begun to treat her. She felt suddenly overwhelmed by disappointment and isolation.

"Well, that's not exactly what I said," she muttered, gloomily.

"I see." He turned away from her. "Rambaldo, could you accompany me up to the house? I'd like to have a word with you."

Rambaldo shifted on the spot. "I can't stay long. I've got other business to attend to."

"I assure you, it will only take a moment."

Faustina rolled her eyes. "*I'll* go back to the house, shall I? Then you can talk about me without inconveniencing yourselves."

Not my most elegant riposte, she thought, turning on her heel. No one called her back.

It shouldn't have mattered this much. She had found out about Rambaldo's existence less than a day ago. It wasn't as though a carefully-constructed escape plan had fallen devastatingly to pieces. It was just another disappointment, another dose of fear that she would never escape this miserable island.

She aimed a kick at the marble steps when she reached the house, then regretted it. The shoes Benedetto had lent her had obviously not been designed with woman-on-architecture violence in mind.

Benedetto stared after her, feeling tired. He'd known that Rambaldo could be trusted not to assist Faustina in an escape without checking with him first, which was why he hadn't gone to any trouble to stop her from meeting him, but once again he felt guilty and frustrated. Saving Faustina's life was turning out to be a thankless, endless task.

Rambaldo waited until Faustina was out of earshot before speaking. "Easy on the eyes, isn't she?"

"Mm." An affirmative noise was as far as he trusted himself to go on that subject.

"Aren't you worried about her being here?"

"Worried?" Benedetto slid a finger under the mask to

scratch his cheek, noting the interested way in which Rambaldo stared at him as he did so, alert for any glimpse of his face.

Rambaldo was a good man, though Benedetto would not have recommended him for his delicacy and tact. Their professional relationship had been very new at the time of the curse: Benedetto had just engaged him to procure some of the items he would need to refurnish the house after his aunt's departure. As luck had had it, Rambaldo had been the first visitor to the island after Benedetto's first failed attempt to leave it. The relief Benedetto had felt at seeing a friendly face, under such trying circumstances, had bound the man to his affections very tightly indeed, and he had been immensely grateful when Rambaldo had offered to act as an agent for him.

Rambaldo was the only person who had seen what was under the mask. He had taken it very well, considering.

"She's a thief," Rambaldo said.

Benedetto was surprised. "How did you know?"

Rambaldo shrugged. "Oh, one hears things."

Benedetto scrutinised him for a moment. The answer had been an unsatisfactory one, but he had too much on his mind at the moment to pursue it. "I caught her in the act," he said, "escaping with that brother of hers. No," he added, seeing Rambaldo open his mouth, "don't worry, you've already apologised for that." Rambaldo had been mortified on hearing about the unpleasantness Giacomo had caused at the card game.

"I *could* take her away, if you like." Rambaldo's voice became conspiratorial. "I'm sure I could convince her to keep quiet about the curse. If she's anything like her brother, a bribe might work, if you think persuasion won't."

Benedetto shook his head. "I'm afraid it's rather more complicated than that. She's under the curse too."

Rambaldo looked surprised. "Really? You mean…" He gestured at his face.

"No." Benedetto shuddered a little as the fur on his neck stood up. "No, I—I'm reasonably sure that part of the curse was just for me. I mean, you've seen her. When I… *changed*, it happened all at once."

"Yes. No overlooking that, was there?" Rambaldo was smiling, his tone blackly humorous, but Benedetto couldn't quite bring himself to smile back.

"Indeed." He coughed and changed the subject. "Did you manage to get everything I asked for?"

"Of course I did." Rambaldo seemed wounded by the question. "I even put out a few feelers for your next card game."

Benedetto grimaced. "I think we'll shelve that, if you don't mind. I've had my fill of cards for the time being."

"All right." He sounded put out.

"What about the books?"

Rambaldo turned his eyes briefly skywards. "I told you, I got everything. You there!" He clicked his fingers at a boy of about fourteen, who had been staring into the water in a dreamy sort of way. "Bring me that parcel." The boy obliged, and Rambaldo deftly removed the string from what turned out to be a stack of books. "Here you go: one *Grimoire*, one *Exploration of Divination*, one *On Charms*—"

"All right," said Benedetto, who was becoming uncomfortably aware that Rambaldo's men had started exchanging glances. "I'm much obliged, thank you."

Perhaps detecting this discomfort, Rambaldo turned back to his men. "Come on, gentlemen, we didn't row those crates over here for our own amusement. I want to see them stacked up neatly in Signor Bellini's hallway in the next five minutes, understood? You're not employed as ornaments." He watched with a hawkish eye as the men set about doing as they had been told, then turned back to face Benedetto. "Are you confident about any of these books, then?" Rambaldo asked. "You haven't had much luck so far—"

"I know." Benedetto cut him off again, before he could develop this theme. Rambaldo was right, but that didn't mean he wanted to hear it.

Rambaldo was looking at him curiously. "Has Signorina Casanova seen it yet? Your face, I mean. And everything."

Benedetto shook his head. "I'm afraid it might scare her into doing something irrational." It wasn't a full explanation, but it was good enough.

"Like trying to escape?"

"Yes." Benedetto sighed. "I didn't say it was working." He put his right hand on the sleeve of his left arm, hesitating. "May I show you something? I—I need to know whether or not I'm losing my mind."

"Of course."

He fumbled awkwardly with his cuff for a moment, then dragged the sleeve up to his elbow. Perhaps it was just the sunlight, but the area of blank, unfurred skin looked even larger this morning. He stared at it for a moment, then turned a slightly desperate gaze on Rambaldo.

"Can you see that?"

"*Zio*," Rambaldo whispered, almost reverently. "You don't think the curse is weakening?"

Benedetto felt every remaining hair on his body stand on end. It was the thought he had been trying to avoid, but to hear it from someone else's lips made that impossible. His skin felt hot, too hot, and he could almost feel the blood beginning to pound through his veins. "No," he replied, doing his best to keep the emotion from his voice. He pulled off his glove and his claws gleamed with reflected light. "Look. It's just that one place. Everything else is…" But he didn't have the words for it now, any more than he had for the last year.

Rambaldo removed his mask, wiping sweat from a furrowed brow as he stared down at Benedetto's arm. His face, though lined, had a youthful, handsome quality to it, and Benedetto felt a stab of familiar but irrational jealousy. It would have been nice to be able to remove a mask that casually, without the risk of causing widespread fear and alarm.

"So you're saying," Rambaldo began, replacing the offending article, "that Signorina Casanova arrived here and, within a few days, this happened?"

Benedetto pulled his sleeve back down and tugged the glove back on, frowning. "You're not suggesting there's a link?"

"You don't think so?" Rambaldo lifted his gaze to meet Benedetto's, looking earnest.

"Well, why should there be?" His voice was shaking a little, despite his best efforts. "The island is not exactly heaving with human activity, I'll grant you, but between your men and the card games, it's not as though her arrival was particularly remarkable." *Not for any reason to do with magic, anyway.*

"She might have some magical abilities?" Rambaldo hazarded.

"I doubt it. She doesn't even believe in magic. She's been quite vocal on the subject."

"Hmm. Well, perhaps you're right. Perhaps, it's another coincidence." Rambaldo nodded slightly to himself. "Although…" But he trailed off.

Benedetto tensed. "What?"

Rambaldo coughed. "Well, you likely won't find this in any of your books but, if you want a little honest, traditional wisdom…"

"Go on." It was becoming difficult not to snap at him.

"Well, there's a long history of curses being broken by love, isn't there? True love, I mean. Maybe your attractive guest is developing a certain tenderness in your direction."

Benedetto laughed out loud. It was more of a bitter bark than a cheery expression of mirth, but he couldn't help himself. If nothing else, it covered his disappointment. For a moment there, he had thought the old man might be on to something. "Love?" he repeated, incredulously.

"Oldest remedy there is," was Rambaldo's solemn response.

It took Benedetto a few moments to organise his

thoughts into something more lucid than a vehement "No".

"I hate to dismiss your input out of hand," he managed, eventually, "but I think not. For one thing, as you say, there's nothing like that in any of the books I've read so far—nothing I've read since I left the nursery, I mean. Of course, I don't claim to be an expert on magic, but I fear that the solution to my current predicament will be much more complicated than that. And, for another, as regards Signorina Casanova's sentiments, I fear you have misread the situation entirely. She despises me."

"Hmm." Rambaldo was looking at him in a way he didn't particularly like. "And what about *your* sentiments? How do you feel about her?"

Benedetto clenched his jaw for a moment. "Let's just say that there is ill-feeling on both sides."

Rambaldo gave a little smirk. "That's a pity," he said, "given that you're stuck with one another."

"Yes." Benedetto had nothing further to add to that.

"Well," said Rambaldo, at length, "I suppose I'd better be getting on."

Benedetto nodded acquiescence as another long, empty day unfolded in his mind's eye. "Very well," he said. "It was good to see you."

"And you, signor." Rambaldo started to make for the boat.

Benedetto called him back. "Wait. I'd like you to bring a few more things next time."

"Signor?" Rambaldo's tone was patient, his masked face giving nothing away.

"Another boat. A small one. Casanova took mine."

Benedetto had used the boat for fishing now and then—close to the island, of course, where the pain was bearable. Besides, not having one made him feel uneasy, especially when escape attempts from Faustina were apparently still a very real concern. He wasn't at all sure that she could be trusted not to try and *swim* back to Venice, now that all other options had been exhausted, and he didn't much fancy swimming after her.

"Very well. Anything else?"

"Yes." Benedetto couldn't quite believe what he was about to say. "I'd like you to find a merchant who deals in artists' supplies. Paints, brushes, that sort of thing. I want the best of everything."

Rambaldo sounded surprised. "Another attempt to discover your inner artist?"

"Not for me." He put his fingers through his hair. "Signorina Casanova. She's a painter."

"Very good, Signor Bellini." Rambaldo gave him an infuriatingly knowing look. "I shall attend to it directly."

Though her march back to the house had gone as well as could be expected, once there Faustina was confounded by the question of what to do with herself next. She couldn't face returning to her room, nor did she want to establish herself in any static activity elsewhere that might leave her vulnerable to being stumbled upon by her jailer. In the end, she decided she might as well complete her exploration of the house. She took the stairs too quickly, on purpose, working out some of her nervous energy if not her frustration, and emerged on the second floor panting and a little calmer. She turned right into a wood-panelled corridor and tried all the doors.

One led to a library—lined, as libraries often were, with books. She scanned their spines, wondering if Benedetto was keeping all the interesting reading material for himself, but these were all fairly dry reference books: dictionaries, glossaries, medical codices, treatises on philosophy. The Bellini—or perhaps even successive generations of Bellinis—who had put these together had had eclectic interests. She felt confident, however, in crediting the two newer-looking bookcases, crammed with volumes dealing with the occult, to Benedetto. Most of the books had covers inscribed with strange symbols and at least one volume was triangular. Benedetto's "research", presumably.

The next room was a bedroom. She was a little surprised to find that she felt uncomfortable in there. Of course, a strange man's bedroom was not a place for a young lady, but neither was his silver cabinet. Concerns of privacy didn't usually trouble Faustina. In any case, there wasn't much to see in the bedroom. It was impeccably neat, of course, and contained only a bed, a few assorted cabinets and sideboards, and a washstand. She backed out again, pulling the door closed behind her.

I wonder where he keeps that extensive collection of clothes? she thought. *To say nothing of the masks…*

That question was answered quickly. The next room turned out to be an extremely well-appointed dressing room. Wardrobes and cabinets lined three of the walls, filled with crisp white shirts and exquisitely-crafted suits, each given plenty of space to hang so that none of the delicate fabrics were crushed. One cabinet displayed masks—at least thirty of them, in a wide range of styles—on special stands.

There was a full-length mirror against the fourth wall. She looked at it curiously for several moments, taken aback—as she had been every time she had seen her reflection since arriving here—by the sight of herself in Benedetto's clothes. In a strange way, she was beginning to feel that they suited her.

She was surprised that Benedetto had a mirror in his quarters. She had assumed that someone who went to so much trouble to stop others looking at his face would want to avoid looking at himself, too. Then again, his appearance obviously mattered to him a great deal. She had noted his careful dress sense already, and this impressive walk-in wardrobe only served to complete the picture.

Back out in the corridor, she noticed something she hadn't before: a row of paintings. She approached them without much interest, at first. There was plenty of art around the palazzo, demonstrative of a wide range of tastes. Much of it was a little fanciful for her: mythic battles, winged babies and so forth—preferable to endless copies of the same horse, but not by much. But these were portraits: staid men in proud poses, largely unencumbered by hovering infants. She checked the inscription on the first: "Ernesto Bellini, 1617."

The others were Bellinis too: five of them in total, each separated from the last by a couple of decades. They were all handsome, to one degree or another. She scanned their serious faces, looking for similarities. The family resemblance was not overwhelming but she began to notice that many of them shared a square jaw that Benedetto might also have had beneath the beard, though they were all clean-shaven. Several of them had his near-black hair. She wondered if they all ran their hands through it when they were anxious. Maybe none of these men had had as much to be anxious about as Benedetto.

The most recent portrait was of "Marcelo Bellini, 1720". *Benedetto's father?* The grey eyes were the same.

Peering now into the backgrounds, she found that the portraits had still more in common. Visible behind each man was a view of an island, this island, with the palazzo casting its shadow over the water of the lagoon. At first glance, each background looked like a copy of the last but, when she looked closer, she started noticing differences. The island evolved a little in each painting: an extension to the east wing here, a bit of remodelling there. There was evolution in the garden, too. The first couple of generations of Bellinis, perhaps with other things on their minds, seemed to have been content with trimming the lawns and planting a couple of trees but, as time went on, the designs became more elaborate. By the time of Marcelo's painting, the courtyards had taken shape, and a number of immaculate flowerbeds appeared to line them. Even this latest painting, however, showed a garden that could scarcely hold a candle to the present one. It was clear where the current master of the house had chosen to make his mark.

The rose tree, she noticed, was conspicuous by its absence.

There was something else hanging on the wall. It was separated from the others by a door, so she hadn't noticed it at first, and a piece of black velvet had been draped over it, leaving only the sides of the ornate gilt frame exposed.

She crossed to it, slowly reaching out for the soft surface of the velvet. There was a part of her, very deep down, that wondered if she ought to leave it alone, to pretend she had never even glimpsed it. But she couldn't do it. She couldn't cope with even one more mystery.

Taking a deep breath, she closed her hand around the velvet. It came away smoothly, melting into a puddle on the floor, and suddenly Faustina was staring into yet another set of painted eyes. They, too, were grey.

This man was young, with long hair scraped back behind his head. His lips were smooth and well-defined, his jaw strong. He was easily the most handsome of the Bellini line, and probably one of the most handsome men she had ever seen.

And that was just it. She *had* seen him.

A voice broke abruptly through her thoughts.

"Ah, Signorina Casanova."

She winced. She hadn't heard Benedetto approach—she had let her guard down, becoming too interested in what she was looking at to maintain an awareness of her surroundings—and she wasn't ready to talk to him yet.

"I hoped I'd find you," he went on, "I wondered if—" He stopped abruptly, his gaze leaping between her and the painting. "Oh."

Faustina stared back at him, uncomfortably aware of her own breathing. She couldn't think of anything to say, only managing what she suspected was a mildly constipated expression.

Benedetto, apparently experiencing no such difficulty, cleared his throat. "Tell me, signorina, do you have any sort of moral code, or do you make every decision purely according to whim?"

For some reason, she felt like crying. She channelled the pressure elsewhere, speaking in what was almost a growl. "What do you mean?"

"Well, of course I know already that you take a very flexible approach to the ownership of property. I'm realising now that you have no respect for privacy, either. I'm just wondering what else I should be worried about."

"Well, that makes two of us." She hoped he wouldn't hear the waver beneath the confidence in her voice. She pointed to the picture, speaking again before he could respond. "Who is this?"

Benedetto narrowed his eyes at her, then took several slow, steady steps in her direction. His gaze still fixed firmly on her, he silently extended a finger, indicating the tiny plaque at the bottom of the frame. Faustina looked at it: *'Benedetto Bellini, 1751'*.

"This is you?" It was what she'd thought, but it raised far more questions than it answered.

"You're very perceptive."

"Why was it hidden?"

"As I thought I'd explained last night, the curse has had something of an adverse effect on my personal appearance." He regarded the portrait for a moment, his jaw clenched. "I don't know if it's apparent, what with the mask and the gloves and everything, but it's not a change

I'm proud of, and I prefer not to face *this*—" it was his turn to gesture at it "—every time I pass along this corridor."

"No, I mean—" she made another attempt to find the right question "—why didn't you tell me who you were?"

"I seem to remember that introductions were made when you first arrived. And I'm not the one who used a fake name."

She rubbed her forehead. She was obviously going to have to try the direct approach. Slowly, she said: "We've met before."

He lowered his arms to his sides. "I sense that you don't mean twenty minutes ago at the jetty." He sounded genuinely puzzled.

He really doesn't remember. Of course, she hadn't recognised him, either. But, even so, it stung a little.

"No. I mean a year ago, at St Mark's Square. You were wearing a goat mask. You bumped into me."

She had been expecting to provoke some sort of reaction, but not necessarily the one she got. Benedetto's mouth fell open. His eyes widened, telegraphing a potent mixture of surprise and abject horror. He grasped at his head, turned away from her for a moment, took several steps back down the corridor and then turned back to stare at her again.

"The stolen bracelet? That was you?"

She reached for her cuff, meaning to pull it back and show him the bracelet, then remembered it had been lost. "Yes. That was me."

"No…" Benedetto was shaking his head and moaning softly. "No, no—Signorina Casanova, do you realise what you've done?"

"What I've done?" The conversation was taking a turn she hadn't anticipated.

He looked at her, his eyes at once wretched and incandescent. "Do you know the name Maristela Sourosin?"

"No." But as she spoke, she realised that there was a familiar ring to it. *Sourosin…*

"She was my fiancée. The bracelet you stole was a gift I sent her."

"Ah." Belatedly, her instincts began to tell her that she was on dangerous ground, and she tensed.

"Maristela and I agreed to meet in secret, in masks, that night, at St Mark's Square. I was to recognise her by the bracelet."

Faustina gave him a look soured by growing alarm. "It didn't occur to you that addressing one another by name might eliminate any confusion?"

"I was being discreet." Benedetto ran a gloved hand over his hair. "To get to know one another with any degree of intimacy before the wedding might have raised eyebrows, if anyone found out."

"So why did you do it?"

"Because I didn't know her. We were virtual strangers, and we were going to have to spend the rest of our lives together. We agreed it was worth the risk of raising eyebrows." He gritted his teeth. "Of course, having word get around that I'd been seen kissing a different woman provoked a slightly stronger response."

"So that's why the engagement was broken," Faustina murmured, almost to herself. "You can't have been too upset by that, surely? I mean, she was a stranger. You didn't know her—"

Benedetto let out a noise like a snarl. "Actually," he snapped, "breaking all established codes of honour, and my aunt's heart, very nearly destroyed everything the Bellini name stood for, but you're right, that's not what I'm upset about."

"Then what?" Faustina returned, profoundly confused. He didn't say anything, just dug his gloved fingertips into his hair. A thought finally occurred to her. "Wait—is this about the curse?"

Benedetto swallowed, slowly lowering his hands as he regained control of himself. Finally, slowly, he nodded.

"That was it? That was what you were being punished for?" In spite of her disbelief in the curse, and her suspicions, Faustina was surprised. "So the night we met—"

"Ruined my life," he said. "Yes."

"You didn't tell me that."

"I know." Benedetto started to turn away. "Can you go back to your room, please?" His tone was brittle.

"Why?" Her eyebrows arched.

"Or the kitchen. Or the garden. I don't care. Just go away."

She wasn't sure she could have moved if she'd wanted to. Her feet felt rooted to the ground. "I want to talk about this."

"Well, I don't." Benedetto's hands curled into fists. His eyes met hers again. They were bright, and furious. "Go away."

"No."

For a moment, she thought he might be about to shout at her, to lunge for the portrait, but all he did was bare his teeth. "Fine," he said. Without another look at either her or the painting, he turned on his heel and walked into the library. He locked the door behind him.

TEN

Faustina stared intently at the page in front of her, her fingers almost a blur as they dragged the leadholder across it in a series of thick, angular lines. It was more of a ferocious scribble than a sketch, but it was transforming, slowly, the seemingly disparate lines weaving themselves together into a coherent whole. She had begun the drawing in an agitated storm of feelings but that had dissipated and now, though she wasn't exactly calm, her mind became a pleasant blank as she lost herself in her work.

The leadholder was a nice piece of equipment. She'd never used one before. Graphite had to be imported from England and was very expensive to get hold of. It was everything she had hoped it would be.

She was sitting on the balcony outside her bedroom, leaning back in a chair with her feet on the parapet and using one of Benedetto's improving books to rest her paper on. She rather suspected that the vigour of her strokes was doing it some damage. She couldn't be completely sorry about that.

It was only as she applied a few final lines of detail and her hand slowed to a halt that she became fully aware of what she had been drawing. It was the face of her stranger. He was posed much as he was in the portrait, his body suggested by a few simple lines, but his expression was softer, happier. She had drawn her inspiration from her memories of their *Carnevale* night together, before any of this bizarre unpleasantness had been conceived of. She could see it all in her own lines: the broad, infectious smile, the confident set of his jaw and, most memorable of all, the glint of light in his grey eyes—eyes that didn't seem to shine now.

It's so strange.

If someone had asked her to guess at the stranger's identity, she would have named virtually every other man in the Veneto region before Benedetto. And yet, now that she knew, it was beginning to make a strange kind of sense. She could see the similarities in his height, build and so on—but, more than that, she had begun to notice little things about him, things that she had forgotten about the stranger. His shy, meditative awkwardness, for example. Even a little of his charisma.

Charisma?

Well, now she could be certain that this new information was colouring her perception of Benedetto. She'd never been in any danger of thinking of him as charismatic before.

A noise caught her attention and she turned, looking

up and to her left to seek the source. On a balcony on the floor above, towards the other end of the palazzo, Benedetto appeared, stalking out to peer over into the garden. On catching sight of her, he stiffened, then stalked right back inside again. Faustina sighed. It would have been comical, but this was her life now. Dodging around a man she had once spent a very pleasant evening with, and who now thought he was some kind of unspeakably hideous monster.

Faustina massaged her forehead.

Do I believe him now?

Well, of course she didn't believe in the curse. She might have… *wavered* a bit, after hearing his story, but that was understandable. She was away from home, away from reality as she knew it, and it had been a very *detailed* story. Now that she'd rested and thought about it, she had returned to her senses and remembered that there was no such thing as magic. But she was coming to the conclusion that *he* really believed in it, and that mattered.

She'd been telling the truth when she'd told Benedetto that she wanted to believe him. And she wanted it even more now that she knew he was her stranger. She didn't want to have been wrong. She had trusted the stranger. It had been foolish, perhaps, on so brief an acquaintance, but she wouldn't have gone with him to the tavern if she hadn't—nor would she have given herself over to that kiss, to two kisses, the memory of which still made her heart flutter a little.

She looked down again at her drawing. The stranger's proud, handsome face regarded her steadily.

There was something else to this revelation. She knew

now, for sure, that Benedetto's life had been very different a year ago. The man she'd met in St Mark's Square had roamed the city freely, his hands and face exposed for all the world to see. In that respect, he could not have been less like the man she blamed for holding her captive, who skulked around his empty palazzo and cringed at his own portrait. Something must have happened to him.

Something like magic.

Not magic, because magic didn't exist. But something like it.

What's like magic?

Believing in it. The answer came to her abruptly.

She stood up, resting the book, paper and leadholder on the chair, and went to lean on the balustrade. Beyond the garden, the surface of the *Laguna Veneta* glittered in the sunlight. The line of ships and other vessels passing between Venice and the mainland had only thickened during the day and now the floating skyline was almost completely obscured by sails. She stared at them absently, thinking.

Had she ever believed in magic? She supposed she might have, as a child—but, as soon as she'd thought to ask questions about it, she'd found the answers unsatisfactory.

Her grandmother had always believed, though. Despite the gentle efforts of Faustina's parents—and, later, Faustina and Giacomo—to dissuade her, *Nonna* had faithfully visited the same self-styled "witch" all her adult life.

And the funny thing was, the witch always made her feel better. Not, Faustina was certain, by any really arcane means. Faustina had seen the witch in action once, and she'd done nothing more for her generous fee than wave her arms around and mutter darkly. And none of that had stopped *Nonna* suffering the aches of old age, or succumbing to illness, or dying. But it had made her *feel* better. No matter how slow, how painful, how impeded by coughs and groans and sneezes her journey to the witch had been, *Nonna* returned every time with renewed vigour in her step and a smile on her face.

And why shouldn't she smile? That was the question *Nonna* had always asked, more serene than defiant, if anyone looked at her askance. Because she was full of magic now, and magic made people better, so how could she feel bad?

Faustina had learned not to question her, just as she'd later learned not to question the belief in magic that made it easier for Chiara to cope with her lot in life. *Nonna* believed in a force that could make her feel better, and that belief *did* make her feel better, so she wasn't exactly wrong.

It's just that the force was the belief itself, not magic.

Faustina turned around, resting her elbows on the balustrade as she looked back at her drawing of Benedetto.

Of course, this is different. Benedetto's belief in magic was a blight on his life, a force for evil. *A curse, in other words.*

Benedetto thought he was under a curse that had turned him into a hideous monster and would harm anyone who touched his rose tree, so he had no choice but to hide his face and isolate himself.

But it's the other way round.

He hid his face and isolated himself, so he might as well be under a curse.

She straightened, stretching. Her shoulders popped and creaked, but she felt suddenly relaxed. She knew what she was dealing with now. *How* she was dealing with it—well, she hadn't answered that yet. But at least now she knew what the question was.

Benedetto was at the fire in the kitchen. Even with his jacket discarded over the back of a chair, it was blazingly hot here, but he didn't mind. He found the kitchen soothing, a utilitarian oasis among the endless grand rooms designed to impress guests that never came. He needed soothing. It had been hours since the confrontation over the portrait but time had yet to make any serious attempt at its widely-touted healing.

Still, by stewing over the incident intently, he had at least managed to organise his feelings somewhat. They fell into a handful of discrete categories: shock, anger and—most confusingly—disappointment. Shock and anger were simple enough to make sense of. While it had been, he could see now, rather naive of him to think that Faustina wouldn't be drawn to a covered portrait like a fly to manure, he couldn't have prepared himself for the revelation that she was the mystery woman from St Mark's Square.

Really, Bellini? put in a deeply sarcastic voice somewhere in his subconscious. *A beautiful, witty woman you couldn't resist who turned out to be a thief? You don't see a link there?*

Well, it was obvious if he put it like that. But that was where the disappointment came in. By disappearing so abruptly from his life, the woman he'd met last *Carnevale* had retained her air of mystery. He had tried—rather desperately, he saw now—to find an explanation for her having the bracelet that put her in a good light. Might she not, he had wondered, simply have bought a very similar bracelet for herself? And then happened to remember an urgent appointment when he'd asked her about it? He would have been satisfied with any indication that the charming creature who had led him to ruin had done so with the best of intentions, no matter how tenuous. Knowing that she was Faustina, and that the incident had been simply a thread in the tapestry of a life of crime, made the illusion difficult to hang on to.

Of course, the ruin wasn't her fault, not really. While it was true that, if Faustina hadn't stolen the bracelet, he might not have ended up under the curse, it was the magician who had cast it and he, Benedetto, who had deserved it.

I deserve this. He repeated that to himself a lot. It helped. If something like this had happened at random, to an undeserving victim, the crushing unfairness and the anger would surely have been impossible to bear. But he had made a mistake, and this was his punishment. It wasn't pleasant, but at least it made sense.

Bending over a little, he squinted into the tiny oven built into the brickwork of the fireplace. His bread had risen nicely. It always did. Baking made sense: you used the right ingredients in the right proportions, combined them with the right method, and you got what you were expecting. It was more than he could say for anything else. Taking up a peel from a rack beside the fire, he slid the flat, paddle-like end under the crisp-crusted brown loaf and extracted it from the oven, savouring the smell.

When he turned to deposit it on the table, he saw Faustina lingering in the doorway. She was staring hungrily at the bread, utterly transfixed by its journey. Either that or, like him, she was avoiding eye contact. He let the bread slide onto a wooden board on the table, then returned the peel to the rack. Out of the corner of his eye, he saw her reach for the bread.

"Not now," he said, brusquely. "It's hot."

She folded her arms. "You're still angry with me, aren't you?"

"The bread has just come out of the oven. It's hot. But if you'd rather burn yourself than take my advice, do please go ahead."

"You know what I mean."

"Do I?" He pulled out a chair and sat on it, then gestured for her to do the same. "You mean, am I angry that you violated my privacy by gawking at that portrait? Or that you stole the bracelet in the first place? Or, let us not forget, that you broke your promise not to try to leave the island for a second time, once again risking your life on the assumption that I am either a liar and a manipulator or unable to tell the difference between fantasy and reality?" He'd almost forgotten that last one.

Faustina sank into a chair with a weary groan. "I'll take that as a yes."

He could feel his fur prickling again. Now that he knew the truth about her, he couldn't look at her without thinking about her in that gown—and worse, remembering what it had been like to kiss her, and the feel of hot skin through silk. It was making it very hard to concentrate. He closed his eyes for a moment, fighting past it. When he opened them again, he kept his gaze fixed firmly on the table.

"Yes," he said, finally, "if you must know, I'm angry with you. I've done nothing but try to keep you safe since you arrived here, and you've done nothing but hate me for it. I don't know what else to do."

Faustina let out a long, slow sigh. "I don't hate you," she muttered.

The words made his stomach flip with disproportionate, if momentary, excitement.

"I mean," she went on, "you're asking me to believe in something that I've never seen any evidence of. I've never *seen* a rose tree turned to glass, or—" She stopped herself, then forged ahead. "But I *know* that there are bad people, people who will manipulate and lie to and hurt other people to get what they want. That's why I was afraid."

Benedetto blinked. "You mean—"

"No, I don't mean thieves like me, before you say that." Sudden irritation sharpened her features. "I would never take anything a person couldn't afford to lose. I'm not quite the monster you think I am."

There was a moment of silence. He wondered if she'd seen him flinch at the word "monster".

"Actually," he said, quietly, "I was going to refer to your brother."

She frowned. "So was I."

Benedetto returned to his study of the table. After another few seconds of silence he said: "I understand why you tried to leave with Rambaldo."

"You do?" Her expression was wary.

"Yes. And, believe it or not, I understand why you don't believe in the curse." She didn't have the dubious benefit of having it in her face—literally. "But what you *don't* understand is that the curse has been a fact of life for me for quite some time now. Your insistence that the curse can't exist is like… I don't know, if someone were to put a cloth over that loaf of bread and tell me there isn't any bread there. I know the bread is there because I've seen it, I can still see the shape it makes under the cloth. But you're saying that there isn't any bread, that there can't possibly be any bread, that there's no such thing as bread. And that's as hard for me to accept as the truth is for you."

"But that's because you're saying the bread is *magical*."

He sighed. "Yes, well, the analogy isn't perfect."

He risked looking up. Faustina was nodding slowly.

"Listen," she said, suddenly shy. "I'm sorry. About your fiancée, I mean."

She looked serious: her eyes focused intently on his, her brow furrowed. It was an unfamiliar expression on her. He'd seen her angry, incredulous, flippant—even, a year and a lifetime ago, flirtatious—but rarely serious. Not for the first time, he wondered what it would have been like, if the woman he'd met that night really had been his fiancée. They'd have had adventures, he knew that much. Days spent getting lost and finding themselves, evenings in whatever questionable nightspot took their fancy—and nights in bed, but not asleep. Somehow, he knew, they'd never have run out of things to talk about.

Maybe he'd have had those things with Maristela. But he hadn't met Maristela. He'd met Faustina. And, while he had plenty to regret about what had happened, he couldn't bring himself to be completely sorry for that.

"Don't be," he replied, softly. "You were right, it was my fault. I could have made sure you were who I thought you were before I spent the evening with you."

He knew why he hadn't. *Because I wanted it to be you.*

It wasn't as though it hadn't struck him as unusual for a noblewoman to take him to that seedy little *osteria*, or drink whatever had been in those tankards, or to kiss him. Twice. Any of those things could have prompted him to be a little suspicious, and they hadn't. He hadn't let them.

"I never said it was your fault." Faustina ran a finger absently along a join in the tabletop. "I still think a curse is an unnecessarily harsh punishment for that. Who do you think this magician is, anyway, to go around cursing people?"

"I don't know. He didn't leave his card."

"Haven't you wondered, though? If I were you, I'd have had people scouring the island for him before the week was out."

"Well, of course, I had Rambaldo make enquiries." It sounded rather weak against what Faustina was imagining. "To tell you the truth, though, I never thought there was much hope of finding him. He can do *magic*, for heaven's sake. He could probably fly to the other side of the world if the whim took him—or hide in plain sight. You know, turn into a vase or something."

"A vase?"

"Or something."

She folded her arms. "Well, I'd have tried anyway. I mean, aren't you angry that someone did this to you?"

Benedetto frowned, giving this thought time to filter through his mind. "No," he said, eventually, "not really." It was the truth—but one he'd never properly thought about before. "I deserved it. It wouldn't have happened otherwise."

"How do you know that?"

"I don't know." That was the truth too.

"So you think, what, that this magician is some unearthly judge of what's right, who goes around doling out punishments to the wicked?"

"Well, I wouldn't have put it in those terms, necessarily, but... yes. Something like that." It was unsettling, having his beliefs probed like this. Perhaps this was what it was like for Faustina, hearing him talk about the curse.

There's no such thing as bread...

Faustina was shaking her head. "All we did was kiss."

"You don't think there's anything wrong with a man engaged to one woman kissing another?"

He imagined it a lot: the moment Maristela had found out. As far as he understood it, the people who'd emerged from a party across the canal had done so in time to see him kiss his mystery woman—Faustina—and were connected to the Sourosins by only a few degrees of separation. The gossip had travelled fast, and he still felt a lurch of guilt when he thought about it reaching Maristela's ear. It was true that they hadn't known one another, never mind been in love, but she had been counting on him and he had let her down. He'd let everyone down.

"But you thought I was her." Faustina balled her fists, exasperated.

"But you weren't."

She stood up. "All right. I mean, that's ridiculous, but all right." Her gaze strayed to the centre of the table. "Do you think the bread's safe to eat yet?"

"Should be. But I was going to make some soup to go with it." The exchange seemed glaringly mundane, after what had passed before, but it was a relief.

"Is there anything I can do?"

"You can bring me some basil in from the garden if you like. It's what's in that bed over by the gate," he added, in response to her quizzical expression.

"I'll just take a bit of this to tide me over." She had torn a chunk off the loaf before he could stop her.

"You know," he said, "in civilised society, it's usually considered preferable to cut bread with a knife."

Faustina swallowed her mouthful, already halfway through the door. "Thank you," she said. "If I ever get back to civilised society, I'll remember that."

Faustina slowly made her way across the herb garden, lingering over the task of selecting and plucking a handful of the bright, wrinkled leaves from the flowerbed

Benedetto had pointed her to. She'd been expecting more of an argument and had a certain amount of built-up tension that she needed to dissipate.

It was difficult to get a really good argument going with Benedetto. He was so rigorously reasonable—aside from the matter of the curse, of course. But even that had a certain internal logic.

You don't have to see the bread to know it's there.

She shook herself. She didn't have time for this. It was time to act on what she thought she'd figured out.

If Benedetto was under a curse because he believed he was then, to break it, she needed him to stop believing. Someone better at persuasion than she was—Giacomo, perhaps—might have been able to talk him out of it, but it was becoming clear that she couldn't. *"But that's impossible"* had seemed like a compelling argument to her, but it was failing to produce any results.

But if his belief in the curse couldn't be broken, maybe something could make him believe that the curse had been broken. He was already looking for a solution in those books of his. Perhaps all he needed was to find one he believed in the way he believed in the curse.

It wasn't much, but it was all she had.

She walked back inside, clutching the leaves.

"Here. Will these do?"

Benedetto reached out to take them from her. The surface of his velvet gloves felt soft and warm, brushing against her palm. "That's perfect," he said, quietly. "Thank you."

Faustina watched his eyelids lower as he looked down at the leaves in his hands. His lashes were long, so that they almost touched the edge of the mask's eye holes.

She could have snatched the mask off him so easily. Just reached out quickly, while he was distracted, and pulled it away. It would take seconds—and then she'd know what, exactly, he was hiding.

She didn't, though. She couldn't.

He'd noticed her staring again. She looked away, quickly.

"Look," she said, "I want to apologise for looking at the painting. I know it wasn't really my place." The words surprised even her. She normally considered that her place was wherever she found herself. But something about that painting, and the way Benedetto had looked at her when she asked him about it, made her feel like she had crossed a line. "I wanted more information and I got it, and I suppose I can't say I'm not glad about that, but it was wrong of me not to at least ask you. I understand why you didn't want me to see it."

"Do you?"

"I think so. I suppose—" She hesitated. There was no easy way to talk about this, but she was in too deep now. "I suppose the painting is of something you've lost, isn't it? Something you don't want to think about."

Benedetto looked away. He stood very still for a moment, then turned towards the counter and carefully lay the basil on it. When he finally spoke again, his voice was hollow and measured. "It's like a death, in a way. Only worse. That is—I know that sounds dramatic. But that man in the picture, the life he had—they're gone. Part of me thinks I should say goodbye—mourn him and move on—but I can't. Because I still believe there's a chance, however remote, that I'll break the curse, that I'll get to be that person again. Sometimes I think that's worse than giving up." He gave a small, sad smile. "Hope isn't all it's cracked up to be."

She didn't know what to say. This was more information, more emotion than Faustina had been ready for, and she couldn't digest it.

He sighed, looking out of the window. "But it's more than that. It's the other portraits. They're reminders too. It's what they're there for. To show how each generation has changed things for the better but lived up to old expectations, to preside over the new generations to make sure they do the same."

She bit her lip. "What expectations?"

"Preserving the past. Securing the future." His lips twisted in a bitter, rueful smile. "That was my one job. Get married. Have heirs. See that the Bellini home, the Bellini fortune, the Bellini name are kept alive. And I failed." He glanced at her. "You're going to tell me how easy it is to be rich again, now, aren't you?"

Faustina shook her head. "No. I can see the value of low expectations. If there's one thing that matters to me, it's freedom." She saw Benedetto wince. "I'm sorry, I didn't mean that as a—I'm sorry." While it was true that she hadn't missed many opportunities to make a dig at him about keeping her here, she really hadn't meant to take that one. She swallowed, and tried honesty. "I suppose I've only ever thought of wealth as providing freedom, not restricting it."

"And I suppose you're right—I don't know enough about what I haven't got to appreciate what I have." He turned back to the window and stared, wistfully, at the sky. "I'll be different, I think, if I ever get back to the city."

A sudden rush of sympathy for him almost choked Faustina. What she blurted out was what she had been planning to say all along, but it came out more abruptly than she'd intended.

"I want to help with your research."

He seemed surprised, but not unpleasantly so. "Don't you think the fact that you don't believe in the curse might hamper you a little?"

"I may not believe, but I can read." She shrugged. "It was just an idea."

"No," he said, quickly, as though his mouth, too, were acting more quickly than his brain, "I'd like that. Thank you."

"We could start right now, if you like. Well, after lunch, I mean."

"Actually," he said, eyeing her a little awkwardly for a moment before crossing the room to fetch a knife, "I was planning to put the research on hold for a few days. Rambaldo's due to bring the livestock any time now, and our work in the garden isn't quite finished yet."

She smiled, a little wryly. "Even despite my excellent assistance?"

"I was going to say *because* of it."

"I take that to mean that you won't want me to come out there with you again." She wondered if he was as glad as she was that they were back to gently needling one another.

"On the contrary," he replied. "If you'd like to come and hamper me again, I'd, uh—" He glanced at her, then looked quickly away, seeming embarrassed. "Well, I'd be glad of your company."

Eleven

The next few days seemed to Faustina to pass very quickly. She and Benedetto fell into a sort of routine: working together from morning to early evening, then stopping to dine together. The work was hard but not unpleasant—Faustina finally felt that she was starting to help more than she hindered—and the conversation was kept reasonably light. It was almost pleasant to lose herself in labour, to simply *be,* with no worries about Ersilia or rent or where her next meal was coming from.

On the second day, along with a crate of disorientated and irritable chickens, Rambaldo brought the most comprehensive and beautiful set of painting supplies Faustina had ever seen. He took away, with Benedetto's permission, a letter she'd written to Chiara. In it, she apologised for her abrupt disappearance and assured her friend that she was safe but, beyond that, not really knowing what to say, she was circumspect. Faustina always worried, when writing to Chiara, that her stepmother might get to the letters first.

On the fourth day, when it rained, she spent the morning in her room with her paints, losing herself in the colours. At lunchtime, however, instinct led her back to the kitchen, where she was surprised to find herself alone. She had been so certain that she would find Benedetto there, preparing the midday meal that she was greatly looking forward to, that she didn't know what to do when she discovered that he wasn't. She hesitated in the middle of the room for a moment. Then, thinking wistfully of coffee, she crossed to the fireplace. The banked fire smouldered away to itself, patiently waiting for someone to feed it. Faustina surveyed the neat pile of evenly-cut logs next to it, then set about transferring some of these into the fireplace along with some kindling. There was a tense moment where it looked as though she might have smothered the embers out altogether but then the kindling caught. She wiped the ashes from her hands and stepped back to admire her handiwork.

"Not bad." A voice from the shadows. She turned to see Benedetto entering the room. His outfit was as fine as ever but she noticed a certain lack of polish. His hair looked ruffled, and his shirt was open a little.

She smiled at him. "Have you only just woken up?" she asked, scrunching her nose. "I've been awake for *hours*."

He half-smiled. "I suppose it must have been one of the palazzo's many other occupants that I heard coming down the stairs a few minutes ago, then."

"Must have been," she said, though her innocent tone

was undermined somewhat by her smirk. "Any chance of something to eat?"

He folded his arms. "I was going to ask you the same thing."

She blinked at him. "What?"

It was his turn to smirk now. "Well, you've been awake and presumably hungry all this time, surely you must have given some thought to lunch?"

"Yes, I thought 'When is Benedetto going to come and make me some lunch?'"

"How very resourceful of you." He made his way into the room, crossing towards the pantry. "How hungry are you?"

Faustina was considering this when her stomach growled. "Dangerously," she told him.

"Then we'd better make it something quick." His voice was now echoing from inside the pantry. He emerged a moment later with a handful of mysterious items wrapped in cloths. "How about *bruschette*?"

"Sounds good to me." Now that she really thought about it, Faustina was hungry enough to eat just about anything.

Benedetto placed his collection of items on the table before handing one of them to Faustina. It turned out to be the remains of a loaf of bread. "Cut that into slices."

She opened her mouth to ask where she could find a knife but she realised that she already knew. She had spent a lot of time in this kitchen by now. "All right," she said.

Benedetto crossed back to the fireplace, checking that the frame over the fire was secure before reaching up to unhook a small pot. "Coffee?"

"Yes, please." She answered without looking up, concentrating on moving the knife slowly back and forth through the slightly-stale bread. She had a feeling that Benedetto would notice any uneven slices—but perhaps be too polite to comment on it, which would be somehow worse than if he did.

She looked up then and found that he was smiling at her. She smiled back quickly then, feeling suddenly embarrassed, dropped her gaze back to the bread. Benedetto turned away to fill the pot with water, and she watched covertly as he hung it over the fire, then did the same with a broad, flat-bottomed pan. She finished cutting the bread as he began to peel a clove of garlic.

"Now what?" she asked.

"There's oil over there," he said, gesturing into a corner. "You must have made *bruschette* before?"

"Of course," she said, automatically defensive. Then, licking her lips, she added, "Well, not recently."

His lips twitched. "Which of us is the over-privileged aristocrat again?"

"You've got me," she said. "I only go as far in the domestic arts as I really have to." Having located a bottle of olive oil, she drizzled a fragrant zigzag across the bottom of the pan. "In mitigation, though, the kitchen at the boarding house is very much Ersilia's domain. Not to be entered if you value your life." She put the bottle down and got out of the way as Benedetto approached the fireplace. "Actually, if you value your life, you'd probably want to give a wide berth to the food, too. Ersilia's signature dish is a *risi e bisi* you could plaster a wall with."

Benedetto lowered the slices of bread into the pan where they sizzled in the oil. "Sounds delicious," he said.

"Yes." Faustina scratched her cheek. "I don't miss the cuisine there, to be honest."

He looked over his shoulder at her. "But you miss other things?"

She nodded, then felt bad. "Of course, as incarceration goes, I'd recommend this kind to anyone."

"On the grounds of the highly entertaining company, I presume?"

"I was thinking more of the food," she said, but she winked. "Though the company could also be worse."

He smiled, but then turned abruptly away. "Watch the bread," he said.

She did as she was told, letting it toast lightly in the oil before turning the slices over. Then she turned once again to watch him. This time he was unwrapping the mysterious parcels, which turned out to contain dried tomatoes and some kind of cured meat—perhaps *prosciutto* or *pancetta*. It was hard to tell from this distance but she found herself uninterested in the details. Whatever it was, it was going to taste good.

There was something arresting about the way Benedetto worked. He was so intent, so methodical—so utterly unlike her. It was fascinating. She found herself noticing small details in the way he moved: slow, precise and deliberate. He bit his lower lip a little in concentration, draining the colour.

He looked up sharply, sending a spasm of surprise down her spine as she tried to look like someone who specifically *hadn't* been staring at him.

"I smell burning," he said.

Faustina turned abruptly on her heel to rescue the bread. "I like it charred," she said, quickly forcing a lightness of tone that did not fully reflect her mood.

Benedetto sounded amused. "That's all right, then."

She brought the toast—only barely blackened—over to him. He assembled the *bruschette,* first rubbing each slice with the peeled clove of garlic, then heaping each one with a generous serving of tomatoes and cold meats. He finished it with a final drizzle of olive oil, then slid half of the slices back across the table towards her on a plate. Faustina prepared the coffee, placing two steaming cups on the table before sitting down. She could get used to cooking as part of a pair: half the work for all of the rewards.

They ate more or less in silence, both concentrating on the food. When they were finished, Faustina looked outside.

"Sun's coming out," she said.

"Yes," he replied, though he wasn't looking out of the window. "So it is."

On the morning they'd agreed to start working on the research together, Benedetto found Faustina in the library, waiting for him behind a stack of his magic books. She was engaged in scribbling feverishly on a loose piece of paper with the leadholder and didn't seem to hear him come in.

He cleared his throat. "*Buon giorno,*" he said, lingering for a moment at the room's threshold.

She looked up. In a subtle movement, though not subtle enough, she slid the piece of paper under the open book in front of her. "*Buon giorno* yourself."

She was smiling. Her face had a sort of simmering intrigue to it when she was angry, but it was nothing compared to the way she looked when she really smiled. It stirred something in him, something it was becoming desperately hard to suppress. Then again, if Rambaldo was right, perhaps he shouldn't suppress it.

No. It was absurd, utterly absurd, to think either that he stood a chance of winning anything stronger than reluctant tolerance from Faustina, or that doing so would break the curse, and he knew he shouldn't be getting his hopes up.

But then how do I explain my arm?

There was more fur missing this morning. Another patch—only a small one—close to his elbow. He had already spent what could easily have been an hour that morning staring at it, prodding at it, trying to convince himself that he was imagining things, but it had stubbornly failed to disappear.

He pushed the thought from his mind as best he could and approached the table. "Very well," he said, "since we're obviously proceeding with maximum efficiency, I feel bound to tell you that I've read all of those already, and have found nothing in them that suits our purpose. I thought we might make a start on these." He indicated the books Rambaldo had brought, stacked up on a side table.

Perhaps we don't need to do this. Perhaps the curse is going away on its own.

Now he really was getting ahead of himself. A couple of bald patches didn't exactly constitute a transformation. If anything, he looked a little worse: a monstrous beast with a touch of mange. Hardly cause for excitement.

And yet…

Faustina stared, incredulous, at the bookcases. "You've read all of these?"

"Yes." He looked around at them, remembering countless desperate, candlelit evenings.

"How long did that take?"

"Well, I started accumulating and studying them as soon as I realised that the curse was real, so about a year." He took a moment to exhale deeply. "I've, ah, had quite a lot of time on my hands."

Faustina's expression was sympathetic, which was somehow almost worse than when she was angry with him. "Yes, I suppose you have."

Benedetto crossed to the new books. He was disappointed with most of them. He'd read many like them already—general-purpose volumes purporting to give a basic grounding in the arcane arts to the fledgling magician, enchanter or soothsayer. The motives of the authors were not always clear: some of them, presumably, knew at least something about magic and were keen to share it, but so great was the variation between them that they could not possibly all have been written in earnest. A distressingly high number of them, in fact, dealt with the art of deception, of creating illusions sufficiently impressive to convince onlookers that something supernatural had taken place. Still others came tantalisingly close to revelations without actually making them—such as the one that advised magicians that, should they ever lose their magic, they might get it back by breaking a spell cast in anger, but did not say *how*.

He handed one of the new books to Faustina. "Here. Try this one."

Faustina turned over *On Charms* in her hands. "What am I looking for?"

"Good question. To be honest, I don't know exactly. Even after reading all these—" he gestured, "—I don't know enough to know what I'm looking for. I'm afraid I haven't been able to come up with anything more sophisticated than simply scouring the pages, looking for anything that seems familiar."

"Familiar?"

"Anything that sounds like this curse—so any references to glass or roses or scratches or—" He stopped himself, but apparently Faustina's mind had been working along similar lines.

"That's going to be difficult, isn't it?"

"What do you mean?"

"I mean, there's something about the curse I don't know. I don't know what it did to you. Besides keeping you trapped here, I mean."

"I see." He flexed his gloved fingers, uneasily. "Any mention of transformations or physical changes to the human body is probably worth looking at. You can just let me know if you see anything like that."

Faustina nodded, frowning slightly as she opened the book. She was silent for a moment but, just as Benedetto was about to turn his attention to his own book, she spoke.

"I wish you didn't feel you had to hide it from me."

He looked up, surprised. The brown eyes that met his were full of curiosity, and a warmth he hadn't seen in them before.

"What do you mean?"

"Well…" She paused for a moment, looking thoughtful. "I mean, it doesn't really matter what you look like, does it? I know this is putting it bluntly but, well, we're stuck together no matter what, aren't we? I'm sure it's nothing I couldn't get used to."

His heart skipped a beat. He wanted to believe her. It would have been wonderful to think that she was right, that what lay beneath his mask and gloves was something one could get used to. But it wasn't. He ought to know.

He ran his gloved hands absently over the surface of the table as he spoke. "I fear, Signorina Casanova, that you are not working your imagination quite hard enough. I can assure you that it is far worse than you suppose. Still," he tried to affect a more cheerful tone, "I appreciate the sentiment. If I could oblige you, I would."

Faustina shrugged, though she looked disheartened. "Well, could we at least dispense with all this 'Signorina Casanova' business? It seems a bit out of place, under the circumstances. I'd much rather you called me Faustina."

"Faustina." He hadn't spoken the name aloud before. He liked the feel of it. "You're right, I suppose. And you can call me Benedetto."

She smiled again. This time, he was surprised to find himself mirroring it.

They returned to their books, but it wasn't long before Benedetto felt compelled to speak again.

"I should warn you," he said, "this could take a while."

She shot him an oblique glance. "It will if you keep talking."

He felt himself blush under the mask. She was right, he was talking a lot. It had been a long time since he had spent any meaningful time with anyone worth talking to, and he was clearly out of practice. "Sorry," he said. "It's just that I've read a lot of these, and often there's nothing of use in an entire book."

"Thank you. I'll try not to approach this task with any kind of optimism."

He snorted. "Yes. I find that helps." He was only half-joking.

He managed to stay quiet after that and, for what might have been an hour or so, only the rustling of pages broke the silence. For his part, Benedetto had to admit to himself that he was not doing his best work. More than once, he caught himself flipping pages without actually having read what was on them. His gaze kept slipping—not, since he was wary of unnerving her, directly to Faustina, but to the window behind her, or the bookshelves. His conscious mind, had its opinion been sought, could have pointed out that he was a gentleman and above such feeble distractions as a glimpse of her in his peripheral vision, but his subconscious acted on its own authority.

Faustina heard the approach first. She looked up abruptly from her book, then stood and went to the window.

"Rambaldo's here," she said.

Hearing the voices now, Benedetto lowered his own book, surprised. He'd forgotten that Rambaldo was due to make another delivery today. That was unusual. Up until now, there had been so little to look forward to that he'd often caught himself counting the hours until Rambaldo's next delivery, just because he was someone to talk to.

He pushed back his chair. "Of course. It should be a bit of a mixed delivery today. He's bringing the pigs and your dresses."

"In different containers, I hope."

He smiled. "I'd better go down and meet him. Are you coming?"

"In a minute. I'll just finish this page."

He left the room. It was only when he was halfway down the stairs that he realised he was whistling.

Whistling?

He couldn't remember the last time he'd done that. But then, he couldn't remember the last time he'd felt like this. Not happy, not exactly. Just… just better than a constant, dull, resigned misery. And, in fact, noticing that was enough to push him over into happiness after all.

"You're in high spirits," was Rambaldo's greeting when Benedetto met him on the gravel path.

He couldn't deny the charge. "Yes," he said, "I suppose I am."

"Perhaps, on reflection, you found a little truth in my remarks, hmm?"

"Well, I—"

"And how *is* Signorina Casanova?"

Benedetto was blushing again. It was the most grateful he'd ever been for the mask. "She's fine. She hasn't tried to escape for, oh, days."

"That's a start, I suppose. And what about the other matter?" He pointed at Benedetto's forearm.

Benedetto self-consciously put a hand to his sleeve. He couldn't pull it up: Rambaldo's men were in sight, unloading a large and faintly-squealing crate onto the jetty. "There's another small patch where the fur seems to have gone," he whispered.

Rambaldo folded his arms. "And you still don't think there's a connection?"

Benedetto shook his head, frowning. "I don't see it. It's too incredible. I've spent all this time looking for a solution, without success, and then one just happens to wash up on the island?"

"Of all the things that have happened to you, *that* seems too incredible?"

"There's no evidence for it."

Rambaldo was pushing this too hard. It was bad enough to find Faustina so intensely… *distracting*, without looking upon her as the means to end the curse.

"Evidence?" The eyes behind Rambaldo's mask were quizzical.

"Well, I mean—" Benedetto looked around for eavesdroppers, then lowered his voice again. "When the curse was cast, there was all this smoke and light—and a glass rose tree that appeared from nowhere, for heaven's sake. There's been nothing like that now."

Rambaldo made a broad gesture with his hands.

"Perhaps smoke and light isn't the only kind of magic. Perhaps it's not even the best kind."

But Benedetto was only half-listening. "Besides," he said, "even if you're right, and it does have something to do with Faustina and her feelings about me, that's hardly cause for excitement. I'm still little better than her jailer, remember? We're being civil enough, because we're stuck with each other, but she'd leave without a backward glance if she could." He sighed, the whistling wind beginning to fall from his sails. "If you're right, if this change—" he gestured at his arm "—is the result of her feelings of lukewarm tolerance toward me, then with time and a bit of luck I suppose we might manage friendship and the whole arm."

"But you don't think she'll love you?"

Benedetto let out a hollow laugh. "No. Friendship is the very best I can hope for, trust me."

Rambaldo shrugged. "It's not for me to argue with you, Signor Bellini." His gaze had strayed over Benedetto's shoulder.

Benedetto turned. Faustina was making her way down the steps towards them. She had on his brown coat and breeches and gold waistcoat today. He realised now that he'd been getting used to seeing her dressed in his clothes. She looked pretty in them, in an easy, relaxed sort of way. Now that he thought about it, he found that he was a little nervous about seeing her in clothes designed specifically to show off a woman's beauty to fullest advantage.

Rambaldo doffed his hat. "Signorina Casanova."

"Signor Rambaldo," she returned, somewhat stiffly.

Then she looked at Benedetto and smiled. "I think you and I have some guests to welcome." She pointed at the crates.

"Yes, and I should be getting along," put in Rambaldo. "Other deliveries to make and so on."

"Rambaldo—" Benedetto began.

Rambaldo put a hand on his arm. "Good luck," he said. "With your 'guests', I mean. *Alla prossima.*"

Benedetto turned to Faustina as his agent walked away. "I don't think we should call them 'guests'," he said. "It's going to feel like rather a violation of etiquette when we eat them."

Faustina shrugged. "I suppose. But calling them 'lunch' just seems hostile."

A thought struck Benedetto. "Excuse me for a moment." He caught Rambaldo at his boat and beckoned him away from his men.

Rambaldo's mask was as passive as always. "Yes, signor?"

"Look, what we were discussing, about the curse..." Benedetto forced himself to breathe. "I—I suppose she *would* have to love me back, wouldn't she?"

"What do you mean?"

"Well, supposing you're right, and it is about, uh—" he swallowed "—love, or... or something. Do you think it's my feelings that would affect the transformation, or hers?"

But then he thought: *well, it can't be mine. If it were, we'd be looking at more than just a couple of bald patches.*

"Never mind," he said. "I think I've answered my own question."

The crate had stopped squealing now, more or less, though it was still possible to make out the slightly disgruntled snufflings of the half-dozen pigs inside it. It had been left outside the enclosure that Faustina and Benedetto had built—or rather, that Benedetto had built while Faustina… *supervised.*

Faustina approached one of the crates cautiously and crouched down in front of it to peer through a gap in the wood. A damp, questing snout came to greet her and she shied back. She'd seen pigs before, of course, at markets—sometimes even alive. But she'd never been this close to one.

"Making friends?" Benedetto walked up behind her.

"You've got to take the company you can get around here," she replied, grinning up at him.

"You mean I'm going to have to compete with the pigs for your attention from now on? That's going to make meeting my daily sarcasm requirements difficult."

Faustina straightened up. "Oh, don't worry," she said, "there's plenty to go around."

As she stood, she felt the page in the pocket of her borrowed breeches crinkle a little. She put a hand in the pocket, pushing it down. She didn't want Benedetto to see it, not yet. This was another little plan—not as complicated as helping to research a way to break a curse she didn't believe in. It was just an attempt to be… well, nice. She wasn't sure it suited her.

They smiled at one another in slightly goofy silence for

a moment. Then, seeming to remember something, Benedetto looked away. "We'd better get the pigs into their new home."

"Right." She frowned. "How do we do that, exactly?"

Benedetto was already starting to pry open the crate. "I'm sure it won't be a problem."

Up until now, Faustina hadn't associated the term "overconfidence" with Benedetto, but the events of the next few seconds gave her cause to rethink this position. Sea travel hadn't agreed with the pigs and they were, it appeared, keen to get their trotters back on *terra firma*. So keen, in fact, that, at the first sight of daylight, they all took it into their little pink heads to stampede. Benedetto caught one but the others scattered, despite what Faustina felt was a valiant attempt on her part to tackle one of them to the ground.

She pushed herself up, spitting grass. "Now what?"

Benedetto leaned over the waist-high fence around the pig pen, divesting himself of his captive before turning back to answer her. "I'll run round to the jetty," he said. "Perhaps Rambaldo and his men are—" But then his gaze strayed to the horizon. "Never mind."

Faustina looked round. Rambaldo's boat was cruising, footloose and pig-free, back towards the city, and well out of earshot. "Ah," she said.

"All right," said Benedetto, having cleared his throat. "New plan. You and I will catch the pigs, preferably before they get into—oh, no."

Once again, Faustina followed his gaze. This time she was looking over towards the nearest gate—an open gate, which led into the courtyard gardens. "Ah," she said again, at the risk of repeating herself.

"I should just stop suggesting things, shouldn't I?" Benedetto muttered.

"Probably," she replied, and then they were both running.

It was Faustina who claimed the next catch. One of the pigs was evidently drawn to shiny things—she could sympathise—and had become distracted by the contents of the fish pond. Faustina scooped it up with a triumphant "Aha!"

Her sense of victory, however, was short-lived. By the time she'd decanted the pig into the pen and returned to the action, sounds of distress were coming from one of the flower gardens. *Human* distress. She hurried towards the noise and found Benedetto swearing over a trampled flowerbed. An overreaction, possibly—but, in his defence, it really was quite thoroughly trampled.

"How did they manage that?" she asked.

"They didn't," he spat, fiercely. "I did. I was about to catch one and didn't look where I was going."

Faustina twitched her lips, looking from Benedetto to the squashed leaves and petals, then back again. "You're angrier about this than you were about being robbed."

She meant it as a joke, but he seemed to take it seriously.

"Being robbed wasn't my fault. This—" he gestured at the ruined plants and swore some more "—this was stupid."

Interesting. She had a feeling she'd just learned something about him. Not an outcome of pig-chasing she'd been expecting.

"How did they get in here? Was that gate open too?"

"They can fit between the bars."

Faustina scrunched her face a little, digesting this information. A squeal distracted her. She looked up, then smiled.

"Well," she said, "almost."

The stuck pig seemed rather sorry for itself as she approached it, and its protestations quickly became the subdued squeaks of a pig resigned to its fate. Clasping it to her chest, Faustina turned back to grin at Benedetto.

"You'd better hurry up," she said. "I'm winning."

He hesitated for a moment, seeming to teeter between his frustration and something else. Something brighter. Then he smiled.

"Not for long," he said.

Over the next hour or so, Faustina learned a lot about apprehending pigs, mostly through a process of elimination. Cajoling them in soft, sweet tones didn't work, and nor did scathing, unrepeatable remarks about their personal hygiene and likely parentage. Vigorous pursuit—for the brief but harrowing period when the pigs had exited the courtyards and done a couple of circuits of the garden wall—was a complete bust. Benedetto had had high hopes for bribing them with food, but that had met with only limited success. One pig succumbed to the charms of his proffered vegetables but Benedetto's celebration at having evened the score was brought to an abrupt halt by the discovery that the remaining two pigs had decided that they liked their vegetables extremely fresh, and were eating them straight from the ground in the kitchen garden.

"The good news," Faustina attempted to point out, "is that they're staying still now."

"I suppose." Benedetto's tone was unique—the dark gloom of a man who knew he could always grow more vegetables, but didn't feel that any new ones would ever truly fill the hole in his heart left by those he'd lost. "What if I stand by the gate, and you sort of herd them towards me?"

"And let you catch them? I think not."

Benedetto shot her a glare, but there was no real malice behind it. "All right. You stand by the gate and I'll herd them."

"Perfect. Victory is mine." She illustrated the point with a little dance.

"Don't do that," he said.

She stuck her tongue out at him.

Benedetto waited for her to get into position, then approached the pigs stealthily—or as stealthily as one could approach a pig while trying not to crush any delicate leaves. They ignored him for a while, or perhaps didn't notice him, so intent was their concentration. But it dawned on them suddenly that something was afoot, and then they were running, their trotters scrabbling for purchase in the loosened earth.

Faustina was ready. She waited, crouched like a tiger—albeit a tired, sweaty tiger who balked at the idea of eating her prey raw once she caught it. Any minute now she would leap, graceful and unstoppable, and—

"Ha!"

She'd never heard Benedetto "Ha!" before.

She blinked, reviewing the last couple of seconds in

her mind's eye. The pigs had been coming towards her. Benedetto had been chasing them. She had been about to grab them and then... they'd slowed. Not much—just enough, on seeing her, for Benedetto to seize them.

Faustina straightened up, softening what she realised was a fairly fierce expression, and smoothed her hair. "Oh," she said. "Well done."

"Victory," Benedetto observed, "appears to be *mine*."

She shrugged. "That doesn't matter," she said, sounding utterly unconvincing. "The important thing is that we caught them."

And then she chased him, armful of pigs and all, all the way back to the pen.

With the pigs secured, the two of them sat down, side by side, on the grass. Overwhelmed by the bliss of rest, Faustina flopped onto her back.

"That was fun," she said.

Benedetto lowered himself backwards, so that he was lying beside her.

"Yes, it was," he replied.

Faustina reached up to her face to brush away a lock of hair. When she dropped her hand back to the ground, it landed on Benedetto's.

Move it away, she urged herself, but the hand stayed put. They lay there together—exhausted, prone, and very nearly hand-in-hand—for several minutes.

It doesn't mean anything, she thought. *We're both tired*.

But then Benedetto turned his head toward her. The eyes behind the mask were bright from the exertion, and they were looking at her as though she were something completely, unwaveringly wonderful.

She looked back at him. She didn't know for how long. When the awkwardness hit them, though, it was like a bucket of ice water.

"Um," she said, and the moment was over.

Benedetto sat up abruptly. "I'm sorry," he muttered. She didn't know what for.

"I should, uh…" She looked around for an excuse.

But Benedetto's mind had obviously been working along similar lines. "I'll head back to the house," he said. "I've got some… things to do." He waved a hand, vaguely.

"I'll, uh, stay here. It's comfortable." Actually, there was a stone digging into her hip, but this didn't seem to be pertinent information.

"Good," said Benedetto. "Um, I mean, it's… good that you're comfortable. I'll see you later."

"Yes," she said, and then he was gone.

Three miles and a world away from the island, Giacomo sat at the exquisite walnut writing desk Bragadin had given him as a surprise gift upon his return to the city. He held a pen in his hand—poised, infrequently dripping, over the inkwell. He was composing a love letter. Giacomo put quite a lot of effort into his love letters but it was a task that paid good dividends since, with careful planning, it was usually possible to make several copies of the same letter and dispatch them to more than one woman.

He hadn't had as much time to devote to the pursuit

lately as he would have liked. Dear old Bragadin had been desperate to hear about his young friend's adventures overseas ever since Giacomo had arrived back in Venice, and it had become too difficult to keep putting him off. Bragadin *had* paid for those adventures, and he had a very gentle, polite but persistent way of reminding Giacomo of it. Giacomo had therefore reluctantly spent the last few days regaling his patron with tales of the Grand Tour, which had rather eaten into his schedule.

He knew he ought to be grateful. After all, he hadn't known for sure, on his journey back to Venice, whether he'd even be welcomed back to Bragadin's house. There was still a lot about magic he didn't know. Giacomo had been born with his power—no one had trained him to use it.

He'd always known there was something special about him. In his childhood, the people around him had put it down to him being unusually charming and spectacularly lucky. For a while, he'd tried to be satisfied with that explanation—after all, that was certainly what it had looked like. More often than not, and sometimes against quite striking odds, things happened the way he wanted them to and people did as he told them. Luck and charm explained that.

But, then, in adolescence, he'd found things they couldn't explain. That he could move objects without touching them, for example—or make them disappear. Make himself hard to see, or impossible to miss. It had been scary at first, exhilarating once he'd got used to it. Lately, though, it had been verging on tedious. Because magic, it turned out, had limitations. Consequences.

Giacomo wasn't a fan of consequences.

Until relatively recently, he hadn't met anyone with powers like his—though he'd been looking. In fact, that was how he'd met Bragadin. After a chance conversation, several years ago, had revealed that the senator was interested in magic, Giacomo had made it his mission to get him alone. Initially—naively—Giacomo had wondered if the old man might know something he didn't. He'd been on the lookout for a mentor, and a rich senator would have fitted the bill perfectly.

Of course, it had turned out that Bragadin knew only what anyone with more money than sense knew about magic—that it was readily available and surprisingly ineffective. But, despite years of disappointment at the hands of mountebanks and pretenders, Bragadin's belief in magic had persisted. Witnessing a modest display of Giacomo's power had delighted him—to the extent that, in retrospect, he might well have offered his friendship, even patronage, without any further encouragement. But Giacomo had been feeling his way with magic then. He still was, now. So he'd pushed it a little further, over the blurry line between natural charm and preternatural magic, between impressing Bragadin with his powers and using them against him. He'd put a sort of spell on the senator. It had been the first time he'd tried a spell like that—and the last.

A knock at the door shook him from his reverie. He lowered his pen and stood.

"Yes?"

A servant entered. "I'm sorry to disturb you, Signor Casanova." He sounded nervous. The servants always did. "You have a visitor."

Giacomo stiffened. He'd had a vision, and it was wearing a black silk gown. "Who is it?"

"A gentleman. One Signor Rambaldo."

"Oh." Giacomo softened his stance a little, now confused rather than uneasy. The name rang a bell, though very quietly. "What does he want?"

"He did not confide in me, signor. Would you have me dismiss him?"

Giacomo considered this, then shook his head. "No," he said. "Show him in." Curiosity had got the better of him.

The servant bowed and withdrew, returning a moment later to deliver the promised Rambaldo. Giacomo recognised the face when the name had eluded him.

"Ah," he said, while his guest was still at the nadir of a very deep bow. "I remember now. You're the fellow that invited me to that card game of Bellini's."

"That's correct, yes." Rambaldo straightened. "Ernesto Rambaldo, your humble servant."

"Well, in that case," Giacomo said, starting to turn back to his desk, "you can serve me by going away. I have nothing to add to what I said to Bellini the last time we met." He wouldn't have admitted it out loud, but this was a complication he hadn't foreseen. He'd forgotten that Benedetto had an agent in the city.

"I'm afraid you have misinterpreted my visit," Rambaldo answered. "I am not here on Signor Bellini's behalf."

Giacomo stopped, surprised. "You're not?"

"No." Rambaldo looked around. The servant had departed. "I may speak freely, I suppose?"

"If you must." Now Giacomo was really confused.

"Very well. I am here as a colleague. A fellow practitioner of the arcane arts."

Giacomo blinked. "You're a magician?" He realised, a moment too late, that he ought first to have denied that *he* was.

"Indeed. May I sit down?"

Giacomo nodded. They sat on armchairs, facing one another.

"Go on, then," said Giacomo. "If you are what you say you are, show me some magic."

Rambaldo gave a wan smile. "Ah," he said. "Well, there, Signor Casanova, you have called my bluff. While I still consider myself a magician, having had—if I may be permitted a moment of vanity—considerable magical ability for most of my life, I find myself currently without it." He licked his lips. "You're aware, I assume, that any magician deemed to have misused his or her magic is liable to have it taken away?"

Giacomo stiffened. "Yes," he said. "By a magician who has already lost theirs."

He was aware, all right. He'd learned that from Leandra. In fact, it was the reason he found himself so frequently in her company. Leandra was a *consequence*.

Giacomo regarded his guest with renewed suspicion. One arcane vulture on his tail was more than enough.

"Well," he continued, standing, "this has been delightful, but I'm afraid I have important business to attend to, so..." He indicated the door in a pointed manner.

Rambaldo remained seated, unruffled. "Don't worry. I don't want your magic. I just want your help."

"And if I don't want to help you?" Giacomo had a horrible feeling he knew where this was going.

"Well, naturally, I've been working on the assumption that you will—being a generous, public-spirited sort of fellow. But, if not, I suppose I might be forced to fall back on certain information in my possession." He cleared his throat. "While *I'm* not interested in your magic, I have no doubt that someone else is."

Giacomo attempted a laugh. "You sound as though you're planning to blackmail me."

Rambaldo crossed his legs, settling more comfortably in his seat. He looked around for a moment before speaking again. "This is a very nice place you've got here. Senator Bragadin seems to treat you with extraordinary generosity."

Giacomo laughed again. This time, borne aloft by relief, it lasted for quite some time. "Oh, my dear fellow! You're talking about the spell I cast on the senator. You're behind the times, I'm afraid. Not only did another magician catch on to that two years ago but, in the time I was abroad, I found a way to wipe my slate clean and secure my magic." He grinned. "On my return, I'm pleased to report, I found that not only was Bragadin's disposition to me as pleasant as it had ever been, but that the spell persisted—leaving him disinclined to believe any wild accusations about me."

"Indeed." Rambaldo's tone was icily calm. "Both your position and your magic were secured—so long as you avoided any further misuse of your power. Which is why, when Benedetto Bellini embarrassed you, you were forced to concoct a plan for revenge that did not involve magic—knowing, as you did, that you were not wholly in the right."

Giacomo swallowed. Rambaldo was remarkably well-informed.

"You've... met Faustina, then?" he asked.

Rambaldo gave a faint smile. "Yes. Our conversation was illuminating. According to her, she knew from the start that attempting to steal from Ca'Bellini was a catastrophe waiting to happen. She'd never have done it on her own."

"I'm very persuasive." Giacomo felt suddenly queasy.

"That's what she said." Rambaldo leaned forward. "But I wonder if even you know, really, where your persuasion ends and your magic begins? Would you swear you didn't cast a spell on her to make her do what you wanted? Would you stake your magic on it?"

Giacomo felt the walls close in around him. The man was echoing his own thoughts. Giacomo took a deep breath.

"How can I be of assistance?"

Rambaldo folded his arms, satisfied. "I knew I could depend on you. It's a simple matter, should barely take a moment of your time. You're planning to go back to the island at some point and help yourself to a few more of Signor Bellini's possessions—and collect Faustina, of course. Correct?"

Giacomo thought for a moment. It was too late for lies. "Actually," he said, "there's a difficulty there. Bellini's told Faustina there's a curse on the island—something to do with a glass rose tree? Faustina doesn't believe in magic, so she thinks it's all so much hogwash, but—"

"She doesn't believe in magic? With a magician for a brother?" Rambaldo's shock was too excessive to be real. "How can that be?"

"Because I've never told her I'm a magician, I suppose." Giacomo tried to keep his tone cool.

"Of course. Because then she'd have treated you with the sort of suspicion that might have stopped her becoming your little vassal when you needed her."

Giacomo looked away. He knew he was being goaded, but the truth was that he did feel at least a *little* guilty about it. Letting Faustina know he was a magician would not have been in his interest, but he could have done *something* about her firm disbelief in magic. Even the smallest dose of healthy superstition might have been enough to stop her from touching a strange glass rose tree out of sheer curiosity.

"If you know so much about it," he said, at length, "perhaps you can tell me—is she under a curse or not?"

Rambaldo considered this for a moment, then smiled. "You've asked just the right question there. There is a curse, but no, she's not under it. Not yet." He got to his feet, so that he could meet Giacomo's gaze. "That's what I'd like you to remedy."

"I'm not sure about this."

It was a day later, and Faustina was lingering outside

the doorway to the library. She couldn't see Benedetto but she knew he was there.

"Not sure about what?" He sounded distracted. She heard pages turning.

"This dress. It's, ah…" She fumbled for the words. The truth was, it was hard to explain what was unsettling her about the dress. It was beautiful: shimmering sky-blue silk with white lace at the elbows and impossibly tiny, incredibly detailed dusky pink flowers embroidered on the bodice. Choosing for herself, she would have opted for something a little more striking and with a less demure colour scheme, but it was still by far the loveliest thing she had ever worn. If it had been offered to her in the city, she would have seized upon it without hesitation.

But I'm not in the city.

"Why don't you come in here so I can see it?" he called.

"You mean, why don't I stop hiding and show you what I look like?"

"Yes."

She smiled to herself. *Did he miss the irony there, or is he ignoring it on purpose?*

She moved to enter the room but found that Benedetto had got up to meet her. They bumped softly into one another, and she stepped back, embarrassed.

"I'm sorry." She smoothed her skirt then looked up at him, shyly. "Well? What do you think?"

He subjected her to a very cursory examination, then turned away and moved back towards the book-strewn desk. "You look… fine." His tone was even, the pause only momentary.

Faustina was disappointed. She hadn't realised it until now, but she had been expecting something more. This was the first time he'd seen her looking her best—well, not quite her best, since she had been forced to do without makeup or hairpins. The natural look, with her dark hair spilling loose over her shoulders, was somewhat at odds with the elegance of the dress. But she knew for a fact that she looked pretty good, and it shouldn't have strained someone with Benedetto's interest in fashion to acknowledge it.

"Thanks," she muttered, hurling herself into a chair. The corset holding her into the dress bit fiercely into her midsection as she sat, souring her mood still further. She hadn't realised how accustomed she had become to the relative comfort of gentlemen's clothing.

It's a good thing I didn't go to all this trouble on his account.

But she had, in a way. She had enjoyed admiring her reflection after putting it on, of course, but most of the fun of a dress this expensive was being noticed in it. As one of the only two people in the building, she was already unmissable. It hardly seemed worth the effort of pouring herself into a beautiful gown like this if her only companion declined to acknowledge it.

Benedetto reached his seat and looked absently down at the book he had been reading, but didn't sit down. "Go on, then," he said. "What's wrong with it?"

"I don't know. It's just that they're all…" She stood up, gesturing down at her skirt. "Like this. Layered with expensive silks and exquisitely embellished and—" she twirled around to demonstrate "*—beautiful*."

Benedetto blinked. "You're right. That does sound awful. I should have the dressmakers flogged."

She rolled her eyes. "Look, I'm just saying, if we were hosting balls here every night then these dresses would be perfect. But we're not. Can you see me helping you in the garden in *this*?"

He appeared to consider this for a moment. "If '*we*' were hosting balls?"

She paused. That hadn't sounded right to her, either. "You know what I mean." She wasn't sure he did. She wasn't sure *she* did, come to that.

Benedetto folded his arms across his chest. "So, you're saying you think it would be possible for these dresses to make you *less* effective with a spade? It's hard to picture."

"Very funny." She sank back into her seat.

Benedetto cleared his throat. "Forgive me," he said. "That was unnecessary. And unfair. I'm sorry."

Faustina looked up. He was giving her that earnest look again, the one he'd had when he told her about the curse on her first night here, the one that begged to be believed.

She shrugged. "That's all right." It wasn't as though her remarks to him had always been the very essence of kindness, either.

He gave a brief, rueful sigh. "I fear I may have got into a bit of a habit of lightly insulting you when I can't think of anything to say."

It caught her in a tender spot: the part of her that housed truths she didn't like to acknowledge. She knew exactly what he was talking about. She'd been doing it herself. Her feelings about him were becoming so confusing that it was impossible to speak in a way that did them justice. Teasing him was easy. Jibes and jokes filled the gaps that, without them, things like *I hate you* or *I like you* would have rushed to fill. She'd used them both ways on Benedetto: the former when she'd become trapped here and resented him for it, the latter a year ago when they'd first met.

She wasn't sure which way she was using them now. Or which way *he* was. The thought was at once surprising, unsettling—and a little exciting.

"Me too," she said, eventually. "Do you think we should stop?"

He looked uncertain. "Perhaps. It's never been my intention to offend you. Well—" He hesitated, then smiled. "Not lately, anyway."

In spite of her own confusion, Faustina smiled back. "Right. And I haven't really been thinking of you as a vile bourgeois oppressor recently, either." She looked away, unfocused, into the middle distance for a moment. "I suppose we each know by now that the other is more than they appear."

Benedetto pulled out his chair and sat down, slowly. "Yes," he said, in one of his cautious, measured tones. "I suppose we do. All the same, though—" His gloved hands idly caressed a book. "Well, it's been kind of fun, sometimes."

She nodded, still smiling. "Yes, it has." She shifted in her seat. "I suppose we could keep doing it, trying as hard as we can to judge whether it's a good time, and apologising if we get it wrong?"

He laughed. "That sounds very sensible."

"I know. I'm surprised too."

They locked eyes for a moment, smiling. Then Benedetto dropped his gaze to the book beneath his hand, and slid it towards her.

"Here," he said, abruptly changing the subject. "I wanted to show you this."

Faustina took hold of the book, pulling it the rest of the way across the table to examine it. A moment later, she let out a low whistle.

"Transformative elixir," she read. *"To take on the shape of an animal, first gather the blood of—"* She broke off. "An animal? There's magic—I mean, whoever wrote this book thought there was magic that can turn a person into an animal?"

Benedetto rubbed his beard. "So it would seem." She knew him well enough by now to know when he was keeping his voice deliberately level.

She frowned, looking him over. She knew she shouldn't ask, but it was impossible to resist. "Is that... relevant to our search?"

He looked away. "Like I said, I've been looking at anything that mentions transformation. After searching for this long, I don't feel I can be too selective about the details."

Faustina looked at him for several pensive moments before deciding to accept this answer. "All right," she said, at length. "But these are the instructions to cast one. And they're disgusting," she added, skimming a list of ingredients that included more in the way of intestines than she would have liked.

"I know. But look at the other page."

She did as instructed. "*To remove the curse, you need only*—wait, this is it? It just says to read this incantation under a full moon. No guts or gore or anything." She looked up at him as the significance of this began to dawn on her. "We can actually try this. The full moon's only a couple of days away."

In spite of her usual irritation in the face of nonsense, she was almost excited. After all, this was what she needed—a means of breaking the curse that Benedetto could believe in. After all his pessimistic talk of year-long searches, she had been expecting a long wait for something like this.

"Certainly," he said, shrugging, when she looked up from the book. "We can try it."

She frowned. "You don't seem very excited."

"I'm not." He leaned back in his chair. "Like I told you, I've been at this a long time. I've found several things that looked as though they might work but didn't—or, at least, didn't work when *I* tried them. That's the problem. I don't know what to look for and I don't know what to do when I think I've found it. This incantation, for example. Will it work when anyone says it? Do you need some kind of magic wand or amulet? Does the book assume some innate magical ability? Is there such a thing? I've no idea. So, if we try this and it doesn't work—and it probably won't—I won't know why. For all I know, I've found the spell that would help already, and just didn't know what to do with it." He straightened. "Although, actually—" But he stopped himself.

"What?"

"Never mind. I suppose what I'm saying is... I've learned not to invest too heavily in things like this. But yes, by all means, let's try it."

Faustina stared at the book, thinking. This put a bit of a damper on her plan. If Benedetto had already started treating potential ways to break the curse with this much scepticism—though saving none of that scepticism for the curse itself—it was looking less than likely that "casting" this "spell" would convince him the curse was broken. Still, it was worth a try. And she found that she wasn't as disappointed by this setback as she might have been. Suddenly, she wasn't in that much of a hurry to leave.

Benedetto pulled the book back towards him. "And, about the dresses—I'll get you something more suitable, if that's what you want. And you can keep wearing my old clothes in the meantime. How does that sound?"

"That sounds good." Faustina smiled. "Thank you. But you're, um—" She hesitated, realising how spoiled she was about to sound.

"What?"

"You're not going to send this one back, are you?" She put a protective hand over her bodice. "It's so pretty. And it looks so good on me!"

"Yes, it does," said Benedetto, absently—then he looked suddenly panic-stricken.

She laughed at him, triumphant. "I knew you thought so."

"Hmm," he said.

TWELVE

Benedetto waited on the carved stone seat by the fish pond, watching the moonlight ripple across the surface of the water. Every now and then it fell still, so that the reflected silver sphere hung for a moment or two, perfect and undisturbed, before a breeze or an errant fin set it dancing again.

He was waiting for a lot of things. For Faustina, ostensibly, but also for his heart to stop racing uncontrollably when he thought about her, for the courage to face the way he felt about her instead of running from it, and for his whole being to stop aching with desperation to touch her.

That last one was the worst. It was physically painful, how much he wanted to touch her. It had reached a peak as they'd lain side-by-side, her skin against his gloves—tantalisingly close but impossibly far away.

She arrived at last, her loose hair swirling in the

breeze. She smiled when he stood up to greet her.

"Sorry I'm late," she said. "I was working on… something." She covered the pause well, but not well enough. She'd almost revealed something she didn't want to. He didn't mind—she could have secrets if she wanted them—but, when she held out the book she'd brought from the library, he saw that her fingers were stained with paint.

"That's all right," he said, accepting the book. "The night is young." It was a strange feeling, the one he got when he looked at her: at once sadness that she was out of his reach and immeasurable delight that she existed in the world at all.

He stood. She watched him expectantly, her eyes flickering between his face—his mask—and the book. Her excitement confused him.

"You're very interested in this, for someone who doesn't believe in magic," he noted.

The question seemed to unbalance her. "That's a good point," she answered, at length. "I suppose it's, I don't know, the atmosphere? You know, an occult tome, the full moon…" She gestured, vaguely. "It's… interesting."

"I suppose so." He looked down at the book. Slowly, he ran a gloved claw along the top of the pages, parting them at the leather bookmark he'd placed inside. He didn't want to do it. He didn't want to stand in front of her and read out some pseudo-arcane nonsense to the heedless air. He'd look a fool.

But, of course, he already looked a fool to her. He'd look an even bigger one if she knew what was on his mind right now.

Better get this over with.

The incantation was a long one—three pages, in the sprawling hand of the self-proclaimed expert who'd recorded it—and unlikely to win any praise from critics of literature. It rhymed in some places but not in others and for several stanzas consisted of a language that Benedetto could not have sworn really existed. Nonetheless, he read it as earnestly as he could.

Nothing happened.

He turned to face Faustina, apologetically. "Like I said, I've tried a lot of these."

"Oh," said Faustina. She looked inexplicably disappointed. "It didn't do anything?"

He shrugged. "I don't think so. I didn't feel anything."

She looked at him, dubiously. "Are you sure you *would* feel it?" Her gaze had strayed, and she was now looking at the pond.

He shuffled, remembering the eruption of pain when the curse had been cast.

But Faustina doesn't trust what she can't see. It was the first thing he'd learned about her.

He sighed. "Do you… want me to check?"

"I won't look. I promise."

He studied her expression for a moment. He could tell when she was being serious. And, for better or worse, he trusted her.

"All right."

She turned her back. Benedetto steeled himself, then knelt beside the pond, offering a silent apology to the fish for the shock he was about to give them.

It didn't take long. He was quick about removing a

mask now and, having made the mildly interesting discovery that his reflection looked even worse with moonlit ripples to distort it, even quicker about putting it back on.

He waited to feel disappointment, but it didn't come. The truth was that, in spite of his self-urging, he had begun to feel quite… hopeful. His arm was almost half-bare now, with a thick band of fur missing from shoulder to wrist, and plenty of other patches, too. It had spread onto his back—and he could swear even that his claws were shrinking. A treacherous part of him was beginning to think that the spells weren't working because he didn't *need* a spell.

"I'm sorry," he said, standing up. "What would you like to—"

But she picked the book up from the ground, where he'd left it. "Let me try."

It was as he listened to Faustina read the incantation—with, it had to be said, surprising gusto—that Benedetto realised exactly how ridiculous he must have sounded when he did it. It was kind of her to level the score.

Nothing continued to happen, with steady alacrity.

Faustina snapped the book shut. He examined her with interest.

"But you weren't *expecting* anything to happen," he pointed out.

"No," she said, "I suppose I wasn't."

He didn't know what to make of that. Was she starting to believe in magic? Or was she just humouring him?

Finally, she brightened. "Oh well," she said. "How about a game of cards?"

He blinked. "Er, yes, all right then. But why the sudden urge?" he added, as he followed her back towards the house.

She stuck out her bottom lip, pretending to think about it. "I don't know. Certainly not because you won at pig-chasing, and I want a chance to even the score. That would be petty."

"Yes." He smiled. "It would."

She held open the kitchen door for him. "Tell you what, though," she said, with an air of forced innocence, as they made for the servants' staircase. "Why don't we make a bet?"

He frowned. "What are the stakes?"

"Oh, I don't know." Her tone was airy—too airy. Benedetto started to get the feeling that he was walking into a trap. "Let's say, oh, I don't know, if you win, I'll help you with whatever your next ridiculous garden project is."

"You'll do that anyway. It's desperately boring here, remember?"

"I think I'm finding ways to amuse myself. Besides, you're missing the point. I'll help you *without complaining*."

Now he had to laugh. "Now, these *are* high stakes. What exactly am I expected to put up to match that?"

It didn't matter. He had a sneaking suspicion that he'd agree to it, whatever it was.

"If I win, I get to give you something. A gift. And you have to accept it—or, well, at least listen while I explain."

He let her overtake him as they entered the first-floor corridor, so that he could fix her with a look of eye-narrowed suspicion. "If I lose, I get a gift? That's the bet?"

She grinned at him, her eyebrows quirked in their now-familiar expression of persiflage. He didn't feel quite as shy around her now—chasing pigs with a person changed things—but that expression was still a little more than he could confidently handle.

Fortunately, inspiration dawned. He cleared his throat. "Very well, then. Shall I get us something to drink?"

"I hoped you'd say that," she said. She produced something from behind her back. A bottle. "I happened to pick this up as we passed through the kitchen."

Benedetto took it from her and examined it. One of his eyebrows arched of its own accord. She had expensive taste. "That's strange," he said. "I don't remember getting out one of my best bottles of wine and leaving it in the kitchen."

"Well, if you must know, I happened to be passing the wine cellar earlier—"

"—The wine cellar you have to walk down a corridor and a flight of stairs that lead nowhere else to get to?"

"—That's the one," she resumed, "and I suppose I must have picked it up and taken it with me, quite by accident."

"How uncharacteristically absent-minded of you," he said. "Are you sure you're ready for this card game?"

She winked. "I suppose we'll find out."

They'd reached the drawing room. Benedetto collected glasses from a sideboard while Faustina retrieved the cards. She shuffled and dealt while he poured.

As he watched her fingers fly, manipulating the cards into fans and concertinas before tossing some of them quickly out into two piles, he couldn't help but make the comparison with her brother. He hadn't noticed many similarities between them, beyond a moderate physical resemblance and a relaxed disdain for social mores, but here her confidence was very familiar.

He decided not to bring it up, but when she asked what he was looking at he couldn't think of a lie.

"That's not surprising," she said, when he told her. "Giacomo taught me to play."

"Oh?" He cocked his head. "Did he teach you to play—" how could he put this? "—The way he does?"

She laughed. "You mean, am I going to cheat?"

There was no way out of this now. "Well, are you?"

"I haven't decided yet." Another wink. They were just as stomach-twirling as her eyebrow-raises.

The game was Briscola, with coins the trump suit. Faustina led confidently with the ace of swords. He could have beaten her with a coin card but decided to hold on to them—for the moment. He played the knave of cups.

Faustina swept the cards in front of her. "Mine, I think."

They each took a good swig of wine and drew new cards from the pack. He found himself watching her closely as she slipped the new card into her hand, scrutinising it with a strategic eye. He wondered briefly if that was how she looked when she plotted her crimes, then realised that the thought made him uncomfortable. Thinking of her as only a thief had been reasonable at first. Now it was just easier than thinking about all the other things she was.

A beautiful, quick-witted, utterly infuriating woman who

despises me.

He stopped himself. He was no longer sure he was right about that. For one thing, even his natural tendency toward negativity and self-deprecation couldn't spin the way she'd been responding to him lately as anything but friendly. She seemed to genuinely enjoy his company. And for another… well, there was the matter of his arm.

He was trying—and it was difficult, very difficult—not to read too much into it. After all, he still had no way of knowing for sure if Rambaldo was telling the truth. It still seemed utterly, totally ridiculous—both to think that magic could be undone by feelings, and that Faustina's had really softened to that extent.

But what else can it be?

They played another couple of hands. Benedetto evened the score, then overtook her. Faustina poured more wine.

"You know," Benedetto said, as they drew new cards again, "you haven't asked me if I'm going to cheat you."

Her eyes held a sort of wine-softened sparkle as she smiled at him over her glass. "Is that something I should be worried about?"

"Your brother was."

She scoffed. "Giacomo. He thinks he can read people. But he isn't as good at a lot of things as he thinks he is. Planning burglaries, for instance."

"It was the mask, or so he said. I think he found it unsettling."

"I don't know," she said. "I think if you're good at reading people, really good, you don't need to see every detail of their face. You can get what you need from their eyes or their voice or even just a feeling you get without realising you're getting it." She looked up from her cards. "I don't mind the mask."

"You don't?"

"No. I know I said I wished you wouldn't hide your face, but it's not that I mind the mask, or that I'm desperate to see what you're hiding. I mean—" She scratched her face, hesitating. "I *am* curious—though of course I know it's none of my business. But what I mean is… I don't mind it. I've seen you masked far more than unmasked. I'm used to it."

Benedetto fiddled with his cards. "I suppose we all spend a lot of our time in masks."

He was thinking about her—about all the ways he'd seen her. Dressed like a noblewoman in St Mark's Square, and a drowned rat in his garden. Looking regal, unreachable in that blue dress, and haloed by candlelight in a loose shirt that somehow made her look more achingly beautiful than anything else.

She looked at him curiously. "Is that a philosophical point, or are you talking about *Carnevale*?"

He felt his fur prickle. There was still enough of it to make that a powerful sensation. "I don't really know what I'm talking about."

She took pity on him and changed the subject as she tossed down another card. "Speaking of masks," she said, "what became of that marvellous goat one?"

He was surprised. "I didn't think you liked it."

"I didn't, at first. But I think it grew on me, over the course of the evening."

"Oh." He didn't know what to make of that. "Then I

suppose you might be disappointed to hear that I got rid of it. It was still in my apartment in the city when I became trapped here, and when I sent Rambaldo to collect my things, I asked him to dispose of it. At the time, I didn't think that was an evening I'd want to remember."

"At the time?"

He inhaled, sharply. "It's complicated. So, er—" He flailed for a moment before landing on a topic change. "What did you do with the bracelet? I'd be surprised if you got much for it."

"I didn't sell it." She rolled her shoulders back, keeping her tone light. "I kept it. Right up until I arrived here, in fact. I lost it swimming ashore."

He frowned. "Why?"

"I don't know, I suppose it broke?"

"No, I mean—why did you keep it?"

She smiled. "It's complicated."

Faustina reclined in her seat, idly rearranging the cards in her hand as she waited for Benedetto. Her suggestion that he might go and get another bottle of wine seemed to have struck him as a good idea so they had put the next trick on hiatus while he went down to the cellar.

She liked him. *Liked* him. It had become indisputable, an unavoidable truth.

That's strange, isn't it?

After all, she had barely seen his face. He was covered from head-to-toe and she had no idea what he looked like now, underneath the mask and gloves—what, if anything, the curse had done to him.

Faustina was no stranger to attraction. She had been drawn to plenty of people in the past, with consequences ranging from the mediocre to the heart-breaking, but always—well, with her eyes open.

That was what this was like. *Falling in love with my eyes closed.*

And maybe it was the bizarre situation, or maybe it was that she was continuing to place too much importance on the night they'd met at St Mark's Square, but she didn't think so. The truth was that Benedetto was courteous and kind and funny, and being with him made her happy.

Wait. Did I just think "falling in love"?

Her cheeks grew hot, and she was glad Benedetto wasn't there to see her blush. Her subconscious was going to have to start warning her before dropping surprises of that magnitude on her.

She lowered her cards slowly to the table and looked around for distractions. Benedetto's footsteps had faded away some minutes ago, and he didn't seem to be returning yet.

His hand of cards lay face-down on the table.

Feeling a little guilty, but also with a little of the familiar thrill of misbehaving, she reached over and lifted them up, examining them. He was—fittingly—well-endowed with coins, though they were mostly low-ranking. She contemplated them for a moment then, affecting an expression of nonchalance despite the empty room, she replaced them. Her next step was to flick through the deck, noting the location of the most useful cards.

This is ridiculous, she thought. But she did it anyway.

She heard distant movement from the direction of the kitchen and, a moment or two later, Benedetto emerged with a bottle.

"It's a good thing I keep that cellar well-stocked," he said. "I can't remember when I've gone through this much wine before."

She smiled, holding out her glass. "If you want me to apologise for bringing a little colour to the place, I'm afraid you're going to be disappointed."

He seemed to take this much more earnestly than she meant it. "Of course I don't." He met her gaze, and she noticed something in his eyes—something undefinable and unfamiliar.

She sighed. "I was joking."

He dropped his gaze, filling his own glass. "I know. I'm sorry, I didn't mean anything. I just… I appreciate the 'colour', as you put it. It's… nice, having you here." He stiffened. "Sorry, I mean, of course it's not 'nice' that you can't leave, and I feel awful about it, but…"

She felt an impulse to reach out to comfort him. A moment later, she was squeezing his hand. "I know," she said. "It's nice being here, too. In a strange way."

His lips quirked briefly into a half-smile before he broke eye contact and dropped into his own chair. "Come on," he said. "I think we had a little card game to finish."

Benedetto played the knave of coins so she played the knight and took the trick. She let him have the next one, so as not to arouse suspicion.

"You know," Benedetto said, collecting his cards, "we

never did establish how you came to arrive here soaking wet and almost naked."

"You're right, we didn't." With her mind starting to become softly hazy, this seemed funny. She laughed. "Giacomo left me in a boat and then shot a hole in it."

When she met his gaze again, she found that Benedetto was gawping at her.

"He… shot at you?"

"Yes. Well, no. He shot at the boat. But, since you mention it, he was shooting very much in my general direction, yes."

Benedetto ran a hand through his hair. "He might have killed you."

Faustina wasn't sure she wanted to talk about Giacomo. "I like it when you do that," she said.

He looked confused. "Do what?"

"Put your hand through your hair like that. You always do that when you're upset. Which is quite a lot, around me."

He lowered his hand slowly, looking at it as though it didn't belong to him. "Do I? I hadn't noticed."

He's played the king of coins, she noted. If her calculations were correct, he should be out of trump cards now. She let a four of clubs go and he took the trick.

"Are you feeling confident?" she asked him.

Benedetto glanced at his stack of collected cards. "Quite confident. Are you?"

"I'm always confident," she said. "Three of coins." She put the card down.

"Ace of coins."

She blinked at it, perplexed. "Where did you get that?"

"The deck?" There was a note of not-completely-unreasonable confusion in his voice.

"Oh."

She took a moment to process this. There were two possibilities. Either she hadn't noted the position of the cards properly—which, she was prepared to admit, was a possibility—or…

"You haven't asked me if I'm going to cheat you."

She'd taken it as a joke.

"You know," she said, "since we're back on the subject of Giacomo, I have a question for you."

"I'm listening."

"That night, when you played cards." She examined her glass before taking another swig. "He thought the mask was helping you to win, unfairly, so he started to cheat. But then, after that, he says you cheated him. Deliberately, I mean."

Benedetto gave a gentle snort. "That's not a question."

"Did you cheat him?"

He smiled. "Does that seem likely to you?"

"Now *that's* not an answer."

"Very well." He frowned. "I suppose it depends what you mean by 'cheat'."

She concentrated. "Did you, in any way, deliberately act to influence the outcome of the game of cards you played with my brother, in a manner not consistent with the rules of the game?"

His smile widened. She hadn't seen him smile like that since that first night, a year ago. It was as striking as she remembered.

"Yes," he said. "Although I prefer to think of it as

beating him at his own game."

She could feel her mouth hanging open. "Benedetto!"

His expression was innocent. "Yes?"

"After all your remarks about my work!" She was reeling.

"Ah, now, let's not get carried away. There's a world of difference between cheating someone who's already cheating you and lying your way into an innocent man's house to steal his silverware."

"But you weren't innocent. You cheated my brother."

He met her gaze steadily, thoughtfully, for a few moments before speaking again. "Did that make you feel better about doing it?"

"Well, yes." It was an honest answer. "Until I found out that Giacomo was cheating *me*, anyway." She attempted a smile, but he didn't return it. That made sense. It wasn't very funny. "Look," she said. "Sometimes you just have to make the best decision you can based on what you know at the time. If the information turns out to be wrong later, that doesn't mean the decision was. Like, for instance, thinking one woman you've never met before is another woman you've never met before, because she's wearing a particular bracelet. And then kissing her." She dropped her gaze. "I'm speaking hypothetically of course."

"Unless," he replied, and she could hear both amusement and tension in his voice, "in this purely hypothetical situation, you really know, deep down, that there is only a very slender chance that the woman dragging you to a deeply suspect *osteria* is really the well-bred society girl you're engaged to, but you let things go on far too long because she's the most beautiful woman you've ever seen and you want to kiss her." He cleared his throat. "Hypothetically."

A feeling like brewing laughter rose inside Faustina, a form of laughter that—instead of emerging from her throat—spread from her chest throughout her entire body, extending, warm and bubbling, down to her toes, the tips of her fingers, up to the very roots of her hair.

She stood up, driven by impulse, slowed only fractionally by rational thought. She took Benedetto's hand without warning. She expected him to react, to stiffen, but he didn't. With anyone else, she'd have pushed up the sleeve, but that would have been wrong, a violation—and she didn't care what he was *usually* hiding beneath his clothes. Instead, she held the hand gently, feeling the sleeve on his forearm to check for hidden cards.

"You won't find anything," he said. Then, with an arch look: "There's such a thing as *over*-preparation, you know."

She peered down at him. "You didn't get that ace from the deck, did you?"

"I'll be happy to answer that," he replied, surprisingly smoothly, "as soon as you tell me what has led you to that conclusion."

He had her there, but she didn't admit it. Instead, she slowly released his hand and took a step backwards.

"That's a lot of trouble to go to just to avoid a present," she told him.

He laughed. "I'm magnanimous in victory," he said. "I'll let you give me a present anyway."

Thirteen

Faustina walked slowly up the palazzo's main staircase towards the second floor, feeling her heart in the back of her throat. She didn't know why she was this nervous.

"You're being very mysterious," Benedetto commented, beside her. "I'm not sure I like it."

She smiled with more confidence than she felt. "You're magnanimous in victory, remember?"

"I knew I'd come to regret that." His hand brushed her elbow and she wondered if it was deliberate.

She'd set the canvas up in the study, before coming to meet him. The painting stood on the desk, leaning up against a stack of books, the way all those faked horses had leaned up on her dressing table back at the boarding house. But this wasn't another drab, joyless copy. This was original: vibrant and real. Both the picture and its subject.

She led the way into the room, using the candle she'd

brought with her from the drawing room to light others, already clustered near enough to the painting to illuminate it. It looked different in candlelight—better, she thought. The soft light suited her painted Benedetto. Like the real thing, he wasn't particularly loud or striking, more subdued and dignified, but with a fierce, bright inner glow that was strangely irresistible.

Her hands were shaking. She couldn't remember when she'd last felt like this.

"All right," she said, once the stage was set. "You can come in."

Benedetto rounded the heavy, carved-wood door somewhat hesitantly. "I have to give you credit," he said, before it was all the way open. "This might be the most apprehensive I've felt in my own—" He broke off on seeing it. "What… what's all this?"

Faustina silently swore. *He hates it*.

"Well, I—" The words started to come too fast, omitting to bring coherence with them. She swallowed and tried again. "Well, I suppose—I mean, you said you hide the painting because you don't like to face what you used to be, what you used to look like. And I just thought—I mean, it's fine if you don't like it, you don't have to hang it up, we can get rid of it or burn it or—" She stopped again, long enough to emit a short, sharp giggle that was both embarrassed and embarrassing. "Anyway, what I mean is, I know you said that you've lost what you had in that picture. But, I mean… A change doesn't have to be a loss. Different doesn't have to be bad." She paused again, catching her breath. "I suppose I just wanted you to know that you can mourn what you've lost, if that's what you need to do, but that what you've still got is still worth having."

Benedetto glanced at her briefly, the expression in his eyes impenetrable, then took one, two steps across the room's threshold, towards the painting.

The overall impression the painting gave, as far as Faustina could tell, was of *greenness.* She'd done that on purpose. The background was made up of an intricate mixture of leaves and soil, buds and petals—fitting for Benedetto, she thought, taken literally, but also a colour and a theme that meant life, new growth, hope. Hope. That was the gift she most wanted to give him, actually, but she didn't know how to do that. All she knew how to do was paint—well, and steal.

She'd dressed him in green, too—the understated olive-green tailcoat that had been, she'd thought at the time, her first impression of him. Then there was the co-ordinating mask, the cravat, the gloves—covering his skin, yes, but immaculate, too, smart and bold and debonair. His clothes were always so much more than an extension of the mask. They were an extension of him. And yet, at the same time, they didn't define him. He was as much himself dressed raggedly—ruggedly—in the clothes he wore for gardening, after all.

Dio. *It's sickening, isn't it, how much I like him?*

Benedetto was still staring. "You—you really did this? For me?"

"Yes." Her cheeks were no longer sufficient to contain her blush, and her ears were on fire. "But, ah, you can appreciate the gesture and still hate the painting! You don't need to pretend."

She was never like this. *What's wrong with me?*

"I don't hate it. Faustina, this is—I don't—thank you. This means a lot to me, that you would—I mean, I look good. I look good in this."

"You do look good," she said.

He took her hands in his, staring down into her eyes with an intensity that made her feel so much more intoxicated than the wine had. "Thank you," he said again. His voice cracked, and he blinked, twice, a little too fast.

She'd put her arms around him before she knew what she was doing. He hugged her back, hesitantly at first but with growing strength. Her cheek was pressed into his chest and she could hear the brisk thump of his heartbeat. She was surprised to find that she didn't want to let go. There was something in this embrace that she had never felt before, something difficult to comprehend but… right, somehow. It was a feeling of security, of complete relaxation, of knowing that for the first time in her life she was exactly where she was supposed to be.

A sudden sound made them both jump. They parted abruptly and each wheeled to face the door of the study.

"What was that?" Benedetto demanded of the darkness outside their pool of candlelight.

"The wind, probably," said Faustina, though she'd never noticed that the palazzo was draughty before now.

A moment later, this theory was destroyed altogether when they heard the distinct, scraping sound of a key turning in a lock.

"What?" Benedetto raced across the room and banged a gloved fist on the door. "What's the meaning of this?

Who's out there?"

No answer came. Nonetheless, Faustina realised she knew who this uninvited guest was—and, if the knot in her stomach was to be believed, he hadn't come alone.

She crossed to the nearest window, one that opened onto a balcony. She fumbled with the catch for a moment then, in a blast of cold night air, it opened. She rushed out, throwing herself at the balustrade and leaning over to crane her neck. Moonlight, the same moonlight they'd hoped to rely on for its magical qualities, now illuminated the shape of a large rowing boat and, beyond it, anchored where the water was deeper, a ship. Faustina couldn't have said for sure that it was the ship Giacomo and Alonso had used to abandon her on the island when all this had begun, but she'd have bet good money on it.

The sound of whispering, borne aloft on a breeze, made her look down. Half a dozen men were standing on and around the front steps, hands thrust in their pockets, looking bored. She saw Alonso among them, and her fears were confirmed. Giacomo wasn't there but, then, he wouldn't have been. He'd have wanted the pleasure of locking them in.

She felt Benedetto step onto the balcony behind her.

"What's ha—"

She shushed him, then pointed down.

The whispered conversation was continuing. Faustina couldn't make out more than the odd word, but it told her at least that these were not seasoned thieves. That made sense. No thief with an ounce of sense would have come out to rob a place with no escape routes, as part of a plan masterminded by Giacomo.

Well, not unless he devoted a full five minutes to persuading them.

She didn't know what it was about Giacomo. People just believed him.

A loud *clunk* indicated that the large bolt on the front door had been drawn back. The hinges creaked as the door swung open. She couldn't see the door itself from up here, but she could imagine Giacomo's smug, smiling face emerging from behind it.

"Come on."

She recognised her brother's voice in the whisper. The men filed into the house.

"Right." Faustina lifted her leg, so that she was already straddling the balustrade when Benedetto put a hand on her shoulder.

"What are you doing?"

She gave him a look of confusion. "They're here to rob you. We have to stop them."

"How?" His hand was still on her, and his often elusive eye contact was fixed and intense.

"I don't know yet. But I'm fairly sure that getting out of this room is the first step."

He was shaking his head. "No. Faustina, think about it. This is fine. They're not planning to do us any harm. They'll take whatever they want and go."

Faustina was hopelessly perplexed now. "Exactly. There are seven of them, they could carry off pretty much anything."

Benedetto took a deep, slow breath, closing his eyes for a moment as he thought about it. Then he opened them and said: "I really don't care. What matters is that we're safe."

He sounded so earnest, so determined, that it was a struggle not to relent. But she couldn't relent. She couldn't just sit patiently here in the drawing room while Giacomo helped himself to whatever took his fancy.

"No," she said. "I'm sorry. I can't let him get away with this. Not this time."

"Faustina, please." Benedetto's hand was still on her shoulder, squeezing a little. "I don't want you to get hurt."

"And I don't want you to get robbed." She stared into his eyes, trying to match the intensity in his expression.

He hesitated, then withdrew the hand. "All right," he said, mounting the balustrade himself. "Let's go."

Faustina took the lead. She'd had plenty of practice at this sort of thing of late, and she'd had a natural knack for it to begin with. Benedetto's palazzo, moreover, was of the type that favoured the vertically-minded burglar, with plenty of archways, carvings and other architectural frills adorning its facade. It was almost too easy.

Benedetto, however, didn't seem to think so. There was something in his grunts, as he attempted to imitate the neat manoeuvre that had transferred Faustina from the balcony to an elaborate cornice below, that seemed to indicate that he was not enjoying himself.

"Are you all right?" she whispered. It wasn't an ideal moment for a conversation, but she wasn't as worried about stealth as she might have been. The men would have been deep inside the house now, probably making plenty of noise of their own.

"No," was Benedetto's rather hoarse reply. "Not

really."

"Come on," she said. "Put your feet on this ledge."

"Remind me again what was wrong with staying in the study?"

"You can do it," she said, ignoring him. "Just lower yourself down."

He did it, though the look he gave her on completion of the stunt was not one of unmitigated friendliness.

"Good," she said. "Now we have to lower ourselves down from here and drop to the ground."

His eyes widened. "Drop to the…?"

"Ground, yes. Watch." Walking her hands down the wall, in order to keep her balance, she eased herself into a crouch. Then she secured a grip on a couple of good, solid lumps in the carved stone and walked her feet down instead. Once she was hanging there, feet-down, she let go. The drop wasn't exactly elegant, and she landed in the flowerbed with the branch of some disgruntled and surprisingly spiky plant up one leg of her trousers, but unhurt.

"See?" she said, disentangling herself.

"Hmm," said Benedetto.

He copied her. It seemed to go well, at first—all that spadework had given him good upper-body strength and he dangled himself from the building as though doing so were a tedious part of his daily routine. But it was at this point that he came unstuck—or, rather, the cornice did. The bit he grabbed had evidently cracked or, perhaps, not unreasonably, had never been designed to support a climber in the first place. He flailed, scrabbled and then fell.

Faustina gasped, leaping forward to fish him out of the flowerbed. "Are you all right?"

"I think so," he muttered, standing, "but that won't have done the clematis any good."

"Never mind the clematis," she began, but she could see that the phrase had stung him. "I mean, worry about the clematis later. We need to do something about Giacomo."

Benedetto tried to brush a smear of soil off his sleeve, but he was so covered in leaves and general detritus that it was a lost cause. "We could destroy their boat and stop them getting away."

"I like the way you're thinking," she said, "but there's an obvious flaw in it: namely, that if they can't get away, they'll have to stay *here*." She thought then, just for a moment, about how desperately pleased she would have been to see a boat not so long ago, and how pathetically she would have pleaded with Giacomo to please, *please* take her away this time, now that he had what he wanted. Things had changed since then.

Benedetto scratched his jaw. "Yes, I take your point."

She looked at him curiously, suddenly distracted. The fall hadn't dislodged his mask, but it had repositioned the high collar of his shirt just enough to allow her to peek past it. It was very difficult to make anything out, but she thought there was a strange texture to the shadows beneath.

He caught her looking and pulled the collar up. "So, what do we do?" He sounded rattled.

Faustina swallowed. "Find Giacomo," she said. "Make him leave." She wished her heart could match the grim confidence in her voice.

"He's got six other people with him. Why should he listen to us?"

"No, he *brought* six other people with him. If I know Giacomo, they're here to do the heavy lifting. Unhooking paintings, scraping the gilt work off the walls, whatever he's got planned. I don't know. Giacomo won't want to get involved in that, though he'll be happy to take a share of the proceeds. I'd be surprised if he's not off by himself, looking for money or jewels or something. He didn't believe me when I said there wasn't anything like that."

Benedetto looked at her askance. "*Jewels*?" He shook his head. "My aunt took all the little trinkets and ornaments and things. I suppose that would have included jewels, if we ever had any."

"What about money, then?"

"Most of it's on paper—in investments, like I told you. There's a bit in the safe."

"Safe?" she repeated. Finally, they were getting somewhere.

"It's in the drawing room," he said. "I'll show you."

Faustina opened her mouth to respond but she was interrupted—by a voice from behind her.

"The drawing room," it said. "Thank you very much."

Faustina wheeled round. Giacomo was standing there, grinning. In fact, it was the grin she saw first: gleaming white in the moonlight.

"Giacomo," she growled, "go home."

"I intend to," he replied. "I just dropped by to collect on a debt. You read the situation very well, though with one key oversight. I know you for the inveterate climber-out of windows you are, dear sister. Family trait, remember?" He looked at Benedetto. "I was surprised by you, though, Bellini. I didn't have you down as much of an acrobat. And—" the grin widened "—I suppose I still don't."

"Casanova—" Benedetto began.

"Not now, dear fellow. I simply haven't the time. Gentlemen," he added.

With horrible prescience, Faustina turned in time to see two men grab Benedetto's arms. He struggled against them and a third, Alonso, joined the fray.

"Giacomo! Stop it!" Her words seemed insufficient so she threw herself at her brother instead. That had more of an effect: Giacomo's stances tended to have more of swagger than of strength about them, and Faustina knocked him to the ground. It was, however, to no avail: the remaining three men stepped forward immediately to pull her away.

Giacomo stood up, looking disgruntled. "Well," he said, "there's no call for that." Then, surveying his band of hirelings, he added: "Which one of you is the locksmith?"

One of the men restraining Benedetto piped up: "Me."

Giacomo nodded. "All right. You three lock Bellini in, oh, I don't know, the wine cellar? Please yourselves. And then you, locksmith, join me upstairs. The rest of you, get my sister to the boat."

"The boat?" Benedetto's voice was taut and furious—angrier than Faustina had ever heard it, and she'd explored the reaches of his emotions pretty thoroughly in their time together. "Casanova, no, you don't know what you're doing!"

"On the contrary." For a moment, Faustina thought she heard a note of uncharacteristic regret in her brother's tone. "I know *exactly* what I'm doing."

The darkness in the cellar was absolute. Benedetto had never been in it without a candle before. It didn't matter, though, not right now. All that mattered now was the door, and that was right in front of his face.

He pounded his fists on it, feeling hopelessly weak. It was just a door. Just a panel of wood, two inches thick. In fact, he knew the dimensions exactly. He'd ordered this door the previous year, while refurbishing the house. The one that had been here before had been thinner, brittle and suffering the effects of woodworm. In his current state of surging fury, he probably could have kicked it down. Not this one, though. This one was solid. He bashed at it anyway—not sure if he was trying to hurt the door or himself.

He felt the echoes of another imprisonment. Was this how Faustina had felt, all that time ago, trapped in the kitchen while he and her brother had stood outside, holding her freedom in their hands?

There was no one outside this door. The men had simply locked it and walked off. And now they were going to take Faustina—not just away from him, but into danger. How long would she survive? The curse wasn't instantly fatal, though his heart broke to think of her in pain, but supposing she didn't—or couldn't—come back?

Supposing he never saw her again?

This is all my fault.

It was too much. All of this was too much. He had spent so long alone with his regret and his guilt and his bitterness—and with no one to talk to that he had almost learned to feel nothing at all. Now he was consumed by feelings, crushed beneath the weight of them.

In the darkness, he seemed to see her. He'd memorised her face—her broad range of smiles, from cynical to delighted, the curve of her cheeks, her smooth, pink lips and her always-laughing eyes.

He knew she didn't love him. His skin was riddled with the truth, blighted with it—but she cared about him, and he had the clear, flawless, precious patches of humanity to prove it.

And I love her.

It may not have counted for much, not in this dark, dusty cellar or even outside, in the cold light of reality, but it meant something to him.

It meant he had something to lose.

Fourteen

With her arms folded and her rear settled uneasily on a scruffy wooden box that seemed to threaten to splinter at any minute, Faustina regarded her captors with ice-cold fury. They were all on the boat, now, except Giacomo and his locksmith.

"You do realise, don't you," she said, "that my brother is the slimiest, sleaziest scoundrel ever to parade around the city dressed in peacock feathers?"

One of the men—a grim-faced type with huge, bare arms, seemingly untroubled by the night chill—let out a wheezing laugh. "Yes," he said. "We quite like that about him."

Faustina rolled her eyes. "All right. But I'd hazard that you like getting paid, too. And Giacomo's not—"

The man—apparently the small group's appointed spokesman—shook his head. "Oh, don't worry," he said. "We'll get paid." He emphasised the point by cracking his knuckles.

It had become clear, over the last twenty minutes or so, that these men didn't intend to harm her—at least, not unless strictly necessary. It was a mixed blessing. On the one hand, "not being harmed" was high on her list of favourite things. But, on the other, she had a feeling that said harm might *become* necessary at any moment.

They hadn't tied her up. That was a bad sign, in Faustina's experience. It meant that they didn't think there was any danger of her getting away.

She heard the crunching of gravel and looked up. Giacomo was making his way towards them with a brisk stride. The locksmith trailed behind him.

"Gentlemen," Giacomo said, cordially, nodding a greeting, "and Faustina. I see you're still the very last word in stylish trouserings."

She glowered at him. "Oh, *do* keel over and die, won't you?"

To her surprise, he didn't retaliate. In fact, he didn't answer her at all. Instead, he waved an imperious hand and addressed his hired help: "Come on, let's go. Haul anchor, or whatever the term is."

"Not so fast, Casanova," said the spokesman. "Tell us what happened. What did you get?"

Giacomo reached into his left coat pocket and withdrew a clinking pouch. "Enough," he replied.

Faustina snorted. "I should check his other pockets before you let him out of your sight, gents."

"I am quite sure my colleagues do not require advice from you, Faustina," said Giacomo.

"I don't know," said the locksmith, quietly. "I think

she's got a point."

Giacomo shot him a look that was only briefly murderous before it became a smile. "Naturally," he said, "I will be only too glad to submit to a search once we're back on the ship, if that would put your minds at ease, but might I suggest that we make haste? Time and tide and all that."

The men exchanged glances, then shrugs. A minute later, they were off.

When they were almost at the ship, and she finally felt no eyes were on her, Faustina attempted to disembark. A large, strong hand closed around her arm. When she looked back at the spokesman, he shook his head.

"Worth a try," she muttered.

Once on board the ship, Faustina found herself borne unceremoniously into a cabin. There was no lock on the door but the two men who stood outside, guarding it, were an adequate replacement. She was just developing a scheme that hinged, regrettably, on her being able to knock both of them unconscious, when Giacomo entered.

"What part of 'keel over and die' was unclear to you?" she demanded, as he closed the door.

"You always used to be so pleased to see me." He crossed the tiny room and sat down on a bunk, facing her.

"I know," she said, in a more subdued tone. His lack of swagger had unbalanced her. "But that was before you lied to me, manipulated me and then abandoned me."

"Do you want me to apologise?"

"I want you to take me back to the island."

"I'm going to." He gave a long, slow sigh. "I'll have to. There's just… something I need to show you first."

"What?" If asked, she'd have said she didn't care, but something in his tone had surprised her.

She recognised the look of shifty unease on his face. It was the look he'd had right before he shot a hole in the *sanpierota*.

"You still don't believe you're trapped, do you?" he murmured. "You still don't believe in magic."

"Of course not." She said it with just a little more confidence than she really felt. "Why?"

In lieu of an answer, Giacomo held up a hand. The cabin door closed—pulled, Faustina assumed, by one of the guards outside.

Giacomo's other hand had disappeared behind his back. When it reappeared, it was holding a rose. One perfect red bloom at the end of a strong, green stem. He held it out to her.

She almost laughed. "What's that for? Because, if it's to buy my forgiveness, you've severely miscalculated. I've had quite enough of roses."

"I know." He spoke stiffly, his eyes on the bloom. "Watch."

She watched, and Giacomo let go of the rose. It hung, indifferent to gravity, as though still grasped in an unseen hand. Giacomo stared past it, watching her intently.

Faustina reached out to touch the flower, conscious of the same mixture of curiosity and bewilderment she'd felt on seeing the glass ones. The stem bent a little as she pressed her fingertips against it, but it resisted the movement. She passed her hand above and below it but felt nothing.

She withdrew her arm. "I don't understand," she

whispered, her voice hoarse. "Are you doing this? How?"

The rose began to turn slowly in the air.

"It's magic," Giacomo said. "Magic is real, and I can use it." To illustrate the point still further, he waved his hand again, and the rose started to make for the ceiling. A single petal detached and floated toward the ground. Giacomo held out his hand beneath it but, just when it seemed that he would catch it, it changed direction, swirling back up again.

Faustina swallowed. "That's—" She wanted to say "impossible", but she couldn't. Her lips wouldn't form the word. In the space of seconds, she found herself re-evaluating everything she'd always believed about the world around her—beliefs that had been somewhat eroded by recent events, and now seemed about to crumble altogether. Chiara's insistence that there was more to existence than could be understood. The glass rose tree that had seemed a trick to her, and a life-changing catastrophe to Benedetto.

Benedetto. Had the best person she knew devoted himself to breaking an imaginary curse—or had she insisted on that because it was easier to cope with than the truth?

She swallowed. "You're a magician."

"Yes," Giacomo said. The rose returned to his hand, and he held it out to her.

With a hesitant half-smile, she took it. She turned it over in her hands. It was so ordinary. So beautiful, but so ordinary. She caressed the petals, so intent on examining it that it was a moment before she realised that Giacomo had spoken again.

"And I'm sorry," he added.

She looked up as the words penetrated. "Wait, what?"

He didn't repeat himself. A moment later, she didn't care. A sudden, searing heat engulfed her palm, causing her to drop the rose into her lap. The pain was focused, a sharp line across her palm. It felt as though she'd seized the business end of a red-hot poker. Staring down, she found that it was radiating from a scratch. A fresh one? She couldn't be sure. She'd have sworn a moment ago that the one the glass rose tree had given her had healed—but then, she'd have sworn magic wasn't real, too.

A thousand questions welled up in her mind, but she couldn't find the words to ask them. The pain was total and absolute. All she could do was feel it.

Finally, gasping, she managed, "What—what is this?"

Giacomo's gaze wavered for a moment. "What do you think it is?"

Her hand twitched, involuntarily, sending a spasm up her arm. She closed her eyes. "The curse. Benedetto's curse. It's real."

She heard Giacomo get to his feet. "I'll take you back to the island," he said. It was the last thing she was aware of before a black mist closed over her.

When she woke, she was lying on the muddy beach. Giacomo and the ship had disappeared, and the world had utterly changed around her.

Benedetto sank down against the wall, his head in his

hands. A half-hour's feverish searching in the dark had produced nothing that would force, smash or pry the door open—not that he had really expected it to. This was a wine cellar. It only contained wine.

He was desperately worried about Faustina, and he was starting to become a little worried for himself, too. Perhaps he'd never get out of here.

Perhaps I don't deserve to. Perhaps this is a punishment.

Wait a minute.

He'd had the thought out of habit. He was simply treading a well-worn path—the one where he made sense of awful things that happened by reasoning that they were no more than he deserved. But this—he really wasn't sure he deserved this. In fact, the more he thought about it, the more he was certain he didn't.

He tipped his head back, waiting for the numb, familiar pain of self-hatred to return. It didn't. What came instead was anger.

He *didn't* deserve this. No one did. He didn't deserve *any* of this.

Apart from the curse, of course.

Unless...

What was it Faustina had said?

Sometimes you just have to make the best decision you can based on what you know.

Hadn't he always done that?

No, he hadn't. But no one had. No one *ever* had. But he'd tried.

He wouldn't have wished this curse on anyone. Not on Faustina, who'd robbed him. Not on Giacomo. Not on the magician, who'd wished it on him.

Faustina seemed to think that he hadn't deserved a punishment at all. He didn't quite agree. He'd broken a promise. He'd deserved to face the consequences. Perhaps he'd even deserved a punishment for the cockiness with which he'd revealed Giacomo's cheating, though he'd have put up a more robust argument for that in whatever metaphysical court of law decided such things. But maybe… maybe this, the curse, the fact that he was trapped in a cellar—maybe those weren't the consequences of *his* mistake. Maybe other people had made mistakes too, and these were the consequences of *those*.

Maybe, sometimes, life just wasn't fair.

He'd never looked at it like that before. The revelation swept through him like a cold breeze—a mental sensation followed rapidly by a physical one, which felt more like a hundred thousand tiny icicles melting on his skin. A moment later, it stopped as suddenly as it had begun. He stood abruptly, blaming the stone wall for his sudden chilliness, so that he was on his feet when he heard someone try the door handle.

"Benedetto? Are you down there?"

His heart leapt.

She's safe.

"Faustina? What—I mean, how—?" But he couldn't decide which questions were important.

"I can't find the key," she shouted.

"There should be a spare in the kitchen," he replied, but an assortment of strange squeaks and scrapes told him that this information was falling on deaf ears.

A minute later, the door was open. It was still night

time, but after the total darkness of the cellar the weak glow of moonlight that haloed Faustina's shape in the doorway was dazzling.

"It's a good door," she said, "but not a very good lock."

He raced up the stairs to her. "You're here," he said.

"I'm here."

They started to embrace, but Faustina pulled away.

"Wait," she said. "I need to tell you something. The curse is real."

"I know." He studied her face. "Wait, you believe—"

"I believe it. I know it. Magic is real. And Giacomo can use it. I saw him. And I felt it—the pain from the curse. It's real. It's all real."

He frowned. "Yes. Are you all right?"

"Yes. I just… I can't believe he got away with it."

"With what?"

"With stealing. With his stupid quest for revenge. With—" She broke off, looking at her hand. "I don't know. Everything."

"I know." He could feel it too: anger at the injustice of the world, and of Giacomo in particular. But there were so many other things to think about.

She looked up at him for a moment, her eyes moist, then buried her face in his chest. Without really knowing what he was doing, he put his arms around her, pressing his cheek to her hair.

"I'm just so glad you're safe," he whispered. "I don't know what I would have done."

Faustina could feel his breath against her scalp, a warm, tingling sensation that seemed to travel down her neck and spread across her back. She tilted her head upwards to look at him again and her cheek met his. She felt the light scratch of his beard as they turned their heads to face one another, impossibly close. Their lips brushed together. It was too obvious to be an accident, too strange to be deliberate. Faustina found herself wishing it would happen again. It did.

This time they fell into it, kissing once, twice, repeatedly. Their mouths opened and his soft, warm tongue traced over hers. She felt his hands move around her body and realised her own were doing the same: one caressing his lower back while the other made its way up to his thick, soft hair.

She didn't want this to stop. It felt good, for one thing, maybe better than anything else she had ever experienced. But, when they stopped, they were going to have to think about what they were doing. Faustina didn't want to do that. She buried her fingers in his hair, pulling him in tighter with both arms, so that she could feel his excitement matching her own. They pushed the kiss deeper still, eagerly exploring one another's bodies with their hands.

They separated just as Faustina was starting to feel light-headed. To her surprise, Benedetto started grabbing at his hands, tearing off his gloves.

She started to ask a question, but surprise silenced her.

Benedetto held up his hands to the moonlight. They were pale and strong with neatly-rounded nails. Faustina realised she was searching them for flaws, trying to work out what awful affliction had led him to keep them hidden, but her gaze was quickly drawn to his face. Behind the mask, his eyes were wide and welling with tears.

"*Dio*," he whispered. "This can't be real."

She didn't know what he was talking about, and started to say so, but the words wouldn't come. Instead, instinct took over. She reached out her hand and touched it to his, fingertip-to-fingertip, palm-to-palm. His skin was soft and smooth and the warmth of it spread into her like the light of dawn flooding the horizon.

His eyes met hers. "So, this is what you feel like." He said it reverently, as though he had just found out some wonderful, beautiful secret. One of the tears spilled over a lower eyelid and trickled out of sight behind the mask.

"This is what I feel like," she replied, and she realised that she was crying too.

He put his other hand to his head. He ran it through his hair once, twice, evidently as nervous as he had ever been. Then, before she knew what was happening, he had seized the bottom of the mask. A violent tug, up and over the top of his head, was all it took to remove it.

Oh.

Faustina stared, openly and unabashed. She had been ready for anything. Almost anything. But somehow, this still took her breath away.

The strangest part was seeing the features she was familiar with—his uneven smile, his warm grey eyes—in a new context, stripped of the mask's framing. But then, the context wasn't completely new. She'd seen this face before—bathed in moonlight at a bridge in the city and immortalised in paint on the wall.

He looked exactly the same, except for the neat, carefully-managed beard, and she rather liked that. There were no scars, no marks, no surprises—which was, in itself, somewhat surprising.

I don't understand. What has he been hiding?

She felt her forehead crease into a frown as she studied him, trying to work out what she was missing. "Benedetto…" she began.

"What?" He threw the mask aside, finally withdrawing his fingers from hers to touch his face with both hands. "Oh." It was just a syllable—a noise, really—but he packed it with more happiness than Faustina had ever heard.

"What does this mean?" she asked him, breathlessly.

"It means it's over," he said. "The curse is broken."

"Does—" She could hardly bear to ask it. "Does that mean—?"

He reached out, taking both of her hands this time. The feeling of his skin on hers was sheer, beautiful bliss.

"It means we're free," he said.

FIFTEEN

Faustina awoke slowly at first. The pinkish light of early-morning sun filtered through her lids and stirred her softly. She didn't open her eyes right away. Instead, she luxuriated in the feeling of warm sheets against her skin, of being utterly, perfectly at ease.

She rolled over, and found the bed beside her cool and empty. She let her eyes flutter open then, squinting against the reflected whiteness of the sheets. She murmured Benedetto's name once or twice, her voice muffled by sleepiness and pillows, but he didn't respond.

That didn't trouble her. It was, after all, a big house, and most of it was well out of earshot. It would have been nice to wake up beside him, the way she had fallen asleep, but there was always the possibility that he had gone to prepare some coffee for them, or something to eat. Who was she to stand in the way of something like that?

She sat up and stretched expansively, watching tiny

dust motes dance in a ray of sunshine. Then she wriggled out from under the sheets and crossed to the balcony door. Benedetto's balcony had an even better view than hers, being a floor higher up, and she could see even further out into the lagoon. She also had what was almost a bird's-eye view of the garden below and, after a moment or two, some movement in it caught her attention.

There he is.

Benedetto was striding through the garden. She smiled, fondly. No doubt there was some complicated and very precise morning routine that had to be followed to the letter every day to ensure that none of the plants got any funny ideas about flowering a day late or putting a leaf out of place. She shook her head, remembering how irritating she had found his attention to detail at first. She was prepared, now, to find it absolutely charming.

He was carrying what looked like a large axe. That piqued her interest.

What's he going to do with that?

He was making for the rose garden. He let the gate slam behind him, bouncing a couple of times before the latch caught. With growing disbelief, she watched him raise the axe, then bring down a swift, devastating blow on the glass rose tree.

A bolt of pure agony shot through her hand.

"No!" she screamed. "Benedetto, what are you doing?" But if he could hear her, he gave no sign. Instead, he lifted the axe again. The stem splintered, scattering glittering shards as a chunk of it fell to the ground.

Faustina turned and ran. Her nightdress clung to her

legs and the cold marble floor bit once again at her bare feet but she ignored them. Having skidded to a halt at the top of the main staircase, she flew down the stairs like some enraged spirit, taking the steps two, three at a time, displaying a surefootedness she would probably have been unable to replicate with conscious effort. Arriving in the main entrance hall, she tore out through the servants' corridor. The kitchen door was open, and she leapt through it and out into the open air. The gardens flashed past, herbs and flowers and fish all blurring together until she reached her destination.

"Stop!" she yelled, finally coming up short in front of the rose tree—or what was left of it. It was in a bad way. Glass fragments littered the flawless grass around the flowerbed, chunks of stem mingling with fallen leaves and petals. They shimmered in the sun, beautiful and dangerous, and a nasty prickling sensation told her that several of them were already embedded in her feet, but the pain was nothing compared to what was in her hand.

Benedetto had the axe raised above his head, ready for another blow, but he lowered it slowly when he saw her. "Faustina! *Zio*, what's the matter?"

"What are you doing? You're destroying it!"

"I know." He was grinning, his strange-yet-familiar face positively radiant with happiness, but she couldn't understand it.

"But the curse—"

"It's broken. Look at me. Look at us. Rambaldo was right, it was love we needed. It's finally over!" His eyes were shining.

Faustina gripped her hand. Pain and confusion set

tears welling in the corners of her eyes. "What are you talking about? It's not broken. I can feel it." She turned up her palm to him, showing the angry red line there.

His face fell, plunging from euphoria to horror. "What are you saying? You're still under the curse?"

She nodded.

"I don't understand. How can that be? I was so sure."

"What do you mean, Rambaldo was right? What did he say?"

Benedetto looked helpless. "He suggested that what was needed to break the curse was love. And since you and I, last night—"

Faustina's heart, already pounding from the sudden run, sped up even further. Fear and panic overwhelmed her. "You knew this would happen?"

"No!" There it was again, that earnest look, the one she'd always found so trustworthy. "But I was sure that if the curse was broken for me, it would be for you, too."

"And now you've destroyed the rose? The only thing that stops this?" She held up her hand. The pain was building to a crescendo now, as bad as it had been on Giacomo's ship and worse.

"Faustina, I had no idea. Please, there must be something I can—"

"Get out of my way." She brushed him aside. She was angry with him and—even though she was still guessing what the implications might be—it wasn't just that he'd destroyed the rose tree. Something else was bothering her, but she couldn't worry about it now. Not with pain gnawing away on every poor, raw nerve in her hand.

She threw herself to the ground. Splinters and shards

embedded themselves in her knees but she couldn't worry about that, either. She scrabbled desperately in the shattered remains until she found what she was looking for: a single glass bloom, a little chipped but mostly whole, still clinging to a stem. Her fingers brushed it and the pain lessened. Squeezing it tightly in sweat-soaked fingers brought the sensation down to a dull, sickening ache. She doubled over, a few tears of relief spilling from her eyes.

"Faustina!" Benedetto's tone was desolate.

Once again, the urge to run had become irresistible—so, once again, she let it take her. "Excuse me," she said, "I—I think I need to be alone."

Sixteen

Two long, desperate hours later, from an upper window of the house where she'd been happiest, Faustina surveyed the most beautiful garden she'd ever seen. She felt sick, and tired. All this time, she'd been certain that the rose tree was an illusion, an expertly-crafted curiosity. Now she was wondering if it might not be the only thing here that was real.

Her right hand clasped the engraved wooden box that had once held the leadholder. She was using it now to keep the last intact rose safe. It numbed the pain, but barely enough.

A noise in the library behind her made her turn. Benedetto had entered, and was surveying the devastation she had caused. She had ripped almost all the magic books from their shelves, scouring the pages for answers. She hadn't found any.

He looked up as she re-entered the room. "Faustina,

are you all right?"

She shrugged, dropping her gaze. Looking at him felt strange.

He took a couple of steps towards her. He moved a little stiffly, as though still adjusting to whatever change had taken place. "Faustina." He repeated her name very gently, almost as though coaxing a frightened animal. "We'll find out what's happened. We'll fix it. I promise."

In spite of her best efforts, the tears came again. "How? You've said it yourself—we don't know how magic works. You've been searching for answers for a year and—" She broke off. That was it. That was what was troubling her most of all. "You knew more than you said you did."

"What do you mean?"

"That thing about falling in love. You knew that if I—" it hurt to say it "—if I loved you—"

"I didn't know anything for sure. It was just an idea. I thought it was ridiculous at first but—"

"But it was worth a try, right? Benedetto, I know how badly you wanted to break this curse. Are you telling me you wouldn't have tried anything, *anything* that might have made that happen?"

He shook his head, his newly-naked face scrunched in desperate confusion. "I don't understand what you're saying."

She turned away.

I should have known.

It had been too good to be true. A beautiful island, a beautiful man—those hours of conversation and banter and pig-chasing that had made her feel the best she'd ever felt. She'd been a fool to believe in it.

"Faustina." He'd moved to stand behind her. "I love you. I'm sorry."

"How do you know?" She didn't turn around. "How do you know you love me? You *had* to love me."

There was silence—a long, cold, empty silence. Then Benedetto said, "I'm going to Venice."

Now she turned. "What?"

"I'm going back to Venice. I'm going to get this curse broken, once and for all."

She shook her head, looking wretched. "You can't. You don't know who the magician is. You don't know how to find him."

"Not yet." He spoke with a steeliness she'd never heard him use before. "But I will. I won't rest until this is over. Your brother's a magician, isn't he? I'll start with him. If he can't fix this, he'll tell me who can."

Faustina stared at him, her eyes searching his for something. It took several heartbeats, but she found it.

"Fine," she said. "I'm coming with you."

"You can't. What about the curse?"

"You destroyed the tree, remember?" She held out the narrow wooden box. "The rose doesn't stop the pain but it numbs it a little. And I can bring it with us."

Benedetto hesitated, but not for long. "Very well," he said. "Let's go."

It was a long journey back to Venice in the little rowing boat Rambaldo had brought. If it hadn't been for his desperation, and how miserable and desolate Faustina looked, sitting opposite him, Benedetto didn't think he would have made it. It wasn't just the physical strain, although it had been a long time since he'd rowed like this and his muscles were making their displeasure known. It was the tide of emotion, the great wave of fear and excitement and sheer, unadulterated panic that slowly but inexorably crashed over him as they neared the city.

Venice. The island city, the most beautiful city in the world. A city that had seemed, some days, like nothing more than a shimmering mirage from Ca'Bellini. The last time he'd been this far from home, the pain in his hand had almost consumed him. Now he felt only the ache in his arms as he pulled the oars—and the one in his chest whenever he looked at Faustina's expression. Though the precious flower in her hand was keeping the worst of that pain at bay, her face was pale and taut with the effort of holding back tears—or a scream.

"Are you all right?" he asked, tentatively. He knew what her answer would be and, when it came—a brief, stiff nod—he acknowledged it without further question, even though he knew it was a lie.

She spoke, finally, as he eased the boat between the walls of a narrow canal that opened onto the lagoon. "We need to go to Santa Marina. Do you remember where that is?"

"Yes." It was coming back to him now. Perhaps it had never gone away. After all, he'd imagined walking these streets often enough over the last year, remembering hasty gondola journeys to business meetings, leisurely morning strolls to meet with friends…

And a moonlit tryst, of course.

He had longed, *yearned* to come back here for so long. Now that he was here, all he could think about was Faustina and the pain the curse, *his* curse, was causing her.

He rowed on. Bridges and buildings glided smoothly through his field of vision, some altered in the year since he had last seen them, most just as he remembered. When they reached Santa Marina, Faustina directed him through a maze of ever-narrower canals.

A woman with black hair and an expression of self-satisfaction strode out of one alleyway and along the canal beside them for several paces, before disappearing down another street. She glanced down at them as she passed and Benedetto thought he saw her sneer, but that could have been his imagination. Glancing at Faustina, he saw that she had been looking the other way and had missed the brief apparition.

They rounded a corner and a grand, ageing palazzo loomed into view.

"This is it?" he asked Faustina. He got another nod in response.

Every impulse he had was crying out to him, begging his limbs to reach out for her, hold her, but that wouldn't make it any better. What they needed now was answers.

They got out of the boat, leaving it moored to a post, and approached the front door. Benedetto raised a fist to knock, but Faustina beat him to it.

The austere butler who answered sized them up for several seconds before speaking. Benedetto was aware, for the first time in several hours, of what he was wearing.

All those months wearing fine clothes with no one to see them, and now I'm calling on a senator in the rags I wear for gardening.

He shook off the incongruous thought.

"I'm sorry," the servant said, "but Senator Bragadin is not receiving visitors today."

"That suits us," Faustina returned, snappishly. "We're here to see Giacomo Casanova."

The butler coloured a little, making to close the door. Faustina, in a movement so quick that Benedetto didn't realise what she was doing until it was done, put her foot in the way.

"There's no Casanova here," said the butler, though not with any degree of confidence.

"That," Faustina countered, "is demonstrably false. I'm Faustina Casanova, his sister, bringing the Casanova count up to at least one. And I'm prepared to wager anything you like that I'd find the second one—well, right over there, actually."

Benedetto followed her gaze. A tall, conciliatory shape skulked out of a shadow in the hallway.

"Ah," it said, "Faustina. It's all right, Natanaele, you can let them in."

"Very good, signor." The butler stood aside as they passed him, then shut the door. A moment later, perhaps sensing a sudden chill in the air, he made himself scarce.

Giacomo licked his lips. "Well," he said. "I must admit, I didn't expect to see you again so soon, my dear sister—not that I'm not overjoyed, of course. And Bellini—" He glanced in Benedetto's direction. "I see you finally found your way off that miserable little island you were so attached to."

Benedetto ground his teeth. Beside him, Faustina glowered. A few silent seconds passed.

"Casanova," Benedetto said, finally. "I hear you're a magician." He did well, he thought, to keep his voice calm, and to not finally give in to the urge to do something to Giacomo that would make his now-fading black eye pale into insignificance.

"Of sorts." Giacomo's eyes flickered.

Faustina was staring rigidly at her brother. "I want your help," she said. Her tone was strange—thick with emotion and so strained that it seemed as if she would fracture at any moment.

Giacomo exhaled slowly. "Yes, I was afraid of that."

Faustina's hands were trembling. "Giacomo. Please."

Giacomo took a step back, attempting to maintain the distance between them. "Yes, well, I'd be delighted to help, obviously, but—"

Benedetto had heard enough. "Casanova, it's clear to me that you don't have any sort of sense of right and wrong, so I shan't bother appealing to it. But I know you have a sense of fairness, however warped, because it's what drove you to seek your 'revenge' against me in the first place. So I ask you, does it seem *fair* to you that your sister, who only came into contact with the curse because she was helping you out of love—"

Faustina glanced at him. "—And a promise of a share of the loot," she muttered.

"And a promise of, ah, 'loot'," Benedetto continued, maintaining his focus, "should be left to suffer terrible, magic-induced pain for the rest of her life as a result?" He stopped himself from pleading. If he'd learned anything about Giacomo, it was that he responded to a challenge.

Giacomo looked between them, bouncing a little on the balls of his feet. He seemed genuinely discomfited, which was a surprise to Benedetto. While his interactions with this magic-wielding swindler had been blissfully few in number, Benedetto knew enough to guess that Giacomo very seldom found himself in a situation that he didn't at least *think* he was in control of.

"Ye-es," Giacomo responded, slowly. "It's not so much a matter of what's fair, so much as—"

"Giacomo." Faustina's eyes were bright with a powerful mixture of tears and fury. "Do this for me. Make this right. And then, if you want—" She swallowed. "I won't ask you for anything again. You never even have to see me again. Giacomo, please."

Benedetto couldn't hold back from her any longer. He reached out and put a hand on her shoulder. Slowly, tentatively, she raised her own hand, the one not holding the rose, to cover his.

Giacomo's eyes darted. For a moment, he seemed to be contemplating escape. Then he sagged.

"I think I'd better introduce you to someone," he said.

It took them barely more than ten minutes to walk from Santa Marina to San Marco but, to Faustina, it seemed like an age. Giacomo had led them from the house and out into the maze of canals in silence and, though there was plenty in her current situation to cause confusion and distress, it was that silence that unsettled her most of all.

Benedetto's hand had found its way into hers. His palm and fingers were warm and rough and held her own just tightly enough to provide a feeling of security. Now and then, she glanced at him, taking in the handsome profile of his face. She really was happy for him, happy that he had his freedom at last. She just wished she understood why she didn't have her own.

Giacomo halted abruptly in front of yet another grand palazzo. He wouldn't meet her questioning gaze so she turned it on the house instead. Almost immediately, she felt an unpleasant tingling in the base of her skull as a memory stirred.

Beside her, Benedetto cleared his throat. "We've stopped," he noted. "What is this place?"

Giacomo didn't answer. Instead, he knocked on the door, giving his name in hushed tones to the servant who answered. A moment later, they were shown inside.

Out of idle habit, Faustina cast her eyes around the hallways and passages. She was looking for valuables, but what she got instead was a deepening sense of *déjà vu*. She didn't like it.

The servant deposited them in the drawing room, then withdrew. The man who entered the room several moments later was wearing a purple mask—one Faustina recognised.

"Rambaldo?" She and Benedetto spoke the name in near-unison.

The man touched his forehead, still smiling. "Signor. Signorina."

"What are you doing here?" Benedetto asked.

Faustina shared his confusion. This couldn't be Rambaldo's home. No one who lived in a palazzo like this would need to earn his money personally escorting pigs and other sundries across the lagoon to Ca'Bellini. And then there was that nagging sense of familiarity…

"I'd prefer, if you don't mind," Rambaldo responded, "to concentrate on what *you* are doing here."

Had he always talked like this? There was something different in his voice now, a bold, strident quality Faustina hadn't noticed before.

"Giacomo brought us." Faustina turned to look at her brother, as did Benedetto and Rambaldo.

Giacomo shifted uneasily on the spot, then addressed Rambaldo. "Actually, there's something I need to tell you—"

The newcomer waved a hand. "Not now, Casanova. I fear your sister's difficulty may be more urgent."

"Rambaldo, what is this?" Confusion and anger fought for dominance in Benedetto's tone. "What's going on?"

"My apologies, signor—and I can only hope you'll understand that they are meant sincerely." He sat up straighter. "Perhaps you'll both indulge me for a moment? I think I might be able to shed a little light on one or two matters, if you'll allow me." He flicked his wrist and something appeared in his previously empty palm. It was a bracelet. The one Faustina had lost. Two strands of pearls cradling a painted rose. He threw it to her and she caught it.

"Oh," she said. She was surprised, but in a weary, dull sort of way. Perhaps it was that she simply didn't have the capacity to react to any more shocks—or perhaps, in the recesses of her mind, this was all starting to make a strange sort of sense. "You're a magician too." She began to turn over the implications. "Like Giacomo."

Rambaldo laughed. "Well, there I have to object. I am not a magician like Giacomo." He glanced over at the object of this derision, who scowled in silence. "But yes, I'm a magician."

Benedetto frowned, the disbelief that Faustina couldn't muster for herself etched all over his face. "But you're a merchant, how can you—?"

In spite of her own shock, she felt sorry for Benedetto. After all, she'd never trusted Rambaldo, but Benedetto had.

Rambaldo winked. "I'd have thought by now you'd have learned something about judging by appearances."

This jogged something in Faustina. Her attention drifted, dragged away by the suspicion that had been forming in her mind ever since they had arrived here. She looked around the room again. She pictured it filled with people—dancing, drinking, making merry. Wearing masks. *Carnevale.*

Faint wisps of memory suddenly coalesced into a clear, inescapable whole. She'd never seen Rambaldo's face…

Benedetto's voice was shaking. "All this time, Rambaldo! You never said a word."

"Probably because he's the one who cast the curse." Faustina heard her own words almost before she'd understood them herself—but when she felt the anger surge through her, she knew she believed them. "Take off the mask," she demanded.

Rambaldo shrugged. "Gladly." He lifted it up and over the top of his head, until it came freely away in his hand. The face behind it was handsome, with bright blue eyes. He looked old enough to be Faustina's father—or, of course, the father of another girl her age.

Benedetto looked desperately between the newly-unmasked man and Faustina. "I don't understand."

Faustina gave a single, grim nod. The man looked very different when not apoplectic with rage and chasing her out of a window, but it was him all right. "Benedetto," she said, quietly, "this is Signor Sourosin. Maristela's father."

"What?" Benedetto looked as pale as a dead man and about half as lively. Faustina suspected that she didn't look much better herself.

She rounded on Rambaldo—or whoever he was. "That's right, isn't it?"

He bowed. "Ernesto Rambaldo Sourosin, at your service. Ernesto to my friends, Rambaldo to what I suppose you'd have to term my victims. I owe you both an apology—and an explanation."

Faustina's hackles rose. "Go on then. Explain everything. Show us that you've been one step ahead all along. Isn't that what wicked sorcerers like to do?"

Rambaldo—Sourosin—looked taken aback. "I fear you may have formed an inaccurate impression of me, signorina. There was no master plan—nor, I flatter myself, any notable wickedness. I confess I have become used to thinking of it as misplaced passion—though I don't defend it."

"Passion?" Benedetto repeated the word, just as Faustina opened her mouth to do the same.

Sourosin gave a rueful sigh. "I love my daughter with all my heart, Benedetto. I have since I first laid eyes on her. The first time I held her in my arms, I promised her—and myself—that I would do anything to shield her from disappointment. I made her a lot of promises. Among them, a husband to take care of her when I'm gone." He lifted his eyes to meet Benedetto's. "It was a promise broken on my behalf."

Benedetto looked away, his expression wretched. He had, Faustina realised, been right and wrong at the same time. He *had* been cursed for what he'd done to Maristela Sourosin, but not by some unknowable cosmic arbiter of good and evil. By a father, seeking revenge on his daughter's behalf.

"You did this to punish us for what happened with Benedetto and Maristela," she said, flatly.

"No." Sourosin folded his arms. "I did it to punish Benedetto for that. You—and please don't take this personally—were more of an afterthought." He looked from one of them to the other and back again. "I suppose I should start at the beginning. Please, all of you, sit down. Can I offer you anything to drink?"

No one answered. Even Giacomo, who had seemed briefly to light up at this offer, thought better of it and sank silently into a chair.

"Very well, then." Sourosin relaxed, hefting his feet onto a footstool. "As I watched you, Signorina Casanova, climb out of my window with the contents of my daughter's jewellery box, I confess that I was deeply tempted to inflict some immediate punishment on you. To turn the necklaces into snakes, for example—I've always had a talent for the transformative stuff—or some other whimsy that would have slowed you down enough to be caught. Or, at the very least, cause you to reconsider some of the choices you were making."

"Why didn't you?" Faustina returned, attempting to cover her confusion with sullenness.

Sourosin sighed. "Well, to understand that, you'll need to understand something about magic—something I believe your brother learned not so very long ago, and to his cost."

Giacomo cleared his throat. "Actually, I need to—"

"Not now, Casanova." Sourosin waved away the interruption. "As I was saying, if you misuse magic, you lose it. The way I understand it, magic is intended as a force for good. Using it for ignoble ends—revenge, for example—causes it to detach, somehow, from the magician. It can then be claimed by another magician who, in turn, has lost his or her own magic. Some magicians lose their magic and claim someone else's a dozen times—though the claiming is difficult, since there aren't many of us and we guard what's ours. Myself, I always considered it a point of pride that mine had stayed with me all my life. I erred on the side of caution, I suppose, never taking any risks. Until—" he gave Benedetto a look "—my daughter's fiancé kissed another woman."

Faustina turned to look at Benedetto. He had his chin in his hands and was staring intently at the floor. He gave no sign of reacting to what he was hearing.

Faustina felt a surge of anger as she turned back to Sourosin. "That was a misunderstanding," she said, leaping to Benedetto's defence. "He thought I was her."

Sourosin inclined his head. "But technically, of course, he shouldn't have been kissing anyone. I do not absolve my daughter—and, indeed, had some strong words for her when I found her attempting to sneak out of my house—but a man of honour would have kept his lips to himself."

Benedetto stirred a little now. "That's true."

Faustina experienced the now-familiar feeling that she was operating on a different level of reality to everyone else in the room. "But they didn't know each other. You wanted them both to marry a total stranger."

"Yes, I see that now." Rambaldo let his gaze wander to the window for a moment. "And Maristela's happy. She's getting married. To someone she *does* know. Seeing her now, I see that what you did—" he looked at Benedetto "—was not so very wrong, and what I did wasn't right. That's why I'd like to apologise."

"To hell with your apology!" Faustina exclaimed, realising only after she'd spoken that she'd interrupted Benedetto, who had also started to speak. "You mean all this time you've been watching us—watching Benedetto—suffer and you could have set us free at any time?"

Sourosin winced. "Not exactly. There are two ways to break a spell cast on a human being. One is for the magician who cast it to reverse it. Regrettably, as I mentioned, misusing my magic left me vulnerable to losing it, and, to cut a long story short, I lost it."

Benedetto looked up. "And the other?"

Sourosin considered for a moment, then looked at Faustina. "Tell me," he said. "Why were you helping Benedetto to look for a way to break the curse when you don't—didn't—believe in magic?"

Faustina hesitated.

What the hell, she thought. There was no sense in hanging on to secrets now.

"Because I was certain magic didn't exist," she said, "and I thought if Benedetto believed in a means of breaking the curse as strongly as he believed in the curse itself, he might believe the curse was broken—"

"—Which would solve the problem of the curse, kind of like breaking it, if curses existed." Rambaldo raised an eyebrow. "Yes?"

Faustina rubbed her forehead. "I think so. I'm not sure anymore." She glanced at Benedetto. "I'm sorry."

"I understand." Benedetto's tone gave nothing away.

That makes one of us, she thought.

Rambaldo continued, "Well, you were right, in a way. Magic does exist, but it depends on belief—at least, it does if you intend to use it on a person. With magic, I could turn objects into other objects, move them, change them, make them dance if I wanted to, but I couldn't do anything to another person they didn't believe I could do." He paused for breath before continuing. "Fortunately, most people are only a waltzing hatstand or two away from believing in magic. You show them that—or, say, a rose tree that turns to glass—and they believe you can do anything. In a way, Signorina Casanova, your reluctance to accept the inexplicable made you immune to magic—except that of your brother."

Faustina shook her head. "No. That's what Giacomo did." She turned to look at Giacomo, who avoided her gaze." He… did something to a rose, and then I felt the curse." She frowned. "Wait—so I wasn't under the curse until Giacomo cursed me?"

Giacomo shook his head, but it was Sourosin who spoke.

"No. That's why I had him reveal himself to you. He and I have—" Sourosin flashed a somewhat Giacomo-like smile "—an understanding. But actually, that wasn't what I was referring to. Up until yesterday, you never thought of your brother as magical—but you believed him capable of persuading anyone to do anything, didn't you?"

Faustina swallowed, still looking at Giacomo. "I… suppose so?"

"And that's why he was able to persuade you, against all logic and reason, to participate in his ridiculous scheme. You've been under a spell all along—just not the one Benedetto thought."

"So, wait…" Faustina returned her attention to Sourosin. "What's the other way to break a curse?"

"Exactly as you thought. To believe it's broken. So I told Benedetto that there was a way to break it—and he believed me, so it was true."

"Falling in love," Faustina murmured.

"Falling, as you say, in love." Rambaldo smiled. "It seems to have worked."

Faustina and Benedetto exchanged glances. It was his turn to look uncomfortable now, and it filled her with an urge to either kiss him or slap him. Maybe both.

Then Benedetto said, "We're dancing around what matters. Faustina's still under the curse. Can you fix that or not?"

Rambaldo shook his head. "No, I can't. Only the magician who cast it can do that, like I said. Casanova?"

Giacomo put a hand to his forehead. Faustina had never seen him look like this—sallow and defeated. Her heart sped up.

Is something wrong?

"Sourosin," Giacomo said, "I really do need to speak to you—"

"And I shall be at your disposal, my dear fellow, just as soon as we've resolved this little matter with your sister." Rambaldo's tone was firm. "Just reverse the spell." He gave Giacomo a look—one which evidently spoke to Giacomo in a way Faustina had never been able to. Giacomo raised a hand and, as suddenly as it had started, the pain in Faustina's palm disappeared.

She felt the tension sag from her body a she released a breath she hadn't realised she was holding. Benedetto turned and took her hand.

"Are you all right?" he asked. "Has the pain gone?"

"Yes." Without really knowing why, she looked down at the slim wooden box in her lap. Pulling her hand free of Benedetto's, she opened the box and stared in disbelief at the contents. It was a rose, a real rose, the petals dry and beginning to curl.

Benedetto was watching her. "It still looked like glass to you, didn't it?"

She nodded.

Benedetto held out his hand again. "Faustina, I'm so

sorry. This morning, when I took an axe to the rose tree—it was just a plant. I thought it was the roses that had changed, not only the way I saw them. I never meant to cause you any pain."

She accepted his hand. "Likewise," she said.

Sourosin was smiling. "It's good to see the two of you together," he said. "Despite everything, I—well, I've come to rather like you, Signor Bellini. I hope someday you'll forgive me."

Benedetto looked at him for several moments before speaking. "I hope so too."

"Well," Sourosin said, "you know where to find me. But for now, I must ask you to leave, if you have no further business here? Giacomo and I have something to discuss."

Back out on the street, Faustina and Benedetto stepped out of the shadow of Ca'Sourosin and let sunlight drench their bodies.

"I don't know about you," Faustina said, "but I feel like my brain's been crushed under something heavy."

"Or as if I've just chased half a dozen pigs." The weariness on Benedetto's face matched her own, but he managed a smile.

"I don't know, I remember the pig chasing being quite good fun." She smiled back.

"Me too. And *that* was…" He trailed off.

She couldn't help him. She didn't have the words either.

They watched the sunlight play across the canal for a minute or two, somehow hand-in-hand again.

Then Benedetto said, "Listen, Faustina, about what

happened in there. If I'm understanding correctly, the curse wouldn't have broken if I hadn't believed in what Rambaldo—I mean, Sourosin—was saying. And in—" He looked down at their clasped hands. "In this. I believe I love you."

She studied him closely. He was beautiful to look at, beautiful all over, but it was those eyes that drew her in. They—and their earnest warmth—had been there all along. They would, she hoped, be with her for a long time yet. She grinned. "I believe I love you, too."

Benedetto sighed. "Thank goodness for that." He put his arms around her, so that his safe, delicious, exhilarating warmth seeped into her skin. "What do we do, then, with our newfound freedom?"

Faustina nuzzled into his chest as endless possibilities washed over her. "Anything we want, I suppose. But, since we're in the city… I've got a friend, Chiara, who'd *love* to finally meet you."

Alone in the drawing room with Sourosin, Giacomo deeply regretted not accepting a drink.

"This doesn't make any sense," he muttered, all-too-conscious of the serene gaze of his companion.

"I shouldn't worry about that," Sourosin returned, mildly.

"I mean," Giacomo went on, trying to ignore him, "my magic's gone. That's what I've been trying to tell you. "Leandra took it. She found out about the curse."

"Is that so?"

"Yes." Giacomo swallowed sudden suspicion. "Somehow, she found out what I'd done to Faustina."

Sourosin shrugged. "Well, I can solve your mystery for you. Faustina didn't know you'd lost your magic, so she still believed you could break the curse—so you could. As for the other matter…" He folded his arms. "There's an awful lot you don't know about magic, isn't there?"

Giacomo grunted. Given the current circumstances, he knew that he wasn't in a position to defend himself against this charge, but that didn't mean he had to agree.

"It seems to me," Sourosin went on, "that what you need is a mentor. Someone with a lifetime's experience with magic."

Giacomo was not exactly overcome with excitement, but he felt a jolt of interest pass through him. It wouldn't hurt to be a little better-informed if—no, *when*—he got his magic back. And he didn't have to like Rambaldo to take whatever he was offering.

He raised an eyebrow. "Someone like you?"

Sourosin shrugged. "My daughter is to be married. Benedetto's curse is broken. I find myself suddenly at a loose end. And I think there's potential in you." The smile grew by a tooth or two. "However deeply buried."

Giacomo bridled at this, but something in Sourosin's manner suppressed the urge to react to this slight. He focused on practical concerns instead. "I'll need to re-acquire some magic first."

"Yes." Sourosin steepled his fingers. "I suppose you'll need a curse to break."

"I suppose so."

Sourosin's eyes misted briefly in thought. "As it happens, I might know of the very thing…"

SEVENTEEN

The sun rose over the lagoon, tinting Ca'Bellini and its magnificent gardens in a soft, blushing pink. It was rather earlier than Faustina would usually have woken up of her own free will, but she hadn't been prepared to let Benedetto have all the fun.

She paused in her work for a moment, passing a grubby hand over her face. It was an ill-considered move, serving only to replace the beads of sweat that had formed on her brow with streaks of dirt, but she didn't care. Summoning all her strength once again, she lifted the spade as high as she could and then drove it viciously into the ground, with the air of a warrior queen impaling a particularly troublesome enemy.

Benedetto was watching her with an air of concern. "Are you all right?" he asked. "We can take a break if you like."

"No, thank you." Faustina swiped a strand of hair out

of her face, spreading the dirt still further, and flashed him a wicked grin. "I'm enjoying myself."

His lips twitched. "I'm glad to hear it. I'll just be, uh, somewhere else, if you need me. Perhaps somewhere with reinforced walls."

She laughed. "All right, point taken. It's just… it feels good, you know? It's like we're tearing it out of our lives."

"I know." Benedetto peered into the jagged-edged hole they had dug, taking in the ruined root structure of what had once been a rose tree. He'd been letting Faustina take the lead this time, since he'd had the pleasure of ripping up much of what had been above the ground. He must have known what she was feeling now. "There's a line between catharsis and grinding the whole garden into soup, though."

"I see what you mean." Faustina lowered the spade again and joined him in surveying the carnage. "Now what?"

Benedetto shrugged. "I hadn't thought that far ahead. We can either fill in the hole, or plant something else here. Another rose tree or—" he seemed to notice her facial expression "—something else. A fruit tree? Maybe oranges—they'd be sweet, like you."

She gave him a look that mixed a flattered smile with a sceptical raising of one eyebrow. "Sweet?" She'd never been called that before.

Benedetto smirked. "No, you're right—I suppose a good sour lemon would be more the sort of thing."

She pursed her lips and brandished the spade at him. "I could always bury *you.* Perhaps you'll grow some charm."

"Bury me? If I stood still for a decade or so, maybe."

"Are you impugning my spadework?"

"No, you've improved a lot." He raised his arms defensively. "But there was a *lot* of room for improvement."

She glowered at him, then they both started laughing. It was good, happy, ringing laughter, laughter that seemed to wash through them, cleaning out the spaces where pain and sadness and resentment had been to make them ready for better things. When it finished, they were in each other's arms.

Faustina tilted her face upwards, meeting Benedetto's gaze. His naked, perfect face was close to hers, so close that she could feel the warmth of his skin. He had that look in his eyes again, the look that said that, despite her faults—or, perhaps, because of them—she was utterly, completely wonderful. She couldn't tell whether her own eyes were saying it back, so she pressed her lips against his and said it with kisses, just to be sure.

THE END

Epilogue

Dawn was also breaking over Murano, an island in the Veneto chiefly occupied by Venice's world-renowned glass makers. Within the next hour or two, furnaces would be stoked and voices raised over the clattering din of a hundred craftsmen at work but, for now, all was silent. Exactly as Giacomo hated it.

He stood, his arms folded, in the alleyway beside a small workshop, scanning the urban landscape for movement. Finally, he saw it. A lone figure in a black cloak, picking his way between the buildings. The man's stride had a self-confidence that his sense of direction couldn't match. He kept hesitating and looking around—seeking something in unfamiliar territory. Giacomo watched him with faint amusement for several moments, then stepped out into the light and put on a smile. "Domenico. *Buon giorno.*"

"I'll give you *buon giorno*." The young man threw back

his hood, so that Giacomo received the full benefit of a slightly groggy glare. "Do you know what time it is? I should be in bed for hours yet."

Giacomo had met Domenico only once before, and couldn't afford to get attached to him—not when he was about to rope him into Sourosin's plan. But, at this, he couldn't help feeling a certain kinship with him. Giacomo, too, was missing his bed. Still, he managed to keep his face impassive.

"Well," he said, moving to brush a little imaginary dirt from his coat, "if winning our little wager is less important to you than sleeping, I'd be happy to collect my winnings now and leave you in peace."

Domenico narrowed his eyes for a moment, then his shoulders sagged. "All right," he conceded. "There'll be plenty of time for a nap once I've relieved you of that purse of moneys you so rashly promised."

Giacomo smirked. "You're sure about this? That was quite a boast you made the other night."

"I stand by it. At least..." He rubbed his forehead. "I think I do. To tell you the truth, some of the details of that night are a little blurry."

"Hmm." Giacomo looked his contact up and down. The details were blurry to him, too, though for a different reason. He didn't like this—following Sourosin's instructions one at a time, without knowing what the overall plan was.

But if this is what it takes to get my magic back...

Domenico lowered his hand. "Go on, then," he said. "Let's see it."

"It's right in there." Giacomo pointed.

Domenico looked at him curiously for a moment before turning his attention to the workshop's small, dust-clouded window and squinting into the darkness beyond. A few seconds later, he let out a low whistle and straightened up.

"You can't be serious," he said.

Giacomo shrugged.

He is, he thought.

"I am," he said.

As Domenico let out a slow, soft groan, Giacomo turned to take a second look at it himself. He couldn't quite make sense of it either.

In the centre of the room, resting on a dusty velvet cushion and twinkling softly in the blooming daylight, there was a single glass slipper.

Read Chiara and Domenico's story in

The Murano Glass Slipper

A Cinderella Retelling

Chiara has always dreamed of finding love. With her family on the brink of financial ruin, though, it's money she really needs. What she gets is Leandra, a seasoned con artist who makes an unconventional fairy godmother. Leandra has a plan, and Chiara's just desperate enough to go along with it.

Occasionally-charming Domenico isn't quite a prince. He's an English earl living a secret, quiet life in Venice, at least until he makes an ill-considered bet with Giacomo Casanova. Now Domenico has a second false identity to maintain, as well as a glass slipper to find. With all that to deal with, he needs to avoid distractions—like the irresistible stranger he keeps running into. The only problem is, he's falling in love with her.

Dancing with Domenico is the best feeling Chiara's ever had and, as Carnevale draws to a close, she realises she's found the man of her dreams. Now all she has to do is break his heart…

To be the first to hear about new releases, sign up for Victoria Leybourne's mailing list at VictoriaLeybourne.com.

Thank you

I am very lucky to have had help and support from some of the world's most excellent people while writing this book.

Boundless appreciation and thanks to, in no particular order: Chriswyn, Céline Malgen, Tushmit, Marita, Rachel and Mum.

All that and more to Carl, my hero.

And thank you to *you*, for reading this book. I was so worried no one would.

All my love,

—*Victoria*

Printed in Great Britain
by Amazon